REBEL SOUL

REBEL SERIES BOOK 1

J.C. HANNIGAN

Cover Design by Chelsea Barnes (CJPB Designs)

Edited by Shawna Gavas (Behind the Writer)

Formatted by J.C. Hannigan

ISBN 978-0-9951911-6-7 (paperback)

ISBN 978-0-9951911-0-5 (ebook)

www.jchannigan.com

This one is for the family.

CHAPTER 1

*J*une 2013
 Tessa
Late afternoon had given way to evening, the sun slowly rolling behind the pine trees to the west and casting pale pinkish-orange light across the expanse of our farm. The heat had yet to dissipate, and my long honey blonde hair—carelessly tossed into a braid and shoved beneath my baseball hat—stuck to the nape of my neck as I worked, mucking out the horse stalls.

I wiped the sweat off my brow and squinted out the open stable doors to the north field, spotting my brothers, Ben and Tommy, wrangling in a panicked heifer that had somehow managed to get caught up in the fence. The heavier jobs fell into their capable hands, but I was responsible for my fair share of work around here, too…and it was never-ending.

My family had owned *Rebel Creek Farm* in McDougall for close to six generations. We primarily raised Hereford and shorthorn beef cattle. With over a hundred cows, three pigs, ten laying chickens, ten meat chickens, and the horses—the work around here never stopped.

I was mainly responsible for handling the kitchen and household duties, the chickens, and the horses.

As the youngest of four, and the only girl to boot, my jobs weren't as unpleasant as the ones that fell on my brothers. Smirking, I watched as Tommy went down in the muddy, cow-pie ridden field. His shouted swears echoed over the field, and I laughed harder at him.

Turning back around, I set to finishing the task at hand, eager to get my chores done so I could get on with tonight, a smile still playing on my lips.

There was an energy around me, and I knew it could be felt all over the county; the rodeo was in town.

The Parry Sound Stampede was renowned around these parts. People came from far and wide during the last week of June, excited to see the smash up derby, bull riders, show horses, and tractor pulls. Even the food trucks that accompanied the traveling rodeo brought foodies from far and wide, and they always left with raving reviews.

Once I'd finished clearing out the rest the stalls, I set the shovel aside and wiped my hands on my old jeans. I had just enough time to shower before meeting my friends at the fair-grounds to watch the smash-up derby.

I left the barn, making my way quickly across the driveway to the farmhouse.

"Are you taking off now, Tess?" my father asked, his deep, stern voice making me pause as I was about to climb up the front porch steps.

I halted, my right foot suspended in the air, and reluctantly turned to face him, sensing that these words weren't going to be quick ones. "Yeah, I'm supposed to meet Elle in an hour. I wanted to shower first," I told him. "I'm sleeping over at her house tonight."

"Right." Dad exhaled deeply, nodding and pursing his lips.

He had a strange look on his face, like there was something more he had to say.

A few seconds went by, and I grew impatient. "Well…if that's all?" I gestured with a tilt of my head toward the house in question.

"I want you to be careful tonight, Tessa." My dad's tired blue eyes met mine, conveying his seriousness. He'd finally found his voice.

I narrowed my eyes, on edge. "It's just the rodeo, Dad. I've been going every year my whole life," I pointed out, trying to keep the tone of rebellion from my voice. It was true; I had been going since before I could walk, and I even competed every year in show jumping. I was no stranger to the rodeo, or to the type of people it brought in. Still, I had a feeling my father's warning had very little to do with the rodeo itself.

Back when I was a tomboy who liked dirt and sports, I was his constant shadow. But then I hit the tender age of sixteen and started developing breasts and curves and crushing on boys, spending more time off the farm than on it—although I'd never slacked off in my duties.

It didn't matter that I was now practically an adult at eighteen years old; my dad still thought of me as his little girl that desperately needed protection from the evil menfolk. It used to enrage me, how my brothers could go out on dates and stay out late, but I couldn't.

My older brother, Tommy, used to joke that it was because *"Once your boobs grow in, your brain falls out."*

The way my father treated my brothers versus the way he treated me was notable, and it was a source of constant conflict. My brothers weren't girls, therefore they didn't need to have the same rules in place.

Ben, Gordon, and Tommy could come and go as they pleased, so long as all their chores got done and they didn't flunk out of school. I had a stricter curfew, and if I didn't obey, not only did I get seriously grounded, but at least two—and sometimes all three—of my brothers would show up wherever I was to "escort me home". The only exception to this rule was if one of my older brothers tagged along, which meant I wasn't allowed to drink or kiss any boys or have a life at all.

I knew he meant well and that he was just trying to protect me from the harshness of the world. Dad just wanted me to focus on school and get a top education. He expected the boys to work on the farm, but he wanted more for me.

Or at least, that's what Grandpa used to tell me. Dad wasn't one to talk about his "feelings", so I didn't know for sure. He was a stern man, and although he was just as stern with my brothers, with me...he was different. More protective.

Grandpa Jack figured it had a little something to do with the fact that I was the first female born to an Armstrong in over two centuries. But *I* figured...most of it had to do with losing my mom.

"I heard Brock Miller is back in town." Dad said gravely, as if this should mean something to me. I arched a brow, waiting for him to explain himself. My father scratched at his thick, deep, copper coloured beard, looking extremely uncomfortable. "He's trouble, Tessa."

The Millers weren't exactly one of the most respected families around here. The rumor mill was always churning with gossip about them. When he was alive, Brent Miller had a reputation for being a somewhat belligerent drunk. Deanna Miller had worked full-time at the water treatment plant, and all three of their kids had gotten into various levels of nuisance over the years.

When he was in high school, Braden always seemed to be in trouble for fighting. He could be harsh and combative at times, but Elle loved him, and I'd be lying if I said Braden hadn't changed a little after he started dating her. He was softer now, and I *knew* he treated my best friend right.

Then there was their sister, Becky—and she had her fair share of troubles, too. She was twenty-two years old and the single mother of a four-year-old boy. The older folks in town still whispered about it, on occasion, although from what I could tell...Becky was doing okay for herself. I knew this by proxy—Elle was smitten with the whole family, although she admitted she didn't know much about Brock.

My brother, Gordon, knew him. They were the same age—twenty-four, and they'd been best friends growing up. Between the ages of fourteen and eighteen, Brock had spent a lot of time here at the farm, helping out and doing odd jobs for some extra cash. My dad hadn't thought he was dangerous back then, or else he wouldn't have let him stay for supper as often as he had.

In all the years he'd been a staple in our household, I'd never spent any time alone with him or even spoke to him aside from the occasional whispered request for a dinner roll.

Back then, I was painfully shy. I was also acutely aware of how good-looking Brock was. It was impossible for anyone to not notice him.

As young as I was, I was enamored by him; bewitched by his easy, dimpled smile and the unusual colour of his blue eyes: like steel and smoke. They were enticing, even from afar.

Brock was the kind of guy that just looked dangerous and he had the reputation to prove it—or so thought everyone else in town.

Me? I didn't know. In all the years I'd indirectly known him, I'd never witness him be unkind to animals or people.

"Come on, Dad." I sighed, almost rolling my eyes. "You used to feed '*that Miller boy*'. He's harmless."

"Harmless people don't go to jail, Tessa." He replied gravely, his eyes serious. I winced, nodding once. My father had a point.

Brock had served eighteen months in jail a couple years back after he was charged with assault causing bodily harm. The details on what happened were fuzzy. Despite how often the

Millers were gossiped about, they were private people and nobody actually knew the proper details of anything.

I don't remember much about the day that the newspapers broke the news of a local man arrested for assault causing bodily harm; I only remembered the look of disappointment on my father's face.

My father, for as serious and tough as he was, had a soft heart. He guessed that Brock didn't have a good home life, so he tried his best to provide a more constructive outlet for him on our farm. He gave Brock a means of making money to put food on their table, since Brock's dad seemed more concerned with drinking their money away at the local bars.

Frankly, I didn't feel it was my business or place to worry about other people's affairs, and since I had no intention of seeing Brock...I didn't particularly appreciate the hold up. I barely put up with having Braden around. While my heart had softened marginally towards the youngest Miller boy, I had absolutely zero desire to awaken that old, awkward crush I'd harbored on his older brother when I was a gangly child.

I sighed, glancing towards the front door of our white farmhouse longingly. I was desperate to wash the smell of animals and manure off me, and eager to get to the rodeo and meet up with my friends.

"I'm serious, Tessa." He added when I didn't respond quickly enough, dragging my attention back to him.

"Dad..." I popped my lips out and huffed with aggravation. My father said that about almost every guy that lived within a one-hundred-mile radius, but for some peculiar reason...this felt different. Annoyance prickled beneath my skin, and so did the need to rebel. I couldn't understand why my father was freaking out about his reappearance or what I had to do with it. Even if he'd been friends with Gordon, Brock Miller had never spoken more than three words to me. I wasn't likely to capture the attention of the notorious Miller boy, but I *was* likely to miss the whole derby if this conversation dragged on any longer. I bit back a sigh and forced myself to relax a little. "I promise I'll stay away from Brock."

Dad nodded gruffly, satisfied with my answer. He waited until I'd climbed up the front porch before heading off to check on the cows.

My dad was about as country as they got. He raised Hereford and shorthorn cattle, just like his father before him, and his grandfather and his great grandfather—dating all the way back a hundred-and-fifty years or so. My brothers and I had grown up knowing what hard work and dedication looked like, and we were put to work as soon as we were old enough to stand and take a few steps.

I loved my dad, even though we didn't see eye to eye on anything lately. It had a lot to do with me being a girl, I think. I tried not to allow my gender to affect things, but I'd be lying if I said it wasn't a factor.

It didn't help that at least once a month, I get so fed up that I would stomp my feet around and throw fits, ranting about the toilet seat being left up or raving about how Gordon never remembered to take his boots off in the mud room, and ended up tracking mud and manure from the fields throughout our entire kitchen.

It was always my job to clean it up. If I didn't, it didn't get done. My brothers and father didn't exactly see messes the way normal people did, so it was up to me to make sure the house was in fine order. To say I resented that role would be an understatement, but like I said…if I didn't do it, it wouldn't get done. I didn't know how they'd manage without me come September. I suppose Sue, Elle's mom, would check in frequently.

Dad understood Ben, Gordon, and Tommy in a way he couldn't understand me. My brothers were easy enough because they were boys. But me? I was a whole different kettle of fish, or

I was when I hit puberty anyway. It was like my dad suddenly didn't know what to do with me.

With my dad and brothers still out in the fields or at work, I had the house to myself and I could shower and prepare for the evening in peace. If Tommy was around, he'd undoubtedly be making fun of me for putting on eyeliner and mascara. He'd point out the lip gloss and too-tight jeans, and he'd likely rat me out to dad just to get me in trouble. I could almost hear his voice in my head. *"Are you seriously going to let Tessa go out like that, Dad?"* He could be almost as overbearing and protective as my father.

Ben irritated me the least out of my brothers, and that was because he lived in town now. Even when he'd lived at the farm, he hadn't been a nark. He was eight years older than me, far too mature to tattle. If anything, he'd been amused by our younger antics in a semi-detached kind of way. Now a newlywed with a baby on the way, Ben was far too focused on his own life with his new wife, and the farm. He was my dad's right-hand man.

Tommy and I were the closest in age, and although he wasn't as overbearing, Gordon could—and *did*—egg him on when we were all together.

I didn't attend parties my brothers would be at because I had learned from experience that they would monitor me all night. The last time I went to a party with my brothers in attendance had been a Canada Day party at the Little's cottage. Elle had just started dating Braden, and my brothers hadn't been fans of that. Their excuse was that they wanted to make sure no "funny business" occurred.

I'd finally gotten the attention of my crush at the time, Corbin Little. He asked me to dance and ended up with a broken nose, courtesy of Tommy, just for copping a feel when we were dancing. I was so livid at Tommy that I was practically seeing red. Gordon drove us home and I couldn't stop yelling at them about what huge jerks they were. Somehow, I ended up grounded for drinking and Tommy and Gordon got a pat on the back for "protecting their sister's virtue".

It was really difficult being the only girl in the house, and not just because of my family's extreme overprotectiveness of me. Growing up, I often felt torn between what I did like and what I should like. I liked hanging out with my friends and didn't mind farm work. I loved horseback riding and I knew how to drive pretty much every all-terrain vehicle known to man. I played football with my brothers and I had helped over a hundred cows give birth. I was a better shot with a bow and arrow than my brothers, and I could aim pretty well with a shotgun too.

I wasn't afraid to get my hands dirty. I liked my old Blazer, my casual wardrobe and my cowboy boots, but I also liked lipstick and makeup and occasionally daydreamed of getting kissed by a man and falling in love. Although in the same breath, the very idea terrified me.

I didn't fit into one category or another, and sometimes… that was maddening.

My best friend's mom, pretty much the only female constant in my life, always said I could still ride horses and dirt bikes and rock lipstick. At the thought of my friend's mom, I smiled. If it weren't for Sue Thompson, I didn't know how I'd survive this world, brought up by these Neanderthals. I went to Sue when I first got my period, crying my eyes out because I was so scared. She taught me about menstruation and she was the one who took me to the walk-in clinic to get birth control, not because I was sexually active, but because my cramps were unbearable and I was too mortified to broach the subject with my old-fashioned father.

Tonight I was wearing a pair of faded blue skinny jeans, my genuine brown leather cowboy boots, and a red plaid blouse over a white tank top. I'd braided my hair in the familiar style I always wore it in just to keep it out of my face. My deep-set amber eyes seemed brighter with the added embellishment of makeup.

My cell phone started to vibrate, and I made my way over to the old desk that had belonged to someone in my family. Almost everything in the house belonged to someone else in my family at some point; I don't think the décor or furniture had changed in a hundred years.

I slid my phone off the surface of the desk, unlocking it with a swipe of my finger to read the message. It was Elle, demanding to know where I was. I texted her back to tell her that I would be there in fifteen minutes before tucking my phone into the back pocket of my jeans.

I grabbed my overnight bag and paused in the kitchen to check the crock pot on the counter. I knew I wasn't going to be home for dinner, but I still wanted my dad and brothers to eat so I'd prepared a stew that had slow-cooked all day. I flicked the switch to low heat before I raced out the front door.

The sun was just setting as I walked to my truck, a 1978 Chevy Blazer K5—almost in mint condition, aside from a dent on the front driver side fender. It was a two-toned white and blue colour, dulled with age. Dad bought it secondhand back in 1988, about a year before my oldest brother had made his unplanned appearance. He drove it for years before caving and finally buying a new truck. Each of my brothers had learned how to drive in this Blazer, and I had too.

My mother had birthed me in it. Not intentionally, of course —they'd *tired* to make it to the hospital in time, but after having babies as big as my brothers, my seven pounds and eight ounces made me slip through the birth canal effortlessly. I came without warning during a summer storm; my parents had barely made it halfway down the driveway when she felt the need to push. Dad stopped the truck and helped her. He caught me, then cut the cord with a utility knife he always had on hand.

Now, this old truck was mine. Considering the history, I

couldn't complain about its elder status. In a way, it made me feel close to her. I didn't get a chance to know her the way my brothers had; I didn't have my own memories of her, just the ones I'd been told over the years.

The door creaked when I opened it, the white and blue leather creaking as I slid in and slipped my key into the ignition. The old engine rumbled to life without complaint, and I put it in reverse.

My heart was pounding with excitement, and I couldn't say why for certain. I knew it had very little to do with the evening before me. It felt more like something in the air; the excitement, the thrill. I just had a good feeling about tonight, and I couldn't wait.

After watching the smash-up derby and hitting up the Midway, we were going to a bush party, the first bush party of the summer without any of my brothers hovering over me like protective mother hens. I thanked the stars that all three of them had other obligations tonight. Hell, I don't even think they knew about it—Elle and I were extremely careful not to talk about it around any of them, or her mom.

Elle had already gotten our tent set up, and she'd managed to score us several cases of beer. Elle assured me it would be safe; it was her boyfriend's family's property, so there wasn't a risk of getting the cops called on us.

I was intent on enjoying my last carefree summer. In September, I would be heading off to college and the fun would have to stop so I could focus on my studies and my goals.

I was enrolled in the veterinarian technician program at Georgian College. The ultimate goal was to work for a couple of years as a veterinarian technician and save up for the Doctor of Veterinary Medicine program at Guelph University. I knew my father couldn't afford the program or the living expenses at Guelph, and I didn't want him to end up stretching our family finances even more than they were already strained. Plus, a part of me wanted to do this on my own.

Barrie was far enough away from Parry Sound that I might actually gain some distance—and independence—from my family, yet close enough that I could easily drive home whenever I missed them. As nutty as they drove me on a day to day basis, I'd never spent longer than a week away from them, and I knew I would miss them. My dad hadn't been thrilled about the idea of me going even that far for school, but the living expenses of Barrie were super cheap, and I'd gotten several scholarships and bursaries.

I was excited for September, excited for all the new possibilities. Better yet, I was excited that my best friend would be at my side. Elle was also enrolled at Georgian College; she was going to take the paramedic course.

This was the moment we'd both been eagerly anticipating for the last four years, when we'd get to be college students together. I could only imagine the different kinds of trouble Elle would attempt to lead me into, but I was hoping I could keep her head on straight.

Volunteers directed me to an available parking spot in the makeshift lots they'd set up on the grassy fields near the fairgrounds. Once I'd parked, I made my way to the front gates, scanning the crowd for familiar faces.

I spotted Elle waiting for me by the ticket booth. She was peering around, looking for me. I couldn't help but smile at the sight of my friend. We'd been best friends since the day she was born, two months after I was born. Her mom, Sue, had been my mother's best friend growing up. Elle had always had my back, and I'd always had hers. We were as close as two people could be, yet we were as different as night and day. She was more of a free spirit than me, and her sense of adventure was never-ending. I worried about consequences for everything, and Elle worried about nothing.

Elle was a few inches shorter than me, thin with curves in all the right places. She had beautiful dark hair, dark eyes, and a mischievous smile that always meant she was up to no good. Sue was very well loved in the area, and that made Elle was one of the town's darlings. She could often get away with anything just by flashing her sweetest, most demure smile. She was definitely a force to be reckoned with, and I'd seen her in action.

Tonight, she was dressed in her black cowgirl hat and the shortest shorts known to mankind; Daisy Duke herself would likely cringe at the amount of thigh showing. She squealed when she caught sight of me and bounced over, throwing her arms around me as if she hadn't seen me in months.

"Jesus, Elle. Did you consider putting on pants tonight?" I joked, shaking my head at her.

"You sound like your dad." She snorted. "Besides, I'll just have to take them off later for Braden."

"Okay, gross." I frowned, my excitement for the night waning at the mention of Elle's boyfriend. Braden wasn't my most favourite person. He'd graduated from high school the year before us, and now worked as a mechanic at Chuck's Garage in town. Although he wasn't very book smart—or at least, hadn't put the effort into school when he was in it himself—he knew his way around an engine block. His talent would have been more impressive if he wasn't such an arrogant prick about it.

Braden annoyed the hell out of me, and I sort of resented him. Before him, Elle and I could talk about literally anything. That girl and I were tight, and we still were...just not when it came to Braden. When they began dating two years ago, she started to get protective and a little defensive about her relationship with him, telling me I needed to get to know him before judging him for his past mistakes. She loved him, and despite my first opinion of him...Braden made her happy. He could be a complete dick to everyone else, but he was sweet and attentive to her.

Besides, I'd known that Braden was going to be a part of Elle's grand plans. After all, we were partying on his property. I just hoped that Elle wouldn't end up ditching me to hang out alone with Braden. The last thing I wanted was to start off my summer feeling like the third wheel to everybody, again.

"Oh relax, Tess. Tonight is going to be amazing," Elle said decidedly, linking her arm through mine and leading me away from the gates.

I pushed down my feelings of discomfort and smiled at my friend. When Elle decided something, it was done and she was usually right. We would have fun tonight, despite Braden's presence.

The number of people at the rodeo was astronomical. It felt as if the entire town was there, along with all the people from the smaller local communities. Twilight fell and the energy around us cracked and sizzled. Elle led me to the bleachers around the show ring, where our friends were saving our seats. Krista Turnkey and Joanna Poole were in our grade and our tight knit circle of friends.

"Hey, Tessa!" Krista grinned, moving closer to Joanna to make room for Elle and me in the packed stands.

"Hey." I smiled back, biting my tongue and resisting the urge to comment on their similar state of undress—Elle might have found it humorous, but they likely wouldn't. Krista and Joanna were both wearing jean shorts and tight tank tops like Elle. They were the kind of girls that loved flaunting their bodies and giggling any time they got hit on. I almost felt out of place sitting amongst them.

The smash-up derby was about to begin, and Elle stood up and cupped her hands around her mouth to scream for Braden. He'd entered the derby, driving an old Sunfire that he and his friends had painted to look like some kind of monster.

Elle dropped down to sit beside me as soon as the squeals of tires announced the beginning of the derby. She clung to my arm, watching with wide eyes as Braden rammed his car into the others with notorious precision and speed.

Every year, Braden entered the smash-up derby and almost every year, he placed in the top three. This year, he came in second place to one of his friends, Ezra Johnson.

An hour later, Elle, Krista, Joanna and I met up with the guys outside of the ring. Elle dropped my arm the second she got close enough to Braden and threw herself into his arms. He grabbed her ass, pulling her against him, and started to kiss her. I rolled my eyes at their nauseating display.

"Hey, Tessy." Braden grinned when he finally came up for air. I glared at him; he knew how much I hated that variation of my name, but it didn't prevent him from using it as often as he could. It was one of many reasons why he annoyed me.

"Hi, Brandon," I retorted, feeling very much like a third grader the moment the words fell from my mouth. I knew it; I was lame.

Braden chuckled, shaking his head at me as if we were in on a private joke. I glowered at him. I didn't want to be in on a private joke with him. Sure—maybe I *was* a little jealous of his constant, well...existence.

"Can you two just try to get along tonight for my benefit?" Elle pouted. "It's my birthday soon!"

"Elle, your birthday isn't until October, *mine's* sooner." I pointed out, arching my brow at her. The corners of my lips perked up in a bemused smile. Elle shrugged.

"Don't worry, babe. I think I'm growing on her," Braden responded, smirking at me.

"Yeah, like a fungus," I muttered back. Braden hadn't heard, or if he did, he didn't care. His lips were busy kissing Elle's neck. He'd already gotten bored with taunting me.

We stayed at the fairgrounds until they shut it down around

eleven. Then we all piled into cars and trucks and headed to the backwoods for the after-party. Much to my chagrin, Elle had insisted on allowing Braden to ride with us, since his truck was in the shop with a blown fuel pump. He proceeded to highjack the radio, turning the channel from my preferred country station to his heavy metal one.

We reached an access road, and my foul mood began to disperse as I drove my Blazer up it. As annoying as Braden was, he had a beautiful oasis in north-west Parry Sound. I wasn't sure how much of it was his, but he'd turned it into a mudding track a few years ago. Unless you knew where to go, you wouldn't find it. I'd only been a handful of times, always with Elle and Braden for bush parties or ATVing, and he still had to direct me on where to go. This time, Braden directed me pass the wide pathway that lead to the track and fifteen minutes north up a freshly built gravel road to a grassy clearing.

The moment we pulled up, we got to work on setting up camp. People had started to arrive, and the tents were going up quickly. Braden, Ezra Johnson, and Peter O'Connor set to work on building a fire. Joanna and Krista were focused on setting up some cordless speakers on the back of Ezra's Chevy, leaving Elle and me to wander around.

The clearing was shaped like a circle, with the access road on the south side of it. Directly across from it was an old but clean looking trailer, and beyond that was a line of trees. Before I could ask who'd brought the camper, Elle was darting off to join Braden at the fire pit in the center of the clearing.

I watched as she leaned into him and whispered in his ear. He grinned, nodding at her with an affectionate smile as she ran her hand along his chest. He wrapped his arms around her waist, pulling her to him and pressing a slow, tender kiss to her lips.

For a moment, a small swell of jealousy pressed down on me. Not because it was Braden, but because I wanted that. I wanted someone to kiss me slowly; I wanted to feel strong arms around me. I wanted intimacy and tender touches.

And maybe...*that* was my real problem with Braden Miller. Misplaced jealousy.

I glanced around the party, noting there wasn't anyone even remotely interesting around. They were all guys that I'd gone to school with—not one of them made my heart beat faster and my palms sweat. Hell, I got a better chemical reaction from shooting a bow and hitting my target than with any of the guys around this small town.

One reason to really wish the summer away: college meant more of a selection.

Elle saw me sulking and reluctantly pulled away from Braden to rejoin me. "What's up?" she asked, frowning at the sullen look on my face.

"Nothing." I sighed.

"I don't buy that," she called me out, jutting her hip out and propping her hand on it with her certain brand of attitude.

I fixed her with a serious stare. "I promise that I'm fine. Just...please tell me we're still sharing a tent and that Braden won't be in it?" I raised my brows, pleading with her.

Elle smiled at me brightly, her white teeth flashing in the moonlight. "Don't worry about it! Braden's sharing a tent with Ezra. Unless you want to share a tent with him..." Elle trailed off, smirking as her hip bumped into mine.

"Um, no. I'm good." I made a face, my memories drawn to the one time when Ezra and I hooked up. It was a year before the Corbin Little incident. I was sixteen and Ezra was seventeen, his license still fresh in his hand when he asked me out to the movies. We'd mutually decided to skip the movie and drive around in his truck, and one thing led to another. Although Ezra was sweet, he wasn't experienced. Neither was I, for that matter. The whole situation was awkward, painful, unpleasant, and completely overrated. Definitely not worth the black eye that Ezra got when Tommy found out. I definitely had no desire to relive that night. "So, whose camper is that?"

She glanced up, looking towards the trailer. A guilty look befell her face. "That's Braden's brother's trailer," she said innocently, shrugging. She wasn't meeting my eyes.

"Braden's brother?" I repeated, blinking slowly.

"Yeah, I think that's him now." Elle grinned, nodding towards the headlights that were focused on us as a truck pulled up. My eyes widened as I took in the older Ford F-150 with huge, monstrous tires and floodlights. He parked carelessly with the other vehicles lining our makeshift party area and got out, leaving the lights pointed directly at our little group.

"Hey, Brock! Glad you could make it." Braden smiled, his entire demeanor changing as his older brother slowly walked up to us. Brock had a dark, grim look on his face, as if this was exactly where he didn't want to be. He was carrying two ten gallon jugs of water effortlessly. He set them down a little ways away from the fire.

"Get the rest of the water from my truck," Brock ordered, his eyes narrowing in on Braden's face.

His voice prompted butterflies to explode in my belly. It was deep, gravelly, and full of authority. Brock had the kind of voice and rugged good looks – that made girls swoon.

My eyes drank him in. His dark hair was longer than it'd been the last time I'd seen him; long enough to touch his shoulders. He wore a worn baseball cap backwards. He had a strong, chiseled jaw, a five o'clock shadow and the most sensual lips I'd ever seen.

I had the most ridiculous urge to step towards him and run my hands through all that hair. The way his Wrangler jeans clung to his muscular thighs made my mouth water. He looked like a damn cover model for some country living magazine.

He was even more attractive and intimidating than I remembered. *Not good, not good at all!* I thought, ignoring my body's intense chemical reaction and desperately seeking a flaw in him that I could latch on to.

Even his clothes made me drool, or perhaps it was the way he wore them. He was dressed in worn work boots and a black long-sleeved t-shirt that clung to the muscles in his chest and outlined his strong arms. Arms that looked capable of hard labor; arms that I'd love to have wrapped around me.

Elle elbowed me sharply, giggling. I hadn't realized I was noticeably gawking at the man standing less than a foot away from me, but I couldn't help it. The guys I was used to seeing around weren't built like Brock. They didn't even come close to being built like Brock.

He glanced over, his brow furrowing as his eyes landed on me. I clamped my jaw shut and tried to force my eyes away from his, but he had some kind of pull on me. I couldn't stop staring at him—and he was staring right back.

His eyes were every bit as intriguing as I remembered, but the easy dimpled smile was definitely not present. Brock Miller looked hostile and every bit as dangerous as they said he was... and still, I couldn't stop staring.

"Yeah, yeah," Braden grumbled, effectively breaking whatever strange spell had overcome us. Brock's eyes tore from my face and he watched as his brother stomped over to his truck. A second later, a menacing deep bark sounded from in the cab. Braden yelped and flew backwards, away from the snarling dog sitting inside. Brock smiled slowly, the dimple appearing just above the left corner of his lip.

He put his fingers to his lips and whistled. The dog leapt from the open window and growled at Braden. Brock whistled once again. Obediently, the dog walked up and sat down at Brock's feet, still watching Braden carefully. The dog was huge and beautiful, a German shepherd mix from the looks of it. Absently, Brock's hand dropped down to pat the dog on the head.

"I hope you're going to control that fucking mutt," Braden seethed, his face red with embarrassment. "I don't want it barking all night."

Brock sent him a single look that had Braden clamping his mouth shut and fetching the rest of the water jugs from the back of the truck. It seemed that Brock had an undeniable power over those around him. Me, Braden, the dog, even Elle watched with wide eyes—silently, which was usually a feat for her.

I grabbed Elle's arm again, dragging her further away from both Brock and Braden. I felt lightheaded, and I didn't like it at all. "Why didn't you tell me he was going to be here? If my father finds out, he's going to flip!"

"Chill out, Tessa. Your father isn't going to find out...I promise." Elle's eyes were filled with sincerity. "And really, there's nothing wrong with Brock."

"Didn't he just get out of jail for aggravated assault?" I retorted, folding my arms across my chest. I was suddenly cold; the good mood I'd been in earlier had long since evaporated in a puff of smoke, replaced with a swirling number of complicated emotions and reactions that I couldn't even begin to sift through.

"It was assault causing bodily harm, and he got out a while ago. But you don't know the reason why." Elle said, as if this should make all the difference in the world. Elle noticed my unimpressed, *are you serious* stare. She smiled sadly. "Tessa, your world is always so black and white. Sometimes, things fall in the grey area. Trust me when I tell you, this is one of those things. *He* is one of those things."

I wrinkled my nose, resenting my friend for calling me out. "Fine, but don't expect me to talk to him. I barely tolerate Braden."

"I know," Elle said without humor. She pursed her lips as if she had more to say. Instead, she forced a smile. "Let's go get a drink."

I HAD BEEN SO excited to finally be able to let loose and get drunk without one of my brothers around to put a stop to the fun. Only, I couldn't. Not at first, anyway. I felt Brock's eyes on me often, and I couldn't believe that I'd finally ditched my brothers only to gain a surrogate one.

I started to get a little chilly. I knew I had a sweater in the cab of my truck, so I told Elle I'd be right back and wandered over to grab it. I yanked the door open, and the hinges creaked loudly. I grabbed my sweater and slammed the door perhaps a little too harshly.

"Well, aren't you the life of the party?" The modulated voice startled me, and I strained my eyes through the darkness trying to find the speaker. Brock stepped out of the shadows, followed by his dog. The dog hadn't left his heels or made a sound since snarling at Braden. When Brock came to a stop at the end of my truck, the dog sat down, watching me with intelligent glowing eyes.

My heart jumped in my chest and my face felt heated. I didn't understand what was coming over me. I'd always been attracted to Brock, sure...but it had never taken my breath away like this before. "Yeah, well. I could say the same about you."

Brock chuckled, but it wasn't unkind like the last time I'd heard him laugh. He leaned against my truck, still looking at me, and took a slow sip of the beer in his hand. My eyes were instantly drawn to his broad shoulders, snug in a tan work jacket. "Yeah, I didn't particularly want to spend my Friday night chaperoning my little brother and his friends. No offence."

"None taken." I frowned. "And for the record, I didn't want

to spend my Friday night being chaperoned by someone's older brother. I have enough of my own, thank you."

Brock's mouth curved into an attractive smile that made the butterflies I'd felt earlier come back full force. There it was, that complete chemical reaction I'd been so desperate to find an hour ago. Now, I wish it would disappear back to wherever it came from.

He tilted his head, studying me as closely as I studied him. "Are you the Armstrong girl? Gordon's little sister?"

"I am," I retorted, straightening my spine so I'd stand taller. Even with my posture as straight as I could get it, Brock still towered over me by at least a head and a half. It bothered me more than I cared to admit that Brock didn't immediately remember who I was.

His eyes traveled down the length of my body slowly. I clung tighter to the sweater in my hands, thrown off by how greatly that simple gaze affected me. "Well, ain't that something."

I narrowed my eyes at him, disliking the fact that I liked the covert way he was looking at me.

That Miller boy, he's trouble, Tessa. My dad's words came back, the ominous forewarning washing over me like a wave.

"Why are you chaperoning anyway?" I asked, the question spilling from my lips before I could prevent it.

"This is my section of property," Brock explained, nodding to the clearing. "My brother has a tendency to do stupid things and let stuff get out of hand. I'm just here to make sure that doesn't happen."

"Oh," I exhaled, unaware that I'd been holding my breath. "I guess that explains the lurking and bummer attitude."

"Guess so," Brock replied, taking another swig of his beer and glancing towards the fire. I almost felt like Brock was trying to dismiss me, and I liked that even less than I liked the fact that he hadn't remembered me.

"Why didn't you just tell him he couldn't throw a party here?" I asked.

Brock looked at me again, and my breath caught somewhere in my esophagus. "Because I'm putting him to work tomorrow as payment."

"Putting him to work for what?"

"You ask a lot of questions." Brock's sensual lips twitched, and I licked mine in response.

"So? Asking questions isn't a bad thing."

"No, it's not," Brock agreed. He considered me for a moment. "I'm building a cabin. I have a friend coming over with the wood miller tomorrow, and Braden is going to help."

"Oh," I said, surprised by his answer.

Brock picked up on my surprise, and the corner of his lip lifted in a taunting smirk. "Did you think I was going to put him to work doing something illegal?"

"No," I said quickly, my eyes narrowing at him. "I just didn't expect you to say you were going to build a cabin. You just got back into town."

"I've had this land for years. It's time I did something with it," Brock muttered. He was still looking at me, and that gaze was doing all kinds of things to my body. My blood felt hot and thick in my veins, and breathing was becoming increasingly harder to do.

"Oh, well. Congratulations, I guess. I, um…I'd better get back," I said, taking a step backwards, away from that molten gaze. "Have fun lurking in the shadows," I added. His lips curved up in the tiniest hint of a smile and I thought I heard the faint sound of him chuckling. I grabbed another beer, taking a long sip of it while I tried to calm the fluttering in my belly.

AFTER MY THIRD BEER, I stopped caring that Brock was there... watching, and I started to have fun. My discomfort at my body's unexpected reaction to Brock Miller disappeared as the party grew from a cluster of six people to a whopping twenty or more. Each time someone else joined the fun, the fire grew and so did the noise level.

The cordless speakers were now pumping country music. Music, laughter and conversations flowed while the fire flickered. I sat beside Elle on a log in front of the fire, watching the antics around me while I started my fourth beer.

I kept catching the guy standing across the fire beside Ezra staring at me. Each time I'd catch him, he'd look away and slowly sip from his beer, half a smile curving the corner of his thin lips upward. I didn't recognize him at all, and his smile didn't have the same effect on me that Brock's had.

I elbowed Elle's side. "Who's that guy?" I demanded, gesturing across the fire when he'd finally looked elsewhere. He must have still been watching me out of the corner of his eye, because his smile grew when I pointed in his direction.

Elle looked up, squinting. "That's Ezra's cousin. I think his name is Chris or something."

"He's not from around here," I pointed out, my brow furrowing as a sense of unease prickled beneath my skin.

"I know." Elle grinned, shoving me playfully with her shoulder. "I think he's here for the rodeo. Why the interest? Do you like him?"

I squinted again, trying to get a closer look. Chris was... average looking. Brown hair, average face, average build. Nothing about him stood out except maybe his clothes. He didn't dress like the guys from around here. Guys from up north wore blue jeans, plaid shirts, or camo. Chris was dressed in DC from head to toe.

I wrinkled my nose. "No, not my type—at all." I couldn't help but think of Brock. I searched the crowd, finally spotting him standing with Braden, taking slow sips of his beer while they inspected the new tires Peter O'Connor had put on his 1994 Bronco.

"Is anyone ever your type?" Elle sighed, her voice pulling my gaze away from Brock's tall form. She rolled her eyes at me and smirked; she'd caught exactly where I'd been looking. Before I could respond, Elle was nudging me again. She pointed to the back of Ezra's truck, where Krista and Joanna were trying to climb up. Ezra took pity on their level of intoxication and helped them up, shaking his head ruefully. It was common knowledge that Ezra had a thing for Krista now. It was definitely evident in the way his hand lingered on the back pocket of her shorts for a fraction of a second too long.

I remained beside Elle on the log, watching as Krista and Joanna danced in the bed of Ezra's truck. They were belting out the lyrics to Carrie Underwood's "Two Black Cadillacs", completely off key. Guys were hooting, loving the show. Elle and I looked at one another and exploded into a fit of giggles.

Then "Bow Chicka Wow Wow" by Meghan Patrick came on, and Elle's laugh faded away. She gave me a knowing look before she grabbed a hold of my hand and yanked me up. "Oh hell no, Elle!" I told her, laughing harder while I shook my head. I was smiling so much that my cheeks actually hurt.

"Yes, hell yes," Elle corrected, waving a finger at me with a devilish grin. "This is our song, and we're actually pretty good at singing it," she pointed out with a wink. I knew that Elle was drunk, and I was pretty gone myself. I knew that I was having fun and I didn't want to stop, and I'd be lying if I said I wasn't fishing for some attention from a certain dark and mysterious guy who evoked strange sensations in the pit of my belly. I caught Brock's eye as I followed Elle towards the truck. The way he looked at me set me on fire. It was so intense I had to turn away, suddenly regretting my decision to follow Elle.

It was too late to back out now; Elle wouldn't hear of it even if I wanted to. Krista and Joanna helped pull us up. "Don't you dare change that, Braden!" Elle shouted, seeing Braden moving towards the speakers. He stopped, raising his beer in surrender, a smirk upon his lips.

Elle threw her arm around my shoulders and gave me an encouraging wink before she started to sing. Elle and I were quite good at singing; we could carry a tune and harmonize together after years of singing into hair brushes in her bedroom during sleepovers. I joined in confidently, along with Krista and Joanna on my left. I had no idea what we sounded like with them, but I didn't care. Everyone else was having a blast, singing along and grinning like they were at an actual concert, not at some bush party with a bunch of drunk girls.

Brock's eyes were fixed on me the entire time, a gentle smile playing on those thick lips. His eyes made my heart rate accelerate and the butterflies take flight. Even when I closed mine, I could still feel the heat of his gaze.

We couldn't even finish singing the song before the four of us dissolved in a fit of laughter. I suddenly had to pee something fierce, and I needed a moment away from those eyes before I did something I'd undoubtedly regret in the morning—like ask Brock Miller if he wanted company in his trailer later. "I need to pee," I told Elle, squeezing her arm. "Come with me!"

"Oh, but I really love this song!" Elle pouted. I shrugged, unconcerned and climbed down off the back of the truck. I lacked grace, but at least I didn't stumble and eat dirt. I wandered towards the bush and walked a little into the bush, safe from any eyes that happened to look in my direction. Not that they'd see me anyway; it was pitch black.

I'd been peeing outside since I was a little kid; I had gotten the art down to perfection. I finished my business quickly and hiked my jeans up, buttoning them with clumsy fingers. I almost giggled, I was drunker than I thought.

The sound of twigs breaking beneath heavy footfalls made me freeze.

"Oh don't pull those up just yet, sweet cheeks," the disembodied voice said, making my blood run cold. I swallowed hard.

"Who is that? Braden...it's not funny. Don't even play." I folded my arms across my chest, trying to keep myself from trembling.

The voice laughed, and the figure stepped forward. The little bit of light that came from the fire in the clearing was almost enough to make out his features. It was the guy that had been standing across from the fire, watching me. Ezra's cousin, Chris.

Dread washed over me, and my skin erupted in goose bumps as he spoke.

"I'm clearly not Braden."

"You're also clearly not funny," I retorted, my voice sounding strong to my ears. This situation had me desperately wishing I wasn't drunk. My mind was moving slower than it usually did.

"I'm not trying to be funny," Chris said, stepping towards me. I didn't like how he was leering. I didn't like the way his tongue darted out and licked across his lips, as if he was hungry and I was food.

"Leave me alone," I ordered, about to whirl around and head back to the group. His arm shot out and grabbed my wrist painfully hard.

"Come on, don't be a cock tease. I saw the way you were looking at me. You want it." His breath smelled like whiskey and cigarettes. Chris was obviously three sheets to the wind.

"I definitely don't," I assured him, trying to wrench my wrist from his grip. He sneered, squeezing tighter and twisting. He yanked me towards him, and I collided with his chest. My head knocked against his chin and he swore before the back of his free hand struck my cheek with a staggering force. I stumbled, seeing stars. I tried to shove him away, but his hands were on me again, grabbing my body and trying to touch me in places I didn't want to be touched.

"Stop!" I tried to shout before his clammy hand clamped over my mouth, silencing my protests.

Tears blurred my vision and I panicked. My brothers and my father had all made sure to teach me a few basic self-defense moves, but it was an entirely different thing to apply what I learned when I was thirteen now that I was in a situation like this. I couldn't recall anything, but I refused to be compliant and still. I thrashed about, trying to elbow and knee him in places, trying to make enough noise that someone at the fire would hear me. But the music was too loud, people were talking and we were too far away. I had a terrible feeling that no one would come.

Chris had my body pressed against the nearest tree, pinning me to it.

In a matter of seconds, he had unbuttoned my jeans and was trying to force his hand down between my legs. I squeezed with all my might, trying to keep his intrusive fingers away. I couldn't speak with his hand clamped over my mouth, but I kept trying to scream. My voice came out in muffled whimpers. I could barely see through the tears, and I tried to shake my head and plead with him to stop. Chris laughed darkly, shoving my head back so it hit the trunk of the tree. I bit my tongue, and instantly a metallic taste filled my mouth; I knew it had to be the taste of my own blood.

Just before the hopeless desperation welled over me, I heard a sinister growling sound that made the hair on the nape of my neck stand up. All I could do was watch as a huge dog darted from the clearing and latched on to Chris's leg. Brock's dog.

Chris released me, swearing as he tried to free his leg from the dog's mouth. He kicked at it with his free foot, but the dog didn't seem to feel the impact at all. He was relentlessly shaking the limb he had. The effort of trying to kick the dog had Chris falling to the ground, but the dog didn't loosen its hold.

My hands gripped into the bark of the tree I was still leaning against and I desperately fought to keep myself from completely collapsing. I knew I should run, but my limbs wouldn't work.

CHAPTER 2

 rock

As the hours passed, the party grew, more and more people appeared in my clearing. The fire grew, the noise level grew, and my patience shrank.

I'd been back in town for a week, and this was my first "public appearance". It had been a long time since I was surrounded by so many people, and I can't say that I was comfortable about it. I was on edge, and I couldn't tell if something was actually off about tonight, or if Tessa Armstrong had just thrown me for a loop.

After our brief conversation by her truck, I'd watched as she returned to the fire and her friends and struggled to make sense of whatever the hell happened to me back there.

The last time I was around Tessa Armstrong, she'd been just shy of sixteen and definitely not the young woman who'd stood before me, amber eyes wide with want. Tessa had always been a pretty girl, but now she was stunning...

Now, I was attracted to her. It took everything I had to not walk up to her and kiss those smart lips until she melted into me. During our conversation, I found myself wanting to know exactly what sounds she'd make when pleasured.

And no good things could come from that. I knew the Armstrong family enough to know that they wouldn't let me anywhere near Tessa. Hell, they wouldn't have let me near her before the label of ex-convict befell my shoulders. I knew this with utmost sincerity: if any of her brothers knew that Tessa was in the same place as me, they'd be here to drag her home.

I needed to keep my distance.

Still, my eyes betrayed me. Time and time again, they'd float over to the fire pit just to catch a glimpse, almost like I was already addicted to the sight of her. After a while, she seemed to relax and even started to have a little fun with her best friend, my brother's girlfriend. I turned to watch her laugh, the way she tossed her head back, her slender throat just begging to be ravished.

What the hell? I shook my head, trying to clear away the overtly sexual thoughts about my former best friend's little sister from my mind.

"You know, it's not a bad thing," my brother remarked, leaning against a parked Bronco. He took a slow sip of his beer, his eyes fixed on my face. Braden looked a lot like I had at his age. Lean, mischievous, that *I-don't-give-a-fuck* attitude I used to wear like armor. He had our mom's thin lips and we both shared the Miller characteristics of dark hair, chiseled features, and a fighter's personality.

"What?" I gave Braden a warning look, hoping it would convey that he'd better not go where I thought he was going to go.

Braden's lips perked up in defiance, and I knew the little shit knew. He just didn't care. His eyes flickered to the fire, to where

Elle and Tessa were sitting. "Tessa. It's not a bad thing. She's actually really cool."

I narrowed my eyes at him. "I'm not interested." My tone booked no room for argument, and anybody else would have backed slowly away and let it be. Not Braden though; he liked to get under my skin about shit like this. His eyes came back to focus on me. They were glassy from the eight beers he'd downed.

"Yes you are. You'd be fucking nuts not to be. Half the guys around here wish they could land Tessa. She's picky though, really fucking picky. And her brothers don't exactly make things easy." One of his friends walked by, and Braden's face lit up with humor. "Fuck, you should have seen what they did to Ezra. Eh, Ezra!" Braden gripped his buddy on the shoulder, buckling over and using his grip to keep himself from falling completely forward.

Ezra looked from me to Braden, apprehension and confusion lining his face. "What?"

"When you fucked Tessa!" Braden laughed, still buckled over with laughter. A swell of jealousy unlike anything I'd experienced before almost consumed me, and I had to work extra hard to keep my face indifferent.

Ezra frowned, irritated that he was bringing it up. "Fuck off," he muttered, shrugging off Braden's hand. He continued walking over to his truck, shaking his head and sending a dark look over his shoulder.

"All three of them showed up to give him a 'talking to'. He ended up with a black eye and I think he pissed himself!"

It was really difficult to keep the smile from teasing up the corners of my lips at the mental image Braden painted, but it became easier when my thoughts focused on the fact that Ezra had fucked Tessa.

Jealousy wasn't something I was accustomed to, especially

jealousy to this extent, over a girl. Well, a woman now, but still. I didn't do jealousy.

Braden straightened up, wiping at his eyes a little to rid the moisture. He actually cried he was laughing so hard. "I don't think that'd be a problem for you though," he remarked, eyeing me warily. "You're fucking jacked."

I exhaled deeply. "I'm not into Tessa," I said, forcing each of my words to drive a point into Braden that I sincerely hoped he'd pick up.

"Whatever. Some other chick then. I highly doubt the mines in Alberta are plentiful in the pootie tang department. I know jail sure as fuck wasn't."

I stiffened at the mention of jail, and for the first time that night, Braden looked almost apologetic. He cleared his throat and took another swig of his beer. "I'm just saying, go get balls deep in some chick. I think it'd help you lighten the fuck up," Braden added, letting his hand drop with the empty beer. He avoided my gaze like the plague, focusing on the first person he saw nearby. "Yo, Peter! Come over here for a minute!"

Peter O'Connor approached, frowning when he saw Braden's boot was positioned against his tailgate. "Boots off, man. I just got that painted!"

"Yeah, yeah. Sorry." Braden waved away Peter's concern, dropping his foot. "Brock was just admiring the Bronco. He wanted to know what kind of work you've put into it."

I didn't let the surprise I felt show. I kept my mask of indifference on and looked at Peter, who seemed to cower slightly before me. It was the common reaction I got since arriving home a week ago. He swallowed hard and started rambling about all the time and money he put into the Bronco.

Normally, engine talk captured my attention. I loved vehicles and the mechanics of how they worked, but my mind was still cloudy with all the shit my brother had said, and with the fact that the last time I saw Braden and his friends, they were far too young to drive, let alone understand how to restore vehicles like the Bronco. But like me and our grandfather before us, Braden was mechanically inclined.

I felt old and out of place. Twenty-four isn't really old by any stretch, but I guess when you go through the things that I went through…it ages you. I had definitely changed a lot since the last time I was here, and maybe Braden was right. Maybe I did need to get laid. It had been a long fucking time since I felt a woman beneath me.

I exhaled, nodding every now and then to keep up the ruse of listening to Peter and Braden as they talked shop. I brought my lukewarm beer to my lips again, still feeling incredibly out of place among these people. My brother's friends, people I'd always known, but not personally. I missed my old friends, my old life. I almost missed the person I was before everything happened, but you can't go back. I could never go back to the person I was four years ago; too many fucked up things had happened since then.

After my dad died, I went a little wild. I rebelled and it was an incredible feeling of freedom, having that man that I hated with every fiber of my body dead and gone. I was free of the guilt of leaving my siblings in that house. I went through a time where I drank a lot at parties just like this one. I had fun, and I enjoyed the attention that was lavished on me from the opposite sex. I used to hook up with willing girls and not care if they developed feelings. All I wanted was to experience the freedom I never had when my old man was around.

When I wasn't partying it up with my friends or getting my old shitty Ford stuck in a mud bog, I spent a lot of time at the Armstrong's farm. I think Gordon's dad took pity on me and put me to work just to try and keep me and Gordon out of trouble. Whatever the reason for hiring me, I was grateful. It was because of that job that I was able to earn enough money working on his farm to help keep food on the table and the wolves at bay.

After applying for and getting a job in the mines, I left for Alberta. The money was decent—good enough to send back to my mom and still have a little left over for myself, and the isolation suited me. I worked there for almost two years before the arrest, working my way up from nipper to driving a haul truck.

Even before the arrest, I'd drifted away from my friends. That's what happens when you move on and pursue different interests; when you aren't forced to see each other often around town.

Gordon and Grady were still in Parry Sound, as far as I knew. I had no clue what Grady was up to; I'd yet to run into him, but I assumed Gordon was still working on his family's cattle farm. Travis, another old friend, was a top charting country singer, living most of the year in Nashville. I hadn't heard from any of them in years—but I hadn't reached out, either.

"Don't get too shitfaced, Braden. We need to be up early tomorrow," I told my brother, frowning as he cracked open his tenth beer. I needed him level headed and awake. Braden rolled his eyes at me.

"Yes, Dad. I'm aware we have to be up early tomorrow," he grumbled. I clenched my jaw, irritated at my brother. I hated when he called me Dad, even though growing up I had filled those shoes to the best of my ability for him. It was still a fucking insult.

"Don't be a dick," I shot back, my gaze drawn again to the fire and the beautiful blonde sitting before it. I forced myself to stop staring and instead looked down at my feet, where my dog was lying. Hunter's body language alarmed me. His head was raised and he was focused on the small cluster of guys hanging out by the bed of Ezra's truck.

Hunter had always been wary of strangers due to his rough start, but he seemed particularly fixated on one guy in particular. He wasn't from around here. With a town as small as Parry Sound, everyone knew everyone else and I definitely didn't know him. He looked like a cidiot, the slang term Gordon used to describe someone that was obviously from the city and most likely an idiot. He was dressed in DC from head to toe. He had a faux hawk and what I could see of his arms were covered in the kind of shitty tattoos you'd expect to get in someone's basement.

I didn't like the vibe he gave off, or the way that he loudly complained about the music selection on more than one occasion since arriving an hour ago. He was boastful, loud, and cocky as hell. I didn't trust him and it was evident that Hunter didn't trust him either.

I especially didn't like the way he was staring at Tessa. I didn't like the greasy way his gaze alternated from watching the two girls shaking their asses to Carrie Underwood to blatantly leering at Tessa.

"Braden," I said lowly, stepping closer towards my brother. "Who's the walking DC advertisement?"

Braden lifted his head, following my gaze. "I don't fucking know. He came with someone, I think."

"I don't like him," I muttered darkly, my brow furrowing.

Braden laughed. "You don't like anybody," he pointed out, shrugging off my concerns. I opened my mouth and promptly closed it when I saw Elle leading Tessa over to Ezra's truck. DC guy's eyes followed her as she climbed into the back beside the other two drunk girls.

A Miranda Lambert song came on, one I hadn't heard before, and Elle started to sing. She was at least better than the two tone-deaf girls beside her.

Tessa hesitated for several long minutes, her eyes searching the crowd for a moment until they found me. I felt my lips turning up in the tiniest hint of a smile when those amber eyes landed on me. She smiled wider in response and joined in.

And shit...she wasn't half bad. Her voice was melodious and the way that her eyelids fluttered closed, her thick lashes resting on her soft cheeks took my breath away. It was as if the music was flowing through her, and it was the most erotic thing I'd ever witnessed. My jeans started to feel extremely uncomfortable. It took everything I had in me to pry my eyes away from her, but not before Braden noticed.

He smirked knowingly, but wisely kept his mouth shut. He must have finally picked up on the fact that I'd had enough of his bullshit prodding; my patience was running out. I wanted everyone to vacate my property stat, but I knew that wasn't going to happen and the last thing I wanted was a bunch of drunken eighteen year olds on the road anyway.

I wanted her to stay. I could watch her sing up there all night.

But Tessa was done singing. She said something to Elle and jumped off the bed of the truck, landing expertly on her feet and heading towards the tree line.

Part of me wanted to follow her, but I didn't. I turned my attention back to Braden and Peter and tried to lose myself in their conversation. But then, Hunter growled lowly, threateningly. He slowly stood up on his feet, his hackles raised and his teeth showing, his eyes focused on the trees.

I frowned, glancing around. I didn't see anything out of the ordinary. People were still dancing and drinking, talking and laughing. Then it dawned on me; the guy decked out in DC clothing, the one that stuck out like a sore thumb, was nowhere to been found.

Neither was Tessa.

I set my beer down and grabbed the nearest flashlight from a stump, whistling once to Hunter. He took off like a shot, leading the way.

He was faster than me. I knew the moment when he reached them, just on the other side of the trees lining the clearing. The snapping and growling that came from Hunter told me that he'd locked in on his target. I wasn't worried; I knew that Hunter wouldn't cause any real damage, not that I'd lose any sleep over it regardless. He'd likely try to immobilize him until I got there.

I shined the flashlight towards the sounds of a scuffle and my dog's threatening growls. DC guy was on the ground, trying to shake his leg free from Hunter's mouth, swearing up a storm. I slowly raised the flashlight, searching around for Tessa.

She was leaning against the tree, her hands gripping the bark like she was afraid to let go. Her amber eyes were full of panic and tears. There was a red mark across her cheek and her lips were stained with blood.

My jaw clenched as a deep rage washed over me. It took everything I had to not give in to the very strong desire I had to teach this piece of shit a lesson. I tried to focus on controlling my breathing and very slowly lowered my flashlight back to the struggle happening on the ground.

"Hunter, stop." I knew that my voice was just as menacing as Hunter's deep throat growling had been. In a lot of ways, I was more dangerous than the dog. DC guy knew it, judging by the fear he wore on his face. Hunter immediately released his leg, but refused to stand down. He was poised, ready to jump again, his teeth bared and a low rumbling came from deep in his chest.

DC guy was struggling to get up, intent on running away. As if he'd get two feet.

"What happened here?" I asked, my jaw clenched to the point of pain.

"Your dog is fucking nuts," DC guy said, spitting on the ground just in front of my feet.

I lowered myself to a crouching position, getting right on his level and aiming the flashlight directly into his eyes. I watched them constrict until the pupils were all I could see. "I'm going to ask you one more time, what happened here?"

"Nothing, we were just having some fun and your stupid dog attacked me!" DC guy's eyes were looking anywhere but at me, a sure sign that he was lying, as if Tessa's appearance wasn't evidence enough.

"Interesting," I said slowly, shining the light on Tessa's face again. She trembled like a leaf. The sight of her like that nearly made me lose the last shred of control I had. "It doesn't look like she's a willing participant in this 'fun' at all. In fact, I'm pretty sure she came out here alone to go to the bathroom and you, being the sick and disgusting fucking pervert you are, decided she was an easy target. A drunk girl going off into the woods alone? Yeah. I could see where you'd make that assumption. I don't know where the fuck you're from, asshole, but around here? We watch out for our girls. I saw Tessa leaving alone, and I saw you watching her. Now, here we are. My dog doesn't attack people for no reason. Chances are, he got here first and saw you hurting an innocent girl, so he put a stop to it because that's what he's trained to do."

I stood up slowly, my eyes still focused on the guy's face, conveying every last bit of rage. It was inevitable that he understood my deadly threat in the words left unspoken.

"She's a fucking cock tease," the guy desperately argued. "She's been making eyes at me all night."

This was the wrong answer. I took one step towards him and grabbed him by his shirt collar, yanking him up. "You don't get to assume a girl's body is yours just because she looked in your direction, shit-stain. No means no, or weren't you taught that back home?" I tilted my head, smiling dangerously.

"I-I'm sorry!" the guy stuttered, the panic evident in his eyes.

"Come," I said, not only to my dog but to Tessa too.

There was only one time where I lost control like this; where the need to pummel every last bit of my rage onto someone had consumed me until I couldn't see straight.

And I'd snapped. I'd done exactly that, and I served time for it.

I needed to get them out of here; I needed to get around people so I didn't lose the last tether to my control and tear this fucking loser apart bit by bit.

Tessa pushed herself shakily away from the tree, following as I dragged the guy out from the bush and towards the fire. If my hands weren't full, I would have carried her. But I wasn't sure my hands could be tender enough for her anyway, not when I wanted to rip this guy apart.

People noticed us approaching, and the conversation and music were quick to die when they realized I was dragging DC guy towards the fire. Braden rushed towards me, alarm on his face. He probably thought I'd gone off the deep end again.

"Brock, what the fuck gives!" he shouted. His expression was angry but I could see the panic beneath his blue eyes. A bunch of the other guys started over, their expressions shocked and cautious. Elle was the first one to spot Tessa, trailing behind me with Hunter at her side. She let out a strangled sounding squeak and hopped down from the back of Ezra's truck, flying past Braden on clumsy legs.

"What happened!" she demanded, nearly tripping over her own feet before she reached Tessa. Braden's eyes followed, taking in her friend's appearance.

I released my hold on the guy and shoved him to the ground. I glared at every person standing around the fire, watching. "Who invited this piece of shit?"

It was so quiet, crickets likely would have been heard if my blood wasn't boiling in my ears. Ezra cleared his throat and stepped closer. "I did."

"Who is he?" I asked, almost needlessly. I didn't give a fuck who he was.

"My cousin...Chris," Ezra answered, looking briefly down to his cousin lying on the ground.

"Well, your cousin just tried to rape Tessa." I spat, my anger boiling over. Ezra looked from his cousin to Tessa, his expression astonished. He opened his mouth and closed it, searching for words he didn't have. Elle was tethered to Tessa, staring at her with a horrified expression on her face. "Get him the fuck off my property before I let the local police department deal with him, or better yet, before *I* deal with him."

Ezra's eyes were dark and angry as he set his beer down and wordlessly walked over. He forced his cousin up by the arm, his head down, ashamed and disgusted, and shoved him into the cab of his truck roughly. The doors slammed, and he took off, expertly weaving around the other vehicles.

Watching them go didn't make the rage boiling inside of me ease up. My hands were at my side, clenched into fists. I stalked back and forth like a wild animal, needing a release for all this pent up energy and anger, but hopeless at getting it out.

"Come on, Tess," Elle said, the sound of her voice breaking through the rage haze was enough to spark my attention. I looked up, watching as they walked gingerly towards their tent. Tessa's movements were pained, and that set me off more.

Braden went to follow, the arrogant smile gone from his face and a look of concern in its place. Elle shook her head at him and he stopped, his hands clenching at his sides before he turned and stomped towards me. We watched as she reached the tent, holding the flap open so Tessa could crawl in.

I put my hand up, silencing Braden before he could speak. I knew he had questions, but I couldn't talk to him yet. Every step Tessa took away from me, the worse I felt. I needed to make sure she was okay, really okay. I needed to make sure that sick fuck hadn't touched her, because if I was too late and if he touched her...there would be no stopping me. I'd be going after him and hunting him down to break every one of his fingers.

I cleared the distance with four long steps, pausing momentarily to grab a bottle of water from a cooler that happened to be in my pathway.

Elle was just about to close the flap, but before she could, I crouched down in front of the tent entrance. Hunter was by my side, his tongue rolling as if he was celebrating a successful game of fetch. To him, he had.

My eyes met Tessa's, and my hands gripped tighter to the bottle of water as I was hit with a thousand different staggering emotions. The need to protect her overwhelmed me. The desire to bring back that smile to her lips and that light behind her amber eyes that had been present just a few short hours ago tore me up inside.

"Are you okay?" I asked, swallowing hard. I was afraid to hear her answer, but at the same time...I needed to.

CHAPTER 3

essa

THE DEPTHS of his steel gray eyes swirled like the dark clouds of a thunderstorm. I could see the warmth and concern, but there were other things too, like heady emotions that I couldn't quite pin-point. The electricity between us sizzled and crackled. It reminded me of that feeling I got just before a serious thunderstorm rolled in. Even the tiny hair follicles on my arms stood up at attention.

I could easily let the world fall away and focus on whatever it was brewing between us, but his question reminded me of what had just transpired…what Brock had rescued me from.

I swallowed hard, my throat raw from crying and trying to scream. "I'm fine," I almost croaked. I dropped my eyes, feeling his unasked question burning a hole through me. "He didn't… you got there in time."

Brock nodded once, his jaw tense. He set the water bottle down inside our tent and stood up. He abruptly changed his mind and crouched down again, staring intently at me. I could feel the burning heat of his gaze, and my eyes rose involuntarily to meet his.

"I'm sorry this happened to you tonight, Tessa. You did nothing to deserve it," he told me, letting the words sink in before finally standing up and walking away.

Elle closed the flap of our tent with a shaky hand and turned to look at me, tears spilling out of her eyes. "Tessa, I am so sorry I wasn't there. I should have gone with you. I should have never let you go alone. I thought..." she trailed off, biting her bottom lip.

"It's not your fault. Normally stuff like that doesn't happen around here." It felt as if each of my limbs weighed a thousand pounds. I was heavy and groggy, and I realized I had yet to process the severity of what had almost happened.

Elle crawled up beside me and wrapped her arms around me, sobbing against my shoulder. "I'm so glad he didn't; I'm so glad you're okay, Tessa. I'm so glad Brock was there. I can't believe I didn't notice that creep following you. I suck as a best friend."

I patted her shoulder wordlessly, too spent to even consider thinking of a response.

I AWOKE EARLY the next morning. My body was still sore and my left eye felt puffy, as if the skin beneath it was swollen. I reached a hand up tentatively and touched it. It was definitely swollen, and it hurt.

Fresh tears flowed down my cheeks. Even though Chris hadn't gotten as far as he could have, I still felt violated and disgusting. I crawled out from our tent, leaving a sleeping Elle to softly snore on her own.

The sun hadn't quite risen yet. It was still early...it probably wasn't even seven o'clock yet. Nobody else seemed to be awake. The fire pit was still smoking a little from last night's fire, and there were beer bottles scattered around the clearing.

I walked on shaky legs to my truck, my body still very sore from trying to fight off Chris's unwanted advances. I walked up and glanced in the square side mirror.

I looked like hell. My hair had mostly fallen out from its braid, and was a tangled mess around my face. My left eye was almost completely swollen shut and there was dried blood in the corners of my mouth, likely from when I bit down on my tongue. I put a fist to my mouth, fresh tears spilling out from my eyes.

There was no way I could go home like this. My dad and my brothers would flip. The 'I told you so' speech would come, along with a severe grounding for disobeying my father's rules. He thought I was at Elle's house for the night; he didn't think I was going to a bush party where boys would be present.

"Tessa?"

I whirled around at the sound of that deep voice. Brock stood at the front of my truck, his dog at his feet. In behind him, his trailer door stood open. He must have seen me from inside, standing here like an idiot crying. I desperately tried to wipe the tears away. The last thing I needed was Brock Miller's pity. "What?"

He watched me for a moment, then sighed and cautiously approached me. He kept his eyes on me the whole time, looking straight into mine as if I was a deer and he was trying not to startle me. "It's okay for you not to be fine. You know that, right? What happened last night was traumatic. You're allowed to feel scared."

"Thanks for your permission," I retorted, averting my eyes so Brock wouldn't see how profoundly his words affected me. I took a shaky breath.

"You're welcome," Brock said, fighting a smile.

"I'm not scared," I told him, crossing my arms defiantly. And I wasn't scared, at least...not anymore. I acknowledged the terrible situation and was thankful that Brock and his dog had shown up in time. I was angry at myself for having gotten drunk in the first place. I was angry that it happened at all. "I'm pissed."

The corner of Brock's mouth perked up. "I bet you are."

I paused, listening to the chorus of snoring coming from the tents around us. I wrung my hands, uncomfortable. I couldn't meet his intense gaze. He seemed to be waiting for me to say something. "Thanks...for, you know..." I finally said, looking down at the German shepherd mix at his heel. The dog tilted his head and wagged his tail.

"Don't mention it," Brock replied, his eyes serious and his jaw clenching as if the memory left a bad taste in his mouth.

I averted my eyes and pursed my lips, drawing in a deep breath through my nostrils. I felt Brock move closer and my heart started to beat frantically.

He stopped less than a foot away, his large hand gently tipping my chin up so he could inspect my face. I knew what he was seeing: the swollen eye, the dried blood caked around my lips, the foolish, drunk girl he'd had to rescue. His jaw clenched and he sighed heavily.

"Come with me," he said, nodding back towards his trailer. "I have something that will help bring down the swelling."

"What?" I was fighting with everything I had to appear unaffected by his touch, but my heart felt like it was about to take flight from my chest at any given moment.

Brock smiled morosely. "I'm no stranger to black eyes, Tessa. Let me help you."

I swallowed hard, nodding once. It was difficult to ignore just how much I liked how he said my name. He spoke it like a caress.

His hand dropped from my chin, breaking me from my thoughts. He led the way back to his trailer and I followed stiffly, bewildered at what was transpiring between us... at least on my end.

The trailer was tiny, but it wasn't cramped. There weren't enough personal items inside for it to feel cramped. I could see a bedroom towards the left, just past the tiny kitchen. His bed was left unmade, his covers carelessly tossed aside, revealing the white sheet beneath. There was a thin door that likely led to the bathroom, and directly to my right was a kitchen table with bench seats that probably doubled as a bed or sofa, true to trailer nature.

Brock gestured for me to sit down at the table and opened one of the storage drawers. He pulled out a clean cloth and gently ran it under the tap. He looked over his shoulder, giving me a small half smile. He seemed a little uncomfortable with me in his space—or maybe with me in general. I flushed, stupidly wondering if his discomfort came from him feeling what I felt.

He walked over, holding the cloth in his hand, and crouched between my legs. My heart jumped in my chest again, just after it had started to settle. The way those steel coloured eyes pierced through me made me feel short of breath. It was the strangest thing...I could have sworn he felt it too. The air between us shifted, becoming denser and warmer as Brock gently wiped at my face, cleaning the blood away. His hands were gentle and definitely not the hands I remembered clenched in anger from last night, the hands that I knew were capable of causing serious damage.

Unable to take the intensity behind his gaze a moment longer, my eyes dropped down to look at those tender hands.

"What happened?" I demanded, noticing the bruising and cuts on his knuckles.

"Don't worry about that," he said, his expression closing off immediately. He stood up quickly, done with washing the blood away, and went back to the kitchen sink. He ran the cloth under it again, this time turning on only the cold water. Then he reached into the ice box in his tiny refrigerator, grabbing a bag of frozen peas. He put the cloth around it and returned, pressing it against my swollen eye firmly.

It was so cold that it hurt, and I instantly tried to wince away from the pressure.

"Don't move," Brock instructed. His voice was gentle again. "I know it's cold, but it'll bring the swelling down."

I bit my lip and tried to focus on breathing. "So...what brings you back to town?" I asked, trying to divert my attention away from the ice cold compress Brock was pressing to my face.

"Lots of things," Brock replied evasively. I blinked up at him with my good eye, unimpressed with his answer. The corners of his lips perked up. "I'm here to build a cabin. I told you that."

"Oh, right. I guess I forgot." I exhaled. The silence stretched on between us, and I bit the inside of my cheek to prevent myself from asking further stupid questions. Brock clearly didn't want to talk to me.

"My mom is sick," he said after several long minutes, when I'd finally given up on making small talk. "She's dying...doesn't have much time left."

"Oh, I'm sorry to hear that..." I muttered, looking back up at him. His expression was still guarded, his jaw tense.

"Yeah, well. That's life—it eventually ends." Brock said gruffly. He pulled the cold compress away for a moment, assessing the swelling. "The swelling is beginning to go down. Another ten minutes with this on and it should almost be as right as rain," he added, pressing it back.

"Thanks," I whispered.

"Do you think you can hold it there? I'm going to make some coffee."

"Yeah, sure," I said quickly, fumbling for the ice pack. My hand brushed against his, and the nerves in my fingertips danced. Goose bumps rose on my arm and I prayed that Brock didn't see them. I watched with my uncovered eye as Brock took one step away from me, ending up right at the counter of his tiny kitchen. He was so tall that his head almost touched the ceiling of the trailer, and he had to duck to avoid hitting the light.

I frowned, trying to figure out exactly what it was about this guy that had me all twisted and clumsy. I didn't do butterflies, usually. Not to this extent. While I daydreamed about the whole falling in love thing, I didn't fall easily and I never had. I crushed on guys, I'd kissed a few and slept with one, but I didn't react like this. That intense, all-consuming burning need to be with someone never came over me like it was now as I sat in Brock's tiny trailer with a bag of frozen peas pressed against my battered face.

The circumstances for this were not ideal. I'd been attacked just last night, for Christ's sake. But my body was still reacting to Brock's mere presence, and I was beginning to panic about it.

"Do you want some? It's instant," Brock added, looking back over his shoulder at me, catching me blatantly staring at him. He grinned, and a dimple appeared in the left corner of his lip. His dark eyes seemed to sparkle. This was a smile that transformed his entire face, making him look playful and approachable and even more desirable than before. This was a smile that knocked the wind out of me.

"Want some what? What's instant?" I blinked, feeling dazed.

"Coffee..." he said slowly. He frowned and assessed me carefully. "Did you hit your head last night? You might have a concussion."

I flushed a deep shade of red. I'd had concussions before, and this definitely wasn't a concussion. "No, I'm fine. I'm just tired. I should go."

Brock tilted his head, considering me. His thick, dark hair fell onto his forehead, and I wanted to get up and run my hands through it. "I don't know if you should drive. I'm still not entirely positive that you don't have a concussion."

"I don't," I sighed, figuring he was probably right about the driving thing. My head did feel like a jack hammer had done a number on it. "I'll wake up Elle."

Setting the bag of peas down on the table, I stood up. I blinked gingerly, surprised that my eye felt better already; less swollen.

"Here, have some of these," Brock said, handing me a bottle of extra strength Advil and a bottle of water. I took two and held out the pill bottle for him to take. His fingers brushed against mine again, an electric shock running up the length of my arm. All I could do was stare.

His hand was large and rough; a man's working hands. Hands had never been my thing, but suddenly I found myself reverently wishing these particular hands would touch me. If I was primed from such a casual brush of his skin against mine, I couldn't help but wonder what would happen if he actually touched me.

I swallowed hard, looking up at him again. Brock's eyes were focused on my face, on my lips. My heart was rattling around in my chest. I stepped back, overwhelmed by the intensity behind his gaze. I needed space. I needed to breathe. "Thanks. For, you know…"

"My pleasure," he replied, giving me half a smile.

I pretty much bolted out of Brock's trailer, away from the heavy air and those intense eyes, away from my stupid, girlish response to him.

When I heard a rustling coming from the tents, I turned to look. Elle was unzipping the flap and spilling out, her eyes frantically looking for me. When she finally saw me, she visibly relaxed. She crawled the rest of the way out of the tent as I approached.

I watched her expression change from relaxed to on edge as she took in my face. "You look better than you did last night. It's still a little swollen though," she remarked, touching my chin and turning my face to look at my cheek and eye. Looking beyond me, her eyes widened a little. "Brock," she said in greeting.

I turned, seeing him a few paces behind me. I hadn't even realized he'd followed me out from the trailer. "Morning." He said, eyes moving from Elle to rest on me.

"Could you tell Braden when he wakes up that I've taken Tessa back to my place to get cleaned up? She's got a show this afternoon and absolutely cannot look like this. I need to break out my best makeup for this job," Elle added, pursing her lips thoughtfully as she studied me.

I groaned, nearly forgetting about the horse show entirely. Every year, I entered the Show Jumper competition with my horse, Scared Spirit. Spirit was a fantastic jumper, and I supposed I was pretty talented too.

Normally, I loved feeling Spirit's powerful body beneath my thighs as we flew over jumps. We usually placed in the top three. Today, jumping was the last thing I wanted to do. I was still shaky from the close encounter last night. Plus, I knew jumping would mean that I'd just have to see my father even sooner. It was tradition for him to help me load up Spirit and accompany me to the show.

Brock focused on my face again and he nodded once. "Yeah, I'll tell him."

***

ELLE DROVE my truck to her place and forced me to sit down on her bed with a cold compress against my cheek and eye for half an hour. Then I showered and got dressed in clean clothes I'd packed the night before. I came back into her room after leaving the bathroom, spotting her fussing over the massive amounts of makeup on her vanity desk.

"Sit," she demanded, pointing at the velvet chair. I obeyed, my feet carrying me across the room. I sat heavily, a sigh escaping my lips. "Don't furrow your brow," Elle scolded, shaking her head. She set to work, adding foundation and contouring. Finally, she blended it all together and added a little mascara and eyeliner. Elle's makeup skills hid the bruising on my cheek completely, and the end result was me looking normal, aside from a hint of swelling.

I pressed a finger against the skin nervously, worried that last night would be written all over my face and that my Dad would just know. I was afraid to go home; afraid to face him. Elle spotted me fretting.

"You can just tell your dad that your allergies are bothering you," she said. "Or, you know…you could tell him the truth."

I frowned at her. "Right, so I can get grounded for the entire duration of summer? Thanks, but no thanks."

"I highly doubt your father will ground you for being attacked," Elle huffed, crossing her arms like a sulking toddler.

"No, but he'd ground me for lying about where I was last night, and for going to an unsupervised party with alcohol and boys," I retorted.

"Woah, woah, woah!" a voice from the doorway startled us both and we jumped. Elle's mother, Sue, was standing in the doorway. The expression on her face clearly said that we were busted.

I swallowed hard, looking back to Elle with a panicked look on my face. She rolled her eyes. "Don't worry about it, Mom. It's under control."

Sue Thompson was not going to let it rest. She crossed her arms and leaned against the doorway, fixing us both with her no bullshit mom-stare that made me want to confess everything. I wondered if my mom would have had that ability if she was still alive.

"What happened last night, girls?" Beneath the calm, I knew she was vibrating with anger. Elle was her only daughter, and she was fiercely protective of her. By proxy, and because I'd been her best friend's daughter, she was equally as protective of me.

Elle sighed heavily, not sensing an out either. "Well, you know how I said we were going to the bush to camp and stuff, right?" she asked. Sue nodded, pursing her lips. Sue knew that we drank and hung out with friends, but in her words, she'd rather know where we were, and she'd rather us know that we could call her in heartbeat. It wasn't her style to be completely clueless to what we were doing, and she'd told us on more than one occasion that what little trouble we got into would never amount to the stuff that she used to do with my mom.

"Go on." Sue gestured with a wave of her hand, growing impatient.

"Well, Ezra invited his cousin and his cousin was a dirt bag who followed Tessa into the woods when she went to pee. And he attacked her but –"

"He did what!" Sue very rarely raised her voice, only right now, she was definitely yelling. She pushed off the door and came towards us, her eyes searching mine. "Why didn't you call me?" she asked Elle accusingly.

"Because nothing really happened. He just hurt her a little –"

"He just hurt her a little," Sue repeated darkly, glaring at Elle. "Eleanor Reese Thompson, I expect better from you." She tipped my chin up, examining me.

"He didn't hurt me like that," I rushed to say. "He was going to, but Braden's brother got there in time and stopped it."

Sue's eyes locked on mine. "Brock Miller was there?" I nodded, my throat dry and scratchy. "And he stopped anything from happening to you? What did he do to the guy?"

"Don't worry, Mom. He didn't do anything, but you could tell he wanted to. He just made Ezra get him off the property before he called the police."

Sue was worrying her lip, probably thinking the same thing

that I was thinking. If Bill Armstrong ever found out about this, I'd be grounded forever. He likely wouldn't let me leave for college with Elle, and Sue knew how much I wanted to go to college. She knew how desperately I wanted independence. She'd been arguing with Dad herself for years about letting me have a little more freedom.

"What did the guy do to you, Tessa?" Sue was at war with herself.

"He just...tried to..." It was difficult to talk with the lump in my throat. I swallowed, trying to break it up. "He hit me when I struggled, and he tried to touch me, but before he could...Brock got there in time. I'm fine, really. He just... scared me."

Admitting that Chris had scared me made me feel weak; it made me want to curl up in a ball and cry. It made me want to run to my mother for comfort. But I didn't have a mother. She was dead.

Sue sensed what I needed, and she wrapped her arms around me tightly, pulling me to her chest. Her hand came up to hold the back of my head. "Oh, honey, it's alright. It'll be okay. You're okay," she said soothingly.

I let her hug me, fighting the urge to cry and break down. "I know, I'll be fine. I'm okay," I repeated, pulling away after several moments. "But if I don't get home soon, I'm going to be late for the show."

Sue had tears in her eyes. She wiped them away with the back of her hand and nodded. Then her expression became stern as she looked from Elle to me. "Next time anything happens, you call me. Got it? I don't care if it's 3 o'clock in the morning, I don't care if you're drunk and I don't care how far I have to drive. You call me."

"Yes, ma'am," Elle and I said in unison, lowering our eyes with shame at the disappointment in her voice.

"Are you going to tell Tessa's dad?" Elle asked, biting her lip.

Her mother sighed heavily and gave me a small, sad smile. "I'm sure that'd cause more trouble than it's worth."

HALF AN HOUR LATER, I finally headed home. After the intense heart to heart in Elle's room, Sue had forced me to eat breakfast at the Thompson house. She wouldn't let me leave until she saw that I'd eaten. I pulled into my long driveway and immediately caught sight of my dad's red F-450 Super Duty parked near the barn. The horse trailer was hitched up to it, but my dad was nowhere in sight.

I exhaled and slammed the driver's door before I cautiously walked into the barn. The scent of horses, hay and leather greeted me. To me, it smelled like home, like comfort.

The barn had eight stalls on either side. Twelve were empty and had been for a long time. When my mother was alive, each stall had a horse. She was a champion show jumper, but her passion was rehabilitating and rescuing mistreated thoroughbreds. I was told that she had a way with horses; that she knew how to fix their broken spirits and mend their tattered hearts. She could make them trust humans again.

Sue had told me these stories, and the rest of the stories I knew about my mom. My father very rarely spoke about her; he almost never walked down memory lane. It used to make me angry, my father's reluctance to share anything about my mother with me. Now, I was old enough to understand just how much he missed her. I was old enough to realize that nothing had filled the void that she'd left when she died, and talking about her was painful for my dad.

When Scared Spirit caught sight of me approaching, he put his face over the stall door and whinnied. I stroked his velvety nose and rested my head against his, my nerves instantly easing in his presence.

Spirit was an eight year old palomino thoroughbred, the son of Artic Wind, who was my mother's competition horse. They had been champion show jumpers. Spirit was the last foal sired by Artic Wind before he died. Aside from the Blazer I'd been born in, Spirit was the last thing and closest connection I had to my mother. He was also an incredibly intuitive horse. When I rode him...I felt as if he was an extension of me, or maybe that I was an extension of him.

Sometimes when I was jumping, I could almost feel my mother watching and smiling down on me. I wondered if she and I would have had the kind of relationship where I could tell her anything, like Elle and Sue.

I couldn't help the tear that escaped, trailing down my cheek and absorbing into Spirit's silky coat. Now was one of those times where I could really use my mother. All I had were pictures and the stories that Sue had told me.

"Everything okay, Tessa?" Dad asked, setting a bucket of grain down and effectively startling me. I blinked away the tears, conscious of the makeup on my face.

"Yeah...I was just thinking about Mom," I responded quietly, knowing that my father wouldn't push or pry if I was at least partially honest.

He exhaled deeply, nodding and turning his gaze to Spirit. He put his hands in his pockets, leaning back on his heels. "Your mother would have been so proud of you, Tessa," he told me, his voice heavy with emotion that I could tell he was desperately trying to keep in check.

"Yeah, well..." I said, straightening my shoulders and pasting on what I hoped was a convincing smile. I didn't want to make my dad sad anymore by forcing him to open up about the woman I never really got a chance to know. "We've got to get Spirit to the track," I said instead.

My dad wasn't the only one that had difficulty opening up.

ON MY DRIVE home from Elle's house, I worried that I would give a lousy performance during the show. My mind was so occupied by everything that had happened during the past eighteen hours. Seeing Brock, my reaction to him, the party, Chris, and finally my thoughts came full circle and landed on Brock again. Even with Brock nowhere near me, the butterflies fluttered around in my stomach at every thought of him. My skin remembered every subtle brush of his, and my lungs still fought for air just as desperately as they struggled when he was actually standing in front of me. It was ridiculous.

I figured it would be impossible to disconnect from those thoughts and focus on the show, but as soon as I stepped into that ring, everything else fell away so that it was just Spirit and me.

I was dressed in my best riding attire. I wore white breeches and a white collared fitted shirt with a beautiful black coat that my brothers had bought me last year for my birthday. My black field boots were shiny and my long, honey blonde hair was tightly braided to my skull and pinned up beneath a hairnet and my equestrian helmet. The black accents complemented the golden coat of my horse.

The jump course was decorated in flowers and foliage by the Agricultural Society. They'd really outdone themselves this year, investing more money into the event than any of the years before. The stands that lined the ring looked jam-packed full of people; the entire town seemed to be there.

Stuff like that used to make me nervous. Now, it just added to the thrill. I closed my eyes, focusing my energy on the feeling of Spirit beneath me. I leaned forward, stroking his long lean neck as we waited for the previous contestant to finish jumping. It was Melanie Clayton. She was a few years older than me, and she was good.

I was better though. Or maybe it was Spirit. Spirit was a better horse; he rarely ever clipped the poles.

"Remarkable jumping from Melanie Clayton and Thunder Crush! Now let's give a warm welcome to contestant number 13, Tessa Armstrong, riding Scared Spirit!" The announcer's voice rang throughout the track, and Spirit and I took off.

I lost myself completely to the sensation of flying over those jumps, focusing on the sound of Spirit's hooves instead of the crowd and the announcer. I seemed to be able to control Spirit with my mind, merely thinking of the direction to change and adding the faintest touch to get him to respond.

Our timing was perfect, and Spirit's hooves didn't knock any poles off. The judges gave me a near perfect score, topping Melanie Clayton's and pushing me to the number one place.

With my breathing labored, I rode Spirit out of the ring. Melanie was scowling, unimpressed with the fact that I'd beat her again. "They might as well just give you the first place ribbon," she snarled, the distain evident in her voice.

I forced a smile. "Who knows, maybe the next contestant will knock me out of first place," I responded, hopping down from my saddle.

"Here's hoping." Melanie snorted, turning around and stalking off. She passed Elle as she headed towards me, and my best friend gave her a foul look.

"God I hate her," she said to me, rolling her eyes. She didn't seem to care that Melanie was still within earshot. She threw her arms around me, hugging me tightly. "You did awesome out there, as always! First place for sure. When do you find out?"

"In fifteen minutes." I shrugged. "Soon as this guy finishes and they tally up the scores to see who won."

"You." Elle grinned. "After you accept your sixth first place ribbon, we're hanging out! Travis Channing is playing tonight and I've got tickets!"

Travis Channing was a twenty-four year old local guy who'd

blown up the country music industry after winning a televised talent show. Travis had gone to school with Gordon and Brock —they'd all been friends, for that matter. I could remember him hanging around on our wraparound porch with them when I was a kid.

"With you?" I arched a brow pointedly. Elle bit her lip, looking very much like she had a secret that she was trying to keep from me. "Elle, don't bullshit me. You know I can tell when you're lying."

"Well…" Elle exhaled, her lips spreading into an excited smile. "It may be me and just a few other people, but it's not like we're going together or anything!" she hurried to explain.

"Like who?" As soon as the question spilled from my lips, I knew the answer.

"Oh you know, the gang. Braden…and Brock," Elle answered, her response sounding more like a question.

"First of all, no. My dad's around here somewhere," I hissed. "Second, I'm not even dressed to hang out."

"We'll go back to your place so you can shower and change," Elle pleaded, her eyes wide. "Please, please, please, please, please!"

"Please what?" My dad's voice startled us both, and we glanced towards him as he approached as if we'd been caught with our hands in the cookie jar before dinner.

"I was just begging Tess to come to the Travis Channing concert tonight," Elle responded easily. "You remember Travis Channing, don't you, Mr. Armstrong? I already have the tickets and my mom won't let me go alone."

"I told you a thousand times, Elle. Call me Bill," my dad said, scratching at his beard as he considered the question. "Now, Tess…you've got some chores to do at home. You're going to need to tend to Spirit and feed the rest of the horses…"

I perked up, thankful that my father's sense of stern responsibility was going to save me from seeing Brock Miller again. I didn't exactly want to be around him right now, not after last night and certainly not when I didn't know how to act or feel around him.

"But that shouldn't take you long, and you're welcome to meet up with Elle again after supper," Dad finished.

"Maybe for supper? And I'll help Tess with the horse stuff?" Elle bartered. My dad looked at her and laughed, shaking his head. She had him wrapped around her finger. My dad was her surrogate father in the same way that her mom was my surrogate mother.

"You're just like your mama, Elle," he told her, putting his hand on her shoulder and squeezing briefly. "You could talk a fish into buying water."

I swallowed my jealousy. Just once, I'd like to hear my dad say that to me with as much comfort and ease. I knew I looked like her; I had her honey blonde hair and her amber eyes. I knew we were similar in a lot of ways; Sue had made sure to tell me that, but my dad's pain over losing her kept him from actually verbalizing the similarities. Today was the first time he'd ever mentioned she'd be proud of me. I understood it, but it still sucked.

"Fine, I'll go," I relented, rolling my eyes.

CHAPTER 4

rock

WHEN I WAS SEVENTEEN, my grandpa on my dad's side died and he left each of my siblings and me a fair bit of land just on the outskirts of Parry Sound. He'd owned 180 acres near a small lake. The terms of Grandpa Miller's will were that the land would be held in trust until we each turned twenty-one. Then, we would be free to do what we wished.

I was still in jail when I turned twenty-one, and then I immediately left for Alberta to reclaim my job and work. I was focused on helping my mom pay back the debt my legal fees had accumulated.

A year ago, I started to think about the property again. The lake was probably where the majority of my good childhood memories took place. My dad had hated it – or maybe he hated my grandpa – and refused to go anywhere near it. It was a safe haven from him. We'd spend as much time as we could there, camping and fishing with Grandpa. He had taught us about nature and the balance.

I started to daydream about going home and building something on my slice of land. I wasn't sure if I wanted to come back permanently, but building something wouldn't hurt regardless. I'd have somewhere to stay, somewhere to escape to when I wanted to visit, but didn't want to stay in that god forsaken town or house.

With the number of hours I worked, it hadn't taken me long at all to pay off the debts. I'd even had a nice cushion saved up, even after sending money home every month to help my family.

They were all pressuring me to come home. This wasn't anything new; Mom was the main supporter of the *Come Home Cause*, but whenever I talked to Becky and Braden, they said the same thing: *You should come home*. Only six months ago, those calls took on a more desperate tone.

One night a little over a month ago, after a particularly grueling day at work, I was in my tiny kitchen heating up a frozen dinner when my phone rang. There was no reception in the makeshift camp town, and I had to depend on the landline to stay in touch with my family. I didn't mind it one bit, but the shrill sound of the phone ringing seemed ominous that night instead of welcoming.

"Hello?" I'd left my dinner abandoned on the counter.

"Brock?" It was Mom. She usually called me twice a week and this was her fifth time. Her voice sounded strange, heavy and weighted with something I couldn't quite put my finger on.

"Hi, Mom. What's up?" I'd asked distractedly, heading back to the counter to resume my task at hand.

"Honey, I'm sick," she had said, her voice breaking over the line.

"What do you mean you're sick?" I demanded, slowly setting the frozen dinner package back down on the counter. In my heart of hearts, I knew that she wasn't talking about having a cold or a flu.

"I have pancreatic cancer," she replied, emotion making her choke on the words. "I'm dying, Brock."

"No." I shook my head indignantly, the words chilling me to the bone and cutting into my heart, like a knife twisting into the flesh. I paced the small shack of a house I'd called home for the last two years, tugging at my hair with my free hand. Hunter whimpered at my feet, reacting to the panicked energy rolling off me in waves. "You can get treatment, can't you? You can beat this. You need to beat this...for Becky, Braden and Aiden. For me too."

Even though I couldn't see her, I knew she was shaking her head. I knew she was crying. She took a shuddering breath. "It's too late, Brock. It's stage four. The doctors have given me three to six months."

"What about chemotherapy?" I pleaded, sinking into the plaid sofa as the energy and will left my limbs. I folded over, hoping to alleviate some of the pain.

"The treatments would only make what little time I have left even more unbearable. I'll get sick, I'll lose my hair –"

"You're concerned with getting sick and losing your hair? Jesus Christ, Mom, you're already sick! You're dying! Aren't you concerned with that?" I interrupted. My words were angry and sharp.

I heard her draw in a shaky breath. "I don't want Aiden to remember me like that...so sick that I turn into a skeleton and all my hair falls out. He won't recognize me, Brock. It will kill me faster to inflict that kind of pain on him."

"So you're just going to give up. You're not even going to fight." The accusation that laced my words was right there, and I knew she heard it. I knew she understood its meaning.

"I regret a lot of things in this life, Brock...but opting to live out my remaining days without worrying about hospital appointments, without fading away to nothing before my loved ones' eyes...that's not one of them," Mom said heavily. "No mother wants to leave her children. I'm so goddamn angry about this, but I want to enjoy what little time I have left. I need you to come home."

So, I took a leave of absence from work and came back.

And I still wasn't ready to face her, to go to the house I'd grown up in, which was why I was throwing every goddamn thing I had into the cabin I was building on my land. I wasn't really planning on staying indefinitely; I just needed to do something, anything that wasn't watching my mom die. Building the cabin I'd been thinking about building for years, seemed like a good thing to do with my time.

Grady McDonnell was over with his portable sawmill, and we were milling all the trees we'd cut down the week before. We still had a lot of work to do over the summer and into the fall, clearing a few of the trees to allow for a view of the lake from the porch. It'd also give me a pathway down to the water.

Braden was helping, partly because I'd told him I wasn't going to let him throw a party on my land unless he did, but also because Braden needed this distraction every bit as much as I needed it.

He was a lot like me. We didn't like to face our problems or talk about the shit that was bugging us. We liked to throw ourselves into distractions, into work. Because he was so much like me, I didn't have to worry about him asking what the fuck my deal was.

Braden didn't ask because he was avoiding the house, too. He was drinking more and attempting to steel himself for the inevitable. We both were. We knew it was going to happen, and we were powerless to stop it. What else could we do?

Becky was the only one of us that actually faced her problems head on, a change that came forth after she'd nearly lost her son. I knew she was livid with me for not going to the house yet. Mom was getting sicker, deteriorating faster, and I'd been dodging her calls.

I was an asshole.

"I need a break and a beer," Braden said, his forehead dripping with sweat. "Do you want one, Grady?"

Grady looked at the huge pile of freshly milled lumber. We'd been going at it hard all morning, my rage from not only my mom's situation but from what had nearly happened to Tessa Armstrong under my watch fueling me.

Another three or four days at this rate and we'd be done ahead of schedule, and I'd have a nice view down the rocky hillside to the lake from the deck.

"I don't normally drink on the job," Grady said apprehensively, looking from the beautifully milled wood pile to the cold Mill Street beer Braden clenched in his hand.

"Go for it," I told him. "This isn't a formal job anyway," I reminded him. Grady and I had struck a deal. I would work for free, and he would give me a wickedly cheap discount. He was also welcome to take all the leftover wood for other projects.

Braden grinned, thrusting a beer into Grady's outstretched hand. "See? Boss man said it was fine." Without asking, he threw one at me. I cracked the cap and took a long swig.

I was hot too, and a break sounded good. I'd long since ditched my sweat soaked t-shirt, but the sun was beating down on us all and the heat was relentless. The condensation rolling off the bottle hit my chest and it cooled me a fraction as it slid down my throat.

"Are you going to the concert tonight?" Grady asked, making conversation. He was sitting down on the wood pile, stretching out his legs.

"What concert?" My brow furrowed.

"Travis is back in town, and he'll be performing at the fairgrounds tonight," Grady explained.

"No shit?" I said thoughtfully, taking another swig from my

beer. I hadn't seen Travis in years, and I'd never heard him perform before. I'd only caught a few of his songs on the radio; there weren't many decent radio stations near the mines, and the ones we did get didn't play newer music.

"I'm going. Elle scored tickets," Braden said. He paused to drink some more beer. "Tessa will be there too," he added with a smirk.

I narrowed my eyes at him in warning. The last thing I needed was for Grady McDonnell to get the wrong idea and go running back to the Armstrong brothers. My life was complicated enough.

"You interested in Tessa?" Grady asked, picking up on Braden's not-so-subtle hint. His dark eyes fixed on my face as he waited for my response. I could have decked my brother then and there.

"No," I answered, keeping my tone neutral and my expression indifferent. "Braden's just on a mission to set up his girlfriend's best friend with someone. I'm definitely not interested."

"Well, you should come tonight anyway. Gordon's gonna be there; the whole gang will be. There's a huge after-party at the Clayton's barn."

"Yeah, you could go get your licking early from Gordon, then Tessa will be free game!" Braden said, cackling at his own joke.

I glared at him. "Seriously, Braden. Shut the fuck up." I shook my head, my irritation at my brother growing tenfold.

Grady grinned, amused by the situation. "Well, either way. Gordon runs his own construction company now; has a few crew members. They build houses and cottages. He'd give you a fair price on building the cabin."

"I'll think about it," I said distractedly.

SHOWERING in my tiny trailer wasn't exactly easy at my height. I was six feet, and I had to crouch down in order for the water to hit my hair. The pressure was shit too, but the trailer served its purpose as a temporary home until I could get the cabin set up. It was definitely a good motivator, if anything.

I knew I'd be welcome to shower at my mom's house, where Becky and Braden still lived, but that would mean going there and facing her. So I sucked it up, crouching beneath the slow stream of water and washing away the hard day of work.

I still hadn't decided on whether I wanted to go to the concert. On one hand, it'd be nice to see everyone again. On the other, I was having a goddamn difficult time getting Tessa out of my head.

My thoughts drifted back to earlier that day, when I saw Tessa leaving her tent through the tiny window over my kitchen sink.

I was about to make myself a cup of coffee, but my hands had stilled, and I found myself watching her for a few moments...just to make sure she was okay. She walked gingerly towards her truck and paused with her hand on the door as if she was considering leaving. She caught sight of her reflection in the mirror and her fist went up to her mouth, tears spilling from those amber eyes. The sight of those tears prompted a lot of heavy emotions in me; anger, guilt, compassion...and something strong and potent that I was afraid to label.

It was a vulnerable moment that I knew she hadn't meant for me, or anyone for that matter, to witness. The urge to fix things took over and before I could talk myself out of it, I was leaving the safety of my trailer and walking towards her.

She hadn't liked that I'd seen her tears, and her sass and attitude towards me when I told her she had a right to feel scared, had me smiling when I shouldn't. *She* had me smiling, and I hadn't smiled like that in years.

Then there was whatever the hell happened in my trailer

when I was trying to tend to her wounds. When she looked up at me and bit her lip, the desire was so potent it took everything I had to not kiss her, although I knew I had several opportunities. Any time our skin touched, she'd inhale sharply. I could practically see her pulse jumping the same way mine was.

She wanted me too.

It was the strangest feeling, watching the tires of her old Blazer spin out as my brother's girlfriend peeled out of the clearing. Normally, I'd be pissed that Elle had torn up the grass, but the only emotion that passed over me was regret. Regret to see Tessa go, regret that she'd been hurt last night and regret that I didn't ask her for her number.

But acting on my strong feelings of desire and even just asking for her number would have been a dick move. She'd been attacked the night before, and having some guy hit on her was probably the farthest thing from her mind. But oh, how I'd wanted to.

The need to get to know this girl was alarming. The desire to be with her was staggering. It was almost acutely painful.

The cold water finally roused me from my thoughts and I finished washing the soap away before turning it off. Another downside to trailer life was that the hot water tank was ridiculously small.

I left the small bathroom, wrapping a towel around my waist, and made my way to the bedroom. My clothes were still tucked away in suitcases. There was no sense in unpacking; I had nowhere to put it anyway. I pulled out a pair of well-worn jeans, a white t-shirt and a plaid button up shirt. It was still warm out, although as soon as the sun faded, it would get chilly.

"What the fuck am I doing?" I muttered, staring at the clothes I'd laid out on my bed. Was I actually considering going to this concert? Was I actually considering putting myself right in front of temptation again? Temptation in the form of someone completely off limits?

But what if he's there? I thought, thinking about that piece of shit asshole that had attacked Tessa last night.

My hands clenched into fists with aggravation. I felt responsible for it, in a way. If only I'd trusted my instincts about that guy. If only I'd trusted Hunter's instincts about him. Hell, if only I had allowed myself to do the one thing I desperately wanted to do, talk to her. Claim her as mine. She would have never been put in that situation. I could have protected her better if I wasn't so busy trying to ignore her existence.

Hunter whimpered from his spot beneath the kitchen table, almost encouraging me with those yellow eyes.

"Fuck it," I sighed, tearing off the towel and stepping into a clean pair of boxer briefs. I dressed quickly, pulling my jeans on and sliding into my boots. I pulled my shirt over my head as I walked out the door. Hunter followed me, dutifully walking over to the chain wrapped around the tree. I always tied him up and left him water when I had to go somewhere without him. If I didn't, he'd tear the inside of my trailer apart. My next project would be a kennel for him once the cabin was completed, but for now this was enough.

I clipped the chain to his collar and patted him on the head before I turned around and walked to my truck.

I didn't bother turning the radio on as I drove, letting the quiet infiltrate my senses. The fairgrounds were packed; it seemed like everyone in town was there to see the concert. I found a parking spot and locked up, joining the stream of people heading towards the brightly lit stage, regretting my decision to come with everything I had. It felt like everyone was staring at me.

I wasn't an idiot; I knew the town gossiped about me and my family. We were that family in town, the family from "the wrong side of the tracks", the family that had never really fit in. My father was an alcoholic that couldn't hold down a job, and we were the kids that couldn't stay out of trouble growing up. If something bad happened, a Miller was likely nearby.

I just took it to a new level with *ex-convict* on my resume.

Before I could turn around and give up on this stupid plan, I heard someone shouting my name. I looked around, catching sight of artificial red hair. Melanie Clayton sauntered up to me, wrapping her arms around me in greeting. I froze, my body tense. She didn't let go for several long moments. When she finally pulled away, I exhaled with relief.

"Hey, stranger," she said, her voice dripping with flirtation. "Grady and Braden said you might show up tonight! I haven't seen you in forever!"

I bit back the cold, detached responses I longed to fire out at her. "Yeah, it's been a while," I said instead.

"You look good," she told me, her eyes lingering on my chest before they slowly made their descent downward. I inwardly sighed. Melanie was one of the first girls I'd slept with, and she'd made her way through every last one of my friends. I definitely didn't want to go down that particular road again.

"Well come on, everyone's waiting for you," she said, reaching for my hand. She led me through the crowd to a cluster of people.

Everyone turned out to be Grady, Braden and two of his friends the other night; Peter, who still looked absolutely terrified to be in my presence, and Ezra, his cousin luckily not in attendance.

Grady lifted his beer and nodded in greeting. "It's good to see you out tonight, man!"

"Yeah," I said, tugging my hand free of Melanie's relentless grip. She pouted like I'd personally offended her, but I ignored her. "Is Gordon not here?" I added, glancing around.

"No, he might show up later tonight," Grady answered. "He had a situation at work to deal with."

"Oh." I nodded once, my eyes restlessly roaming.

"Tessa will be here soon." Braden smirked. I glared at him and Melanie shot a look at me, her eyebrows furrowed.

"Why the fuck would you care if Tessa is coming?" she demanded, as if she had any right to the answer. This pissed me off and made me want to tell her that I fucking cared because Tessa was gorgeous and classy and everything she wasn't. But I bit my tongue, knowing it would cause unnecessary drama and knowing I couldn't act on my feelings anyway.

"Ease up, Melanie." Braden cackled. "No need to flash your crazy bitch card so soon. Brock doesn't like crazy bitches."

"Whatever." Melanie tossed her hair over her shoulder, her expression as sour as her mood. I moved away, my irritation growing tenfold.

"I need a beer," I grumbled. I motioned with my head for Braden to follow me. Luckily, he picked up on the hint. We headed towards the beer tent, my silence stony.

"What crawled up your ass?" Braden scowled, sensing my aggravation.

"You need to fucking quit it with this Tessa shit, Braden. It isn't going to happen."

"Why the hell not?" he demanded. "I saw how you two looked at each other. I know I'm not university material, but I can tell when two people want each other; so what's the problem?"

I stopped walking. It was out of character for Braden to question me on my motives, or lack thereof. "Because," I responded slowly, "I don't have time to get involved, and I can't anyway. Besides, do you really think the Armstrong brothers will let me get anywhere near her? I'm an ex-convict, Braden."

"You can't be afraid of them." He shook his head, a wry grin on his face. "You could take all three of them at once; fucking look at you."

"That's not the point." I sighed, massaging the stubble on my jaw with my hand. "I have enough shit to deal with right now; I don't need to add to it."

The expression on Braden's face was akin to the one he used to wear when we were younger and I told him he couldn't tag along with me and my friends: it was an expression of crushing disappointment.

"Why is it so important to you anyway?" I asked, my voice gentle.

"Forget about it." Braden waved away my question. "Let's just get the fucking beer."

Braden's attitude perplexed me. I couldn't figure out why he was so invested in the whole Tessa thing, but I knew he wouldn't talk to me about it. Braden didn't talk to anybody about the thoughts in his head. He was so stubborn; so much like me, so much like our old man.

CHAPTER 5

 essa

TRUE TO ELLE'S WORD, I won the first place ribbon. A scowling Melanie came in second place, and a girl from Carling won third.

My dad and I loaded up Spirit and I returned to my farm with Elle. She helped me with my evening chores, just like she promised. I think she helped more or less so I wouldn't bail on her.

By seven o'clock, we were pulling out of my driveway, heading back to the fairgrounds for the Travis Channing concert. I was dressed in a pair of dark denim jeans, a cream tank top and an off the shoulder light brown knitted sweater.

Elle was dressed in painted on floral tights, high heeled boots and a tight white tank top with a pale blue jean jacket. She wore her hair down under her black cowgirl hat. I had a matching one in brown that Elle had bought me a couple summers before. It sat on the seat between us, with me undecided as to whether I wanted to wear it. I always thought cowboy hats were a little too overkill, but Elle insisted they were fun.

I parked my truck and gave Elle a leveled look, about to open my mouth to complain.

"Hang on," Elle said with a slight frown. She shuffled closer to me and gently began to pull free the pins that held my braided hair in place. The braids fell against my shoulders, heavy and long, and Elle tugged the elastic bands out. She finished running her fingers through my hair and pulled back with a smile. "Perfect! Let's go." She grinned brightly. Her primping had made me nervous, and I couldn't get my jaw to loosen enough to voice my concerns. We climbed out of my truck and entered through the front gates, heading towards the stage and the beer tent.

"I don't know about this." I stared at the brightly lit stage and the swarm of people before it. Travis Channing was set to go on in ten minutes, if that.

"Oh, Tessa," Elle sighed heavily. She clucked her tongue, shaking her head. I felt her arm link with mine, and she pulled me closer to her so I could hear her voice over the crowd. "I've been your best friend for literally my whole life, I was pretty much *born* for the role. I know when you like someone, and I know you like Brock Miller. You are forever complaining about how boring life is and how you can't wait for college because nothing exciting ever happens around here. Then when something exciting does happen, you run scared."

I exhaled. "I'm not running scared, I'm being realistic."

"Realistic is hardly any fun." Elle rolled her eyes, repressing a smile. "Try not to make a big deal about this. It's just a concert; Brock probably doesn't even know we're coming. He's here with Braden."

I couldn't help but feel a swoop of disappointment in the pit of my belly. Brock wasn't expecting us to join him and his brother. This whole charade was an ill-hatched and impulsive plan of Elle's to force us in each other's company again. "Great," I muttered, drawing in a shaky breath.

Elle jumped with glee. "See! You like him so much you're upset that he doesn't know we're going to show up. I knew it! I told Braden this was an awesome idea!"

"Braden's in on it?" I came to a stop, my jaw wide with disbelief.

"Oh don't give me that look." Elle refused to allow me to dampen her spirits. "Braden just said Brock seemed taken with you."

"Taken with me? What are we, in the 1920s?" I rolled my eyes, biting down on my lip to keep from smiling.

While I was totally not okay with this idea of hers, equal parts of excitement and dread rolled around within me at the prospect of seeing Brock again, and the small hope that he was interested in me took root. I couldn't help but analyze exactly how I had felt when I saw him at the bush party, and any moment after that we had spent alone. I remembered the affect his voice and presence had on me. But I also couldn't help worrying that all he'd see when he looked at me was that naïve drunk girl he had to rescue because she was too stupid to stick to the buddy system at a party.

I didn't have time to dwell on it though, as my eyes fell across the space and landed on Brock's tall build. He was standing with Braden surrounded by what appeared to be a huge group. Peter, Krista, Ezra, Joanna, and a couple of Gordon and Brock's old friends: Grady McDonnell, and Steve Winters. My eyes widened with surprise when I noticed Melanie Clayton standing beside Brock, but that surprise faded quickly, replaced with nervous anticipation when my eyes moved on to Brock.

He had his back to me, and I took a moment to really appreciate the view. He was dressed in jeans and a white t-shirt that hugged the curves and dips of his muscles like a second skin.

The contrast of the white shirt against his tanned complexion was breathtaking, and he wore Wranglers even better from behind. As if he felt my presence, Brock turned his head and looked over his shoulder, directly at me, catching me staring.

I could feel my cheeks heating up.

Melanie's dark eyes landed on me and she sent me a vengeful smirk. She tossed her thick red hair over her shoulder and stepped closer to Brock, practically hanging off his arm as she batted her lashes at him. Brock looked down at the contact and gave her a patient smile before detangling his arm from her grasp. I couldn't help the swell of satisfaction at the sight of him turning her down, not that it meant anything for me. Still, it was nice to see the smug smile fade from Melanie's lips.

"Hey, babe." Elle grinned, stepping up to Braden for a kiss. Braden obliged, kissing her deeply as his arm snaked around her waist. Breaking the kiss a moment later, he grinned playfully at me from over the top of Elle's head.

"Tessa, so good to see you. You look hot as fuck tonight," he said, his voice full of double meaning as he smirked towards his brother. Brock said nothing; he just stonily took a sip from the beer he was holding, his eyes narrowing darkly. "Wouldn't you say, Brock?"

Brock didn't respond. Although he didn't speak, those steel-coloured eyes were caressing me as they slowly travelled the length of my body, finally pausing to rest on my lips.

"Thanks?" I blinked, my thoughts disoriented. The heat of Brock's gaze was doing strange things to me. I felt lightheaded, almost dizzy. Nervous butterflies exploded in my belly and my legs threatened to give out as Brock's eyes rose to lock on mine.

I opened my mouth, about to say something, anything else, when Melanie's face appeared around Brock's body. "Oh, yeah. I think I saw that top on clearance at Walmart. It's cute, I guess... for Walmart," she said, smirking at me.

I arched a brow, my heart pounding in my chest. "You could

spend all the money in the world on clothes, Melanie, but they wouldn't make your ugly personality any prettier," I responded, keeping my tone airy and light.

"DAMN!" Braden cackled, delighted. I stole a look at Brock, and he was trying to suppress a grin. Melanie glared at me, turning her head to the stage.

"Hello, Parry Sound!" Travis's appealing voice fell across the crowd that had gathered before the stage, and mostly everyone stopped their conversations. Brock's intense eye-contact finally broke, and I instantly felt empty. The crowd hooted and whistled, and Travis walked along the stage, chuckling at their exuberance. "It's been a while!"

The crowd continued making a ruckus, and Travis grinned almost bashfully, peering out from under his red trucker hat. "I'm glad to back, so many familiar faces in the crowd!" He crooned, earning a series of cheers and hoots from the audience. "Alright, well I'm going to kick things off with my first single, Trucks and Stuff!"

Elle cheered loudly at my side, bumping her hip into mine. Elle loved concerts. She loved to lose herself in the energy around her.

I tried to relax and enjoy, but between worrying about whether Ezra's cousin was going to show up and trying to ignore Brock's presence as he stood less than five feet away from me, it was difficult. Relaxing was completely out of the question and Brock wasn't even looking in my direction. He was focused intently on the stage.

Melanie was still standing close to him and every so often, she would stand on her tippy toes to speak into his ear. Each time she did this, she looked over his broad shoulder at me and smirked.

I tried my hardest to put on a good face and enjoy myself, but I was feeling spent. Especially when Travis called it a night and told everyone he'd be at the Clayton's barn for the after-party. Melanie stood taller, extending a royal smile to our group of friends, almost as if she was the Queen of England herself.

"No, Elle. I don't want to go to Melanie's," I hissed, tugging on Elle's arms.

"Do you think I want to go?" Elle rolled her eyes dramatically. "Hell no! I hate Melanie as much as you do. But Travis is going to be there, and so is everyone else!" Elle said this last part while gesturing toward Brock. I couldn't help but follow her line of sight, my eyes locking on Brock's. My breath caught in my throat as he held my gaze for several long minutes before finally breaking away to answer something that Grady McDonnell said to him.

"Fine," I muttered, dropping my shoulders in defeat.

"Awesome!" She grinned, practically bouncing on her heels. We started to follow the crowd out towards the parking lot. She looped her arm through mine, tugging me towards her. Krista and Joanna walked just ahead of us, chattering amongst themselves about how amazing the concert had been. The guys, and Melanie, were ahead of Krista and Joanna. Elle fell back slightly so we could continue our conversation without running the risk of anyone else overhearing. "Braden said Brock would drive us," she added.

"I have my truck," I pointed out.

"You're missing the point," Elle murmured, smiling wickedly. She gestured towards Brock again and winked.

"I really don't think that's going to happen." I sighed, my eyes zeroing in on Melanie's close proximity to him. "Besides, I'm not even sure I *want* anything to happen."

"Lies," Elle said with confidence. "You do want something to happen, which is why you're here. And furthermore, I've never seen you back down from a challenge before. What's up with you?" Elle looked at me pointedly.

I took a deep, steadying breath. Elle wasn't an over-analyzer like I was. She let things roll off her shoulders. She didn't worry about the what ifs like I always did. She wouldn't understand why I was still out of sorts after the almost-attack.

"I'm just tired," I said instead of explaining myself. "I'm sure I'll get my second wind soon enough."

"Any chance you'd give me a lift?" Melanie was saying loudly, gazing at Brock with adoration and twirling her hair with her finger. She was even doing that ridiculous duck-face pout that almost every girl in and around my age thought was cute.

Brock hesitated, glancing from me to Melanie. "Yeah, I guess that'd be alright."

"I don't think so, you're in the back. Brothers get shotgun, bitches ride in the back," Braden sneered, blocking the passenger side door. He winked at Elle and she laughed.

Melanie was seething with anger, but Brock said nothing as he walked around to the driver's side. Our eyes met as I passed. I felt tethered to him, as if his gaze had a physical hold on me.

Elle motioned to Brock's truck with a slight nod of her head and a smile. I shook my head and frowned, stubbornly climbing into my unlocked truck. I didn't keep anything worthwhile in my cab, so I never had to worry about locking it up.

"So if neither one of us likes Melanie, tell me why we're going to her stupid party? I don't care if she provides all the alcohol. I've had enough of Melanie Clayton today," I grumbled, putting my truck in reverse and pulling out of the fairground parking lot.

Elle was checking her reflection in the visor mirror. She turned her head slowly to the side and smacked her lips loudly. She was purposely taking her sweet time to answer; she knew how much it drove me nuts. I gritted my teeth, biting my tongue, and forced myself to be patient.

"I've already answered you. We're going because Travis Channing is going to be there. How many people can say they've been to a barn party with a Billboard topping country singer?" Elle arched a brow at me. "Besides, Melanie needs a reality check. Did you see how she was all over Brock? Pathetic!"

I resisted the urge to huff in aggravation. Yeah, I saw, and it was part of the reason why I was so miserable. I opened my mouth to speak, but Elle cut me off.

"He's so not into her. He practically flinched any time she happened to 'accidentally' brush up against him."

"Oh really? If he's *so not into her*, why is he driving her?" I grumbled, irritated with my excessive feelings of jealousy.

"Because she asked him." Elle rolled her eyes. "Braden's there, so nothing will happen. He made her sit in the back and Brock didn't argue."

I sighed, turning onto the county road the Claytons' farm was on, following the trail of brake lights. It seemed like every single person at the concert was headed there. "Elle, I really don't want to be here. This is a terrible idea."

"Why?" Elle twisted her body to face me, her gaze scrutinizing me. She could read me like nobody else. Lying to her was pointless, even if I wanted to lie to her, which I didn't. Elle was my best friend, my closest companion.

"A thousand reasons." I bit my lip, slowing as the trail of brake lights ahead of me lit up as cars one by one turned down the Claytons' driveway. "One, or all, of my brothers could show up. Ezra's cousin could be there."

"If Ezra's cousin is dumb enough to show up, I guess it would be a good thing for your brothers to be there," Elle pointed out. "Besides, you're not in high school anymore. You're eighteen and you're going to college in a couple of months. There's really no reason for them to be fun blockers anymore."

"There may be no reason, but they still will be," I grumbled. "Besides…it's not just about them, or even Ezra's cousin…" I trailed off, sighing heavily as I turned onto the dirt driveway.

"Then what's going on?" Elle demanded, crossing her arms

and fixing me with a piercing stare. I pulled up behind some random car and put my truck in park, killing the engine.

I took a deep breath, trying to organize my thoughts. "I'm in over my head here. I've never felt the way I feel about him before...and nothing's even happened yet. I don't like feeling out of control like this. And I don't like that it's with him."

"Why not?" Elle whispered, her eyes still fixated on my face.

"He seems complicated," I answered, biting my bottom lip. "He seems intense and I don't know if I can survive him."

Elle was quiet, contemplating my answer.

Throughout high school, it was Elle who crushed hard, Elle who was obsessed and Elle who fell. I played the devil's advocate. I soothed her broken heart every time a jerk stomped all over it. Sure, I'd had a few minor crushes here and there, but nothing cures a crush like watching the boy you like run off with his tail between his legs after a "friendly chat" with your brothers.

"Maybe you're not supposed to survive him," she said softly after several long minutes. She raised her eyes to meet mine. "Maybe he's the one."

I snorted. Elle always bought that fairytale crap; she believed in Prince Charming and true love, in passion and soul mates.

Elle loved without regret, without question and without any reservations. Elle's father had taken off when she was six. She was raised by a tough woman who didn't think twice about playing both roles. I grew up watching my father long for the missing piece of his heart. We both grew up seeing what love and loss left behind, only we had completely different reactions.

My best friend held fast to the belief that there was a one great love for everyone, and she was in a hurry to have it.

I, on the other hand, wasn't so sure about love. Even if it was real, even if there was such a thing as soul mates and happily-ever-afters...I still feared the whole package. I suppose I was afraid. I didn't want to be left behind by love, and I knew it could happen. Death wasn't the only culprit, but it was the most final and the most searing.

"Let's just pretend for a moment that Brock likes me, and I like him, and we...start something. There's still the fact that my dad specifically said to stay away from him," I added, opening my door. I couldn't stay inside the cab a moment longer.

Elle climbed out and slammed her door, looking at me over the cab of the truck. "He'd tell you to stay away from anyone with a penis."

I said nothing as Elle led the way into the large barn. Music was already blaring, making the wooden rafters shake.

Barn parties at the Clayton's house were always over the top. They had a lot of money, with several barns on their farm. This particular barn was actually dedicated to being the "party barn". The Claytons allowed couples from all over to get married in it too. It was a sought after venue by brides in Muskoka. There was a fully stocked bar, but it was usually completely off limits and reserved for the events that Mrs. Clayton organized.

It was a twenty dollar cover charge to get in. I arched a brow, shaking my head. It wasn't surprising at all that Mr. and Mrs. Clayton had found a way to make an over-priced dollar.

Still, they'd really outdone themselves this time. Twinkle lights were everywhere, illuminating the makeshift dance floor. Speakers were pulsing and bodies were swaying. I took a steadying breath, scanning the crowd, searching for the one person I had no right to look for.

I bit my lip, trying to talk myself out of this silly infatuation. Brock and I could never work. Besides, I was headed off to college soon. There wasn't any time to start anything, not that Brock Miller was interested.

Still, disappointment crushed down on my foolish heart when my eyes finally landed on him. He was dancing with Melanie, or rather, she was grinding up against him and wiggling her hips like some exotic dancer from a hip hop video.

Elle saw the look on my face and quickly steered me in the opposite direction, towards the bar.

"I'm not drinking tonight," I argued, trying to tug my hand free of her death grip. "I honestly just want to go home."

"The hell you are, and you're going to need a little liquid courage." Elle raised her eyebrows at me over her shoulder, still dragging me. "There's no way in hell you'll get over yourself without it."

"I drove tonight," I pointed out.

There was an overwhelming number of people hanging out by the bar. Elle elbowed her way in, with me following close behind. "And I'll be your designated driver. Not an ounce of alcohol shall pass these beautiful lips." She winked. She had already decided how tonight was going to play out, and arguing with her was pointless.

We came to a stop in front of the black walnut bar. I arched my brow at Elle, impressed. There was an attractive guy behind the bar mixing drinks. His dark brown eyes met Elle's and he grinned, sliding the frothy beers he'd just finished pouring to the customer beside us before looking at us. "What can I get you lovely ladies?"

"Can I get two Red Headed Slut shots please?" she ordered, leaning over the bar. I knew she was giving the poor bartender a generous view of her ample cleavage. He didn't even bother asking her for ID; he just went about preparing the shots.

That's how it was with Elle. She never got carded, and when she did, she had a pretty believable fake ID. I had one too, that Elle was forced to hang on to at all times because I could only imagine what kind of trouble I'd get into if my father found a fake ID in my room. I'd probably be grounded until I was fifty.

I sighed, taking the shot from her hand. I tossed it back in one gulp, the combination of Jager, cranberry juice and peach schnapps assaulting my taste buds. She smiled, relieved that I wasn't going to fight her on this. Her grin widened as she shoved the other shot to me and ordered another.

"Elle! You said you weren't drinking!" I protested, my eyebrows knitting together.

"Relax, I'm not. It's for you. You're going to shoot them, and then we're going to go dance!" Elle nodded towards the shot glass still in my hand. I rolled my eyes and did as she commanded. The idea of numbing all the thoughts in my head right now sounded pretty damn good. I knew Brock was somewhere on the dance floor, with Melanie of all people.

I never liked Melanie. She was always standoffish and rude to me, even when she was dating Gordon. She was condescending and petty, selfish and haughty. Plus, she cheated on Gordon. Not that Gordon had cared; he was thankful for the excuse to break up with her, but still. Anyone who cheated on one of my brothers landed a well-earned place on my shit list.

"Stop thinking about that tramp," Elle ordered, handing me the final shot. I tossed it back, feeling tipsy. The alcohol barely burned as it slid down the back of my throat, a sign that I was definitely going to regret having three shots in so little time.

I closed my eyes for a moment and allowed the alcohol to wash over me like a comforting blanket. I wasn't drunk like I'd been the other night, but I was feeling light and free.

"Dirt Road Anthem" by Jason Aldean was playing as Elle grabbed my hand and tugged me out to the dance floor.

Dancing was something Elle and I had always done together. We garnered each other nicely, and we knew we fetched a lot of attention when we danced in public. I tossed my hair over my shoulders, spinning around with my hands up over my head, singing the lyrics along with her.

My eyes roamed the bodies on the dance floor, searching for that one person that I craved. I didn't see Brock, or Melanie for that matter, and it only made me feel worse. "Dirt Road Anthem" faded off and Blake Shelton's "Sangria" kicked on, the lyrics doing nothing to free my mind of its current thoughts.

"I need another shot," I told Elle, tugging her back towards the bar. "Another Red Headed Slut," I ordered when I'd captured the bartender's attention.

"Do you have ID?" he asked, arching a brow. Elle stepped out and handed him our fake IDs. He didn't seem to care about their authenticity. Shrugging, he slid me another shot. I tossed it back, scowling at Elle.

"I told you this was a terrible idea."

"What, you're not having any fun at all?" Elle pouted, seeming hurt by my foul attitude.

"Not really. Where's Braden?" What I wanted to ask was *'Where's Brock?'* Elle knew and smiled. "He texted me, said he was having a smoke. Brock's with him," she answered.

Before I could respond, someone put their hand on my hip. I turned my head, glaring daggers at the person, about to light into them before I realized who it was.

"Excuse me, darling, I just need to get a drink," Travis Channing drawled, his emerald eyes sparkling at me. They slowly roamed my face and dropped down the rest of my body with slow appreciation. His hand was still on my hip.

I was gaping like a fish, my mouth opening and closing. Travis didn't seem bothered by my inability to communicate. The corner of his lip lifted up in a charming smile. He broke eye contact to order a Jack Daniels, then dropped his gaze back down to my lips.

"What's your name?"

"Tessa," I muttered, frowning slightly. "Tessa Armstrong," I emphasized my last name purposely.

"Shit." Travis chuckled, withdrawing his hand as recognition crossed his features. He took another slow look. "You grew up."

"People tend to do that," I responded, looking towards Elle for help. She was every bit as shocked as I was. I could honestly say this was the first time a celebrity had touched me, even if it was some guy that grew up around here and fished with my brother in high school.

He laughed, like I'd told the funniest joke ever. "Well Tessa Armstrong, do you want to dance?" he asked.

I contemplated his question. It wasn't every day that someone asked me to dance at a party; most of the guys in this town had learned the hard way. My thoughts briefly drifted over to Brock before I inwardly scolded myself for caring. He hadn't shown any interest in me all night, and I refused to be that girl that waited around.

"Alright," I said, shrugging. Elle's eyes widened and she repressed a smile, watching as I allowed Travis to lead me to the dance floor.

He put his hands on my hips and pulled me against his body, swaying in time to Tim McGraw's Diamond Rings and Old Barstools.

All I could think about while I danced with the Travis Channing was Brock; Brock's reluctant smile, Brock's gray eyes. The way I felt when I was around him, the way I felt like everything could fall away, but him and me.

Travis was taller than me by nearly five inches. He had wavy, dark blond hair that couldn't quite decide if it was curly or straight. It teased his shirt collar and fell in a charming swoop over his forehead. He was lean and fit, but he didn't ooze the delectable masculinity that Brock did. By all counts, I should have been attracted to Travis, and I probably would have been at least enamored with him…had Brock not invaded my senses.

"Were you at the concert?" Travis's voice stirred my thoughts away from Brock and I tried to focus on his face. The alcohol in my system made that normally easy task a little challenging.

"Yeah, I was there. It was good," I shrugged.

Travis grinned. "Just good?"

"Sorry, it was the most amazing thing I have ever had the

pleasure of witnessing, ever. My ear drums will never be the same again," I corrected sarcastically, smirking. Travis blinked at me for a moment, and then he threw back his head and laughed.

"Shit Tessa, you're the realest girl I've met in a long time." He sounded astonished by this fact.

"That's really sad." I frowned. "Especially considering we've already met before, so that doesn't even really count."

The corners of Travis's lips perked up as he tried to repress a grin. His hands began to roam my hips, feeling the skin through the thin fabric of my shirt. I was disappointed to not feel a rush of desire, so disappointed that I stopped dancing and closed my eyes.

"What's wrong?" Travis asked, his hands hesitating. I eyed him regretfully for a moment, wishing that I'd feel that chemical reaction I felt whenever I was in close proximity of Brock. I felt...nothing. Crickets. Silence.

"Nothing," I said, trying to will the disappointment from my voice and face. To my great relief, the song finally ended. "Thanks for the dance, Travis! It was great seeing you again." I stepped out of Travis's embrace, leaving him on the dance floor looking confused.

Elle was still waiting for me at the bar, her eyes wide with excitement. "So how was it?"

"It wasn't." I shrugged, tossing back another shot that she'd gotten for me in my absence.

"Little sister, that better not have been alcohol." I froze for a moment, the shot glass hovering just above the bar table, and slowly turned to see Gordon and Tommy approaching. Ben, thankfully, had grown bored with such displays. At twenty-seven years old, he was busy with the farm and his wife. She was due in a couple of months with their first child.

If only Gordon and Tommy would settle down and leave me alone.

"You guys are ridiculous," Elle remarked, smiling a little as she shook her head. "Are you going to follow Tessa along to college too, make sure that she doesn't drink there either?"

"We just might have to." Gordon frowned, scratching at his fair beard thoughtfully and exchanging a look with Tommy, who flashed a mischievous grin at him before looking back at me.

"I've always wanted to go to college," Tommy remarked, stroking his chin thoughtfully.

"You hate school," I frowned.

"Yeah, but I love driving my little sister crazy." He smiled larger, and despite my irritation at them both—I laughed and rolled my eyes.

"You know, you could try minding your own business. I recall the both of you doing far worse things at eighteen than drinking at a party."

"That's different," Gordon argued with a slight smile on his face. He was about to keep talking, but I raised my hand.

"Shut up, Gordon." I sighed. "I really am quite tired of your hypocritical bullshit. If you're both going to insist on being your usual selves, I'll just go elsewhere." I straightened up, about to push past them and head outside, when my eyes locked with Brock's. He was walking over with Braden, but paused when our eyes connected. My heart rate increased in tempo, and my throat suddenly felt very dry.

My brothers saw me gaping like a fish, and turned around to see who I was staring at.

CHAPTER 6

rock

EVERY GODDAMN TIME she looked me at with those wide, beautiful eyes, I forgot where we were. I forgot who I was and who she was. I forgot every damn little detail I was supposed to remember because I was completely lost within their amber depths.

The entire world seemed to fall away; the barn, the people. I forgot about the fact that two of Tessa's brothers were standing right in front of her. I forgot that I'd just watched her dance with another man, one of my former best friends at that, and bit back waves of jealousy so intense, I could barely see straight.

It was a bad idea to come out tonight, I thought, inhaling deeply.

"Brock!" Gordon's voice boomed across the space between us, snapping me out of the spell of her. I blinked, focusing on his face. Gordon had changed a lot in the last four years. He'd gotten a little taller and had finally grown a thick, dark blond beard. I think our entire final year of high school was spent with Gordon trying to grow a beard, and carefully grooming the tiny goatee he'd been able to sprout. He was still wearing the faded green John Deere baseball cap.

"Hey, man. How's it going?" I nodded at him.

"Jesus Christ, they weren't kidding when they said you've bulked up!" He shook his head, mystified. "You're a goddamn tank now!"

"Yeah, well..." I always felt uncomfortable when people brought up this fact. Yeah, I've bulked up in recent years. There was little else for me to do in jail, and even less for me to do in Alberta when I wasn't working. I only had one friend there, a guy named Grayson. We had gravitated toward each other because we the youngest on the crew. He was dealing with his own stuff though, and he had one foot in the door at being a full-blown alcoholic. When he went to the bars, I went to the gym.

"You still mining?" Gordon asked. He turned around for a moment to order a round of beers, and then looked back at me expectantly.

"Yes," I answered slowly.

"Where abouts?"

"Alberta, north of Lake Wabamun. Took some time off."

I could tell that Tessa was listening hard, hungrily eating up any information I gave.

"Oh, so you aren't home for good then?" Gordon questioned, handing me a beer.

"Nope." I accepted it, even though I'd long since lost my thirst for alcohol tonight. I swallowed back a sip anyway. "Just here dealing with some family stuff."

"I heard, man. I'm sorry." Sympathy crossed Gordon's face. I arched a brow in question. My mom hadn't exactly been forth-coming about her battle with cancer, or at least I hadn't thought she had. She kept it from me long enough. "Ben's wife, Katie, is good friends with your sister." he explained.

"Yeah, well…" I cleared my throat, looking for my brother. Braden was standing behind Elle, pulling her against him and studiously ignoring the conversation happening in front of him. "What's new with you?"

"Not much." Gordon shrugged. "Working with a small crew of guys doing renovations and custom builds—mainly cottages. Ben's still helping the old man on the farm full-time. Tommy's there too, most of the time. Kind of still all hands-on deck there still. It'll be interesting when Tessa goes off to college in the fall."

I nodded, trying unsuccessfully to ignore the spike of interest I felt at Tessa's name. I glanced up, catching her looking at me. "What are you taking?" I asked, purposely drawing her into the conversation.

She bit down on her lip, an action that drove me wild. "The vet tech program at Georgian," she answered, almost meekly. Gone was the sassy little spitfire. I had a feeling it had everything to do with her brothers.

"Nice." I allowed the tiniest hint of a smile to grace my lips before turning my attention back to Gordon. "Have you seen Travis yet?"

"No, we just got here."

"Oh, you missed him pawing Tessa on the dance floor, then," Braden helpfully supplied with a smirk. I bit the inside of my cheek, scowling at the reminder and the jealousy I felt. Elle elbowed him, but it was too late.

"What?" Gordon frowned, glaring over his shoulder at his sister. "Travis put his hands on you, Tessa?"

"Oh give it up," Tessa growled, rolling her eyes. "We danced, that's it, you goddamn Neanderthal!" She was pissed, and it was evident in the way her amber eyes flashed with contempt. She pushed through her brothers and stormed away. She was followed closely by Elle who shook her head in disappointment at my dipshit brother.

"What?" Braden chuckled, raising his arms up as if he truly didn't know what he'd done wrong.

"I think we need to have a word with our old friend Travis, what do you think Tommy? Brock?" Gordon's eyes danced between mischief and amusement. Tommy nodded eagerly in agreement, and they both looked at me for my answer.

I took a sip of my beer, stalling, ever so careful to not let my eyes waiver from Gordon's face. Part of me found it absolutely fucking ironic that he wanted me to help back him in this, when I was battling my own attraction to his sister. If he could hear the carnal thoughts I had about her, I highly doubt he'd be inviting me along in to 'chat' with Travis. "I think Tessa is a big girl, and she can handle herself."

"Oh I know she can handle herself," Gordon said carefully, his eyes locked on mine. "I just want to make sure that my friends remember she is still completely off limits."

My hand stilled for a moment, the beer I was slowly lowering suspended in the air. I was bristling on the inside, but outside I remained stoic and indifferent.

"If you feel like you need to pass out that reminder again, by all means, go talk to Travis. But I won't be cracking my knuckles in the background. Not my fight, brother."

Gordon was still for a moment, and then he started to laugh. A deep belly laugh that was almost unsettling. He clapped his hand on my shoulder again, giving it a little squeeze. "I can respect that. You want to keep your nose clean, I get it. It was good seeing you again, Brock."

"You too, Gordon." I nodded, watching as the two middle Armstrong brothers walked off to find Travis.

"Whoa, that was fucking intense," Braden remarked, his eyebrows raised. "I see what you mean."

"You just had to stir the fucking pot, didn't you?" I growled, slamming the barely touched beer down on the bar. He shrugged, like it couldn't be helped, and picked it up.

I stalked out of the barn. I'd had enough of the bullshit drama and I wanted to leave. Several people were hanging out in front of the barn, smoking cigarettes and talking. Elle and Tessa were sitting on the log fence that separated the driveway from the field. Elle was rubbing Tessa's shoulders, talking gently to her. I'd have to pass them to get to where I'd parked my truck.

Elle looked up and spotted me. She whispered to Tessa, and those amber eyes landed on me, rendering me absolutely powerless to anything else. Tessa said something back and then slid slowly off the log, walking purposely towards me.

"Take me back to your place," she said, coming to a stop in front of me. I could barely concentrate on anything, save for the creamy colour of her collar bone and neck. Her sweater hung off her shoulder, leaving more of that heavenly looking skin exposed. I swallowed hard.

"What?"

"Take me back to your place," she repeated, her eyes fixated on my face. "I want to go home with you."

"Why?" My ability to string two words together at a time had apparently disappeared, along with any control I ought to have.

"Because I want to," she said simply, shrugging. She sunk her teeth into her lower lip. "And I think you want me to. I don't think you're going to let anybody else tell you what you can and can't have."

Tessa's thick lashes fluttered against her cheeks as she lowered her gaze, clearly seeing the affect that her words had on me. My pants were straining, and my breathing had deepened as I desperately fought my urges.

She was right. I normally wasn't one to let someone tell me what I could and couldn't have. But this was different. This wasn't just any girl asking me to take her home. This was Tessa Armstrong; the sister of one of my old best friends, the daughter of a man that I knew would skin me alive if I touched her. She was off limits in every sense of the word, but I'd never wanted anybody more than I wanted her.

"Let's go," Tessa said, her hand reaching out and grabbing mine. She led me down the driveway, away from the people. Her hand felt small, soft and warm in mine. Holding her hand was like touching light, like coming alive again after years of being dead. I never wanted to let go.

Which is exactly why I had to.

I cleared my throat, releasing her hand so I could dig through my pockets for my keys. I found them, hitting unlock and opening the passenger door for her. She climbed in without help; a girl like Tessa didn't need assistance getting into a lifted truck, and that in itself was the hugest fucking turn on. Most girls that I'd been with would have waited until I helped them in. Not her.

I closed the door, walking around to the driver's side while gnawing on the inside of my cheek. I was in serious fucking trouble. I got behind the wheel, but before I could slide the key into the ignition, Tessa was scooting over to me. Her thigh brushed against mine, the scent of her skin invaded my nostrils. She smelled like lavender and honeysuckle, and I wanted to taste her more than I wanted my next breath.

There's only so much a man can do when a beautiful girl presses herself against him. There's only so much a man can do when she runs her hand along his chest and peers into his eyes with wanton desire and bites her bottom lip. My hands acted on their own accord to cup Tessa's face. I used my thumb to tug gently on her bottom lip, freeing it from her teeth.

She closed her eyes and sighed, her lips parting invitingly, and there wasn't anything else I could do. I was hopeless. She had me under a spell. My lips found hers, gently at first, tasting her. *I just want one taste*, I told myself.

Then Tessa took control, deepening the kiss while she brought her right leg over my lap to straddle me. I groaned, the feeling of her tongue sliding into my mouth and pairing with mine almost too much to bear. Her hands were on my chest, feeling the hard muscles and the frantic beating of my heart, and she moved against me, grinding against my groin. Two pairs of denim against my hard as fuck cock was torture, and I would have given anything in that moment to be in her.

"Let's get out of here," she whispered huskily, giving me a playful nip on my bottom lip before she fluidly moved away and buckled up. She sent me a daring grin and arched her brow, wondering why I hadn't stomped on the gas immediately.

I swallowed hard, trying to adjust myself as I started up my truck and pulled away from the barn.

It was dark. The clock on my dashboard read one o'clock in the morning. Nobody was on the road, and I had to concentrate completely on driving and not pulling off to have my way with her. I was still painfully hard, still acutely aware of her right beside me.

"How drunk are you?" I asked, my voice sounding rough from need.

"Not that drunk," Tessa answered, sending me a playful look. "I'm sober enough to know what I want."

"And what do you want?"

"You. I want to feel you inside me," she replied, her words easily becoming my undoing. I swallowed hard again, my throat dry.

I said nothing for several moments, turning onto the road that led to the Armstrong farm. "Wait, I thought we were going to your place?" She was sober enough to pay attention to her surroundings.

We'd reached her driveway now, and I drove up it quickly, the dust flying out beneath my tires. I needed to get her here before I changed my mind and took her back to my trailer. I put the truck in park, leaving it idling.

She looked at me, those wide eyes full of hurt. "Don't you want me, Brock?"

I turned to face her, tipping her chin up to force her eyes to meet mine. "Yes, Tessa. I want you really fucking bad." I was ninety percent sure that this whole experience was going to give me the worst case of blue balls I'd ever had.

"Then why'd you bring me back here?" she demanded, hurt and anger flashing in her eyes.

"Because you deserve better than a quick fuck in my truck on some back road, Tessa, and I intend on giving it to you," I told her, my voice heavy with desire.

"What if I want that, Brock?" she asked. "What if I want a quick fuck on some back road?"

Whenever she talked dirty like that, my vision wavered and all I wanted to do was kiss her until everything melted away. I would have too, if the porch light hadn't turned on and if Bill Armstrong hadn't stepped out in his plaid pajamas wearing the most menacing look I'd ever seen a man wear.

"I don't want to be a decision you regret in the morning," I said lowly, my hand falling away from her chin.

Tessa's mouth opened and closed as she struggled to find something to say. She was so captivated by my words and me that she didn't even realize her dad was out front until he walked up to my truck and opened the passenger door.

She startled, struggling with her seatbelt.

"Brock Miller." The way that Bill said my name seemed to be a threat.

"Mr. Armstrong." I nodded, watching as Tessa stumbled out of the truck. She looked at me over her shoulder, biting her lip once, her eyes swirling with confusion and want.

As I watched her walk up the front steps with her dad, I instantly regretted my decision to bring her home. I should have just brought her back to my trailer like she wanted. I should have just let her sleep it off in my bed, then drove her to

Elle's in the morning. I shouldn't have made a decision for her, even if my heart had been in the right place. I truly hadn't wanted to be something that she woke up to regret in the morning.

I'd also known that I wouldn't have been able to resist her. The thought of her in my bed was enough to drive me insane with need, having her actually in my bed and being unable to touch her...that would have fucking killed me.

CHAPTER 7

essa

My father marched me up the front steps and into the house. I made a move to head up the stairs to my room, but his voice halted me.

"Table, now," he said sternly, pointing to the kitchen. The old oak table was reserved for family meals and what Dad liked to call 'family meetings', which were basically sit downs where he disbursed punishments and talked about things that needed to be done around the farm.

I had a feeling that tonight he wouldn't be talking about the things that needed to be done around the farm.

Obediently, I walked into the kitchen and sat down at the table. Dad paced the length of the kitchen several times before he leaned over the table, pressing his palms down on it as if he had to ground himself.

"I thought I told you to stay away from that Miller boy." He was angry, and the disappointment was evident in his voice.

My thoughts were still swirling around on the words that Brock had said before he left, and I hadn't listened to a thing my father said.

"Tessa, did you hear me?" Dad repeated, speaking a little louder now. I looked up, blinking. "I thought I told you to stay away from Brock Miller."

"Yeah, you did tell me to stay away from him, but you also told me to stay away from every other guy that's ever liked me, and you know, anybody with a penis," I tossed out casually, as if saying a sentence with the word 'penis' to your father was a typical thing for an eighteen-year-old girl to do, for me to do. *Damnit, I must be drunk,* I thought, giggling out loud at the shocked look on my father's face.

Dad didn't look like he found any of this humorous. I sighed deeply. "Look, Dad. I'm eighteen. I'm not a little girl anymore and you really can't treat me like one. I'm going to occasionally hang out, and maybe even kiss boys. You probably won't like them, either. But it's my decision who I choose to see. Besides, I'm not even seeing Brock. He gave me a ride home from Melanie's, that's all."

"Where were your brothers?" Dad demanded, his jaw clenching with aggravation.

"They were striking the fear of God into Travis Channing," I said, my tone bored. I even went as far as looking at my nails.

"Why were they doing that?"

"Because Travis danced with me, and they were just doing what you taught them to do," I responded. "If anyone touches Tessa, make sure you teach them a lesson!" I added, mimicking my dad's deep voice.

"I never taught them that." Dad frowned.

I stared at him, blinking slowly. I didn't even have to open my mouth to prove my point; both Tommy and Gordon stumbled into the house laughing.

"The look on Travis's face was hilarious! He really thought

you were going to sock him." Tommy was cackling. They both came into the kitchen and froze, seeing Dad and I sitting around the table.

"The prodigal sons return with news of their triumphant battle." I sighed, rolling my eyes. "This is exactly what I'm talking about. I can't even dance with a guy without everyone around here losing their goddamn marbles. It's driving me insane! Tommy and Gordon have both been dating since before they were sixteen!"

"Tessa, you know that isn't true," my father argued.

"You almost decked Brock for driving me home, Dad," I pointed out.

"Wait, Brock drove you home?" Gordon's eyes flashed with anger.

"Sit down, the both of you," Dad demanded. Gordon and Tommy exchanged a look with one another as they sat down in their usual spots at the table.

My father paced from the table to the kitchen counter and back again, rubbing his bearded chin with his fingers. Occasionally, he would glance from Tommy and Gordon to me.

He came back to the table and pulled his chair out, sitting down and fixing me with a serious stare. "You're right. You are eighteen years old and I need to stop treating you like a child, but you're still under my roof and I won't see you making poor decisions. I have rules that you'll need to abide by, even if you're going to college in the fall. I told you to stay away from Brock Miller because he has a criminal record, not because I want you to stay away from every guy out there. I expect you to heed my advice, and I expect you not to be alone with that Miller boy again. Do I make myself clear, Tessa?"

"Yes, Dad." I sighed, my shoulders slumping in defeat. I wasn't about to admit my intense feelings for Brock, not to my father and especially not with my brothers sitting right there.

"Boys, what's this I hear about you striking the fear of God into Travis Channing for dancing with Tessa?" Dad switched his focus to my brothers, fixing them both with a stern look.

"He was pawing her on the dance floor, and –"

"Improper use of the term 'pawing'," I interrupted, as if we were in a courtroom and not sitting around the kitchen table in the middle of the night. "We were dancing; people have to touch each other to dance. It's kind of how it's done."

"Whatever." Gordon frowned. "He's supposed to be my friend, and my friends know not to go there."

"If your sister wanted to dance with Travis, and willingly did so; there's no reason for you to go put the fear of God in him, friend of yours or not," Dad lectured. I smirked, finally feeling those scales tip a little bit in my favor.

THE NEXT MORNING, my father woke me up two hours earlier than usual. It was his way of punishing me for drinking the night before. The Armstrong offspring didn't get to nurse hangovers or sleep in until noon; they had to get up at first dawn and get their chores done. By eight o'clock, I'd already given the horses a good brushing before setting them out in the fields and mucking out all the stalls in the barn.

After my chores in the barn were completed, I set out to the hen house to collect some eggs for breakfast. Dad always insisted on having laying hens so he could have farm fresh eggs whenever he wanted them. It was my job to raise the hens, and it had been since I was a little girl.

I thought about Brock while I worked, placing each freshly laid egg in the basket. I thought about the things he said to me, about the way he made me feel. He unlocked urges in me that I never knew I had before. He made me want to act in a way I didn't typically act.

I wanted to know everything there was to know about

Brock Miller. I wanted to know about his past, I wanted to know about his dreams for the future. I wanted to fall into him, fall into that feeling I had whenever I was around him, and never come up for air. It was dangerous, it was stupid, but there it was.

I walked into the kitchen, humming to myself distractedly.

"Someone's looking chipper this morning." Elle's voice startled me and I almost dropped the basket.

"Jesus, Elle. Some warning next time." I carefully set the basket down on the counter. "What are you doing here?"

"Dropping off your truck," she responded, joining me at the counter. She leaned up against it, crossing her bare arms. Elle was wearing her signature shorter-than-hell shorts, a tight tank top and sandals. Her long dark hair was pulled up in a messy bun, and although her face was free of makeup, she still looked like a damn celebrity. I was certain I looked like absolute shit. My hair was a curly, tangled mess from last night, and I still hadn't had time to shower. I definitely didn't look fresh and radiant, like my best friend. She pulled herself up onto the countertop while I set to washing the eggs. "And checking in on you to see how last night went?" she added, her voice quiet.

She swung her slender legs back and forth, waiting for me to answer. I glanced around the kitchen, declaring it empty. "It didn't," I whispered, my brow furrowing. "I thought it was going to…we kissed, and it was amazing but…"

"But what?" Elle whispered, her eyes wide and impatient.

"He drove me here and told me I deserved more than a quick…you know, in his truck, and that he intended on giving it to me," I responded, keeping my voice so low that Elle had to lean forward to hear me.

She whistled lowly. "Wow. That's intense," she bit her lip, repressing a grin. "Holy shit, that's romance novel stuff right there."

I blinked at her blankly and then shook my head. "I don't

really know what it means or anything, and I doubt I'll find out..."

"Why the hell not?" she demanded, her voice rising indignantly.

"Shh!" I hissed, glancing around again. The kitchen remained empty. Gordon had left for work hours ago, and Ben and Tommy were busy with their own chores. My dad was also outside somewhere, working. The house was empty, but it still didn't prevent me from being totally paranoid. "When he dropped me off last night, Dad came out. He lectured me about being around him and told me I wasn't allowed to be alone with him again."

"Why?" Elle pouted, displeased by this development.

"Because Brock has a criminal record." I sighed. "Because my dad thinks that he's dangerous."

"Oh." She frowned, chewing on her tongue thoughtfully. "Well, Brock isn't dangerous. At least, not to innocent people."

"What does that mean?"

"Nothing. Don't worry about it," Elle rushed to say. "All I mean is that he isn't dangerous."

"I don't think he is either," I said thoughtfully, thinking back to how Brock had reacted to Chris attacking me. Then I thought about how he'd acted the next day, in his trailer, and again in his truck. I didn't believe for one minute that he'd hurt me. I worried my lip while I thought, barely seeing the eggs in front of me as I set to washing and cracking them in a frying pan.

"Why do I feel like there's more you aren't telling me?" Elle asked, arching a delicate brow.

"Oh! Right, there is. So...I pointed out that I'm eighteen now and how unfair it is I can't even date without everyone acting like total cavemen around here. Dad was going to argue about it, but then Tommy and Gordon came in bragging about the whole Travis thing."

Elle's eyebrows shot up to her hairline. "And?"

"And he agreed with me. He gave them shit. I think that's going to change but..." I trailed off, sighing.

"But what? Damnit, Tessa you are the worst for dramatic pauses," my best friend grumbled, crossing her arms and sulking.

"But I'm still not going to be allowed to see Brock," I added, Elle's pout made me smile a little. "He said he's going to stop treating me like a child, but I still have to follow the rules while under his roof, and one of those rules is that I can't be around 'that Miller boy'."

"Are you going to sneak out and see him anyway?" she whispered mischievously, winking.

"I might." I smiled, my heart thrumming at that possibility. "But first I have to make breakfast and shower. Are you going to sit there, or are you actually going to help me?"

"Fine, fine." She hopped off the countertop. "I'll make the bacon."

I ate quickly before I hopped in the shower. I didn't have time to wash my hair, so I ran my fingers through it in an attempt to separate the curls. Then I dressed in a pair of clean shorts and a button up, plaid top.

Elle was sitting on my bed, waiting for me.

"What are your plans today?" I asked, pausing in front of my mirror. The small bruise on my cheek was starting to fade, but I was going to still need makeup to hide it before it healed completely. Otherwise, I'd have to answer questions that I didn't particularly feel like answering.

"Braden and I are going to the rodeo again. You should come!" she answered, watching while I set to work. "Ugh, let me."

Elle was better at making skin look flawless. I never really had a purpose to learn before, but Elle had struggled with acne —especially a few years ago. My skin was naturally creamy and smooth, my Nordic features, courtesy of my mother's side, were sharp yet delicate.

"I don't know, I should probably job hunt today." I sighed, closing my eyes and letting my best friend work her magic.

"You could hand out a few resumes and then we could go," Elle suggested. "We aren't leaving until this afternoon anyway. The strongman competition is this afternoon, and Mom's doing the chili cook-off again. She could use some extra hands," she added, wiggling her eyebrows at me. She knew how much I loved her mom's homemade chili.

"I'll think about it. I don't even know if I'll be allowed out of the house."

"You will. Your dad didn't seem too angry at breakfast this morning. Then again…" I opened my eyes to look at her. She was grinning mischievously at me. "He doesn't know what's brewing between you two," she added with a wink.

I rolled my eyes. "Whatever." I grabbed a stack of freshly printed resumes and my phone. "Do you know if anyone is hiring?"

"You could try the grocery store and Tim Horton's in town, but…" Elle shrugged. "It'll be hard. It's already summer time. They probably filled those job postings months ago."

"Yeah." I sighed. I really wanted to get a part-time job this summer, just to have some extra cash on hand come September.

We walked out of my room and down the old wooden stairs, flying out the front door like our feet were on fire. Dad was walking up the steps, and we came to an abrupt stop in front of him. He caught sight of the papers in my hand. "More resumes?"

"Yeah, there are some places in town that might be hiring," I answered, holding them up for him to inspect. "I'm going to drop Elle off and then do a little job hunting if that's okay?"

Dad looked between us, chewing on the toothpick in his mouth. Chewing on toothpicks was a habit he'd picked up after he quit smoking six years ago. "Alright," he finally said.

"Could Tessa come with me to the chili cook-off tonight, Bill? Mom could use the extra hands."

"I suppose that'd be fine." Dad nodded once, the corner of his lip twitching with a repressed smile.

"See you in a bit," I added, standing on my tippy toes to kiss his cheek.

"See you later. Say hi to your mama, Elle," Dad said as we raced down the front steps towards my truck that Elle had parked haphazardly in the middle of everything, true to her unconcerned nature.

"I will!" she called over her shoulder. When we were buckled in and flying down the driveway, she turned to look at me with a devilish glint in her brown eyes. "So, that was easy. You basically have the whole day now."

"Basically." I bit my lip, thoughts of Brock rising to obscure thoughts of being responsible.

"Tell me more about this kiss," she demanded as I turned onto the road. She had the passenger window all the way down and she'd discarded her sandals on the floor so her feet could half hang out the window. It always made me nervous when she did this, but complaining about it never made her stop.

"It was…I don't know." I sighed, a small smile tugging up the corners of my lips. "It was incredible. I felt it everywhere, in every nerve ending and in my bones. It was intense."

Elle sighed too, a happy, blissful sigh. "That's a kiss of true love," she remarked, grinning at me.

"I never said that," the smile vanished from my face. "I just said it was a really, really good kiss."

"Uh-huh." She smirked.

I narrowed my eyes at her. "It's lust. He made me want more, and I want it, but I'm not in love with him. That's stupid, Elle."

"No it's not," she argued, still smiling. "When you find *'the one'*, it's instantaneous."

"Ugh." I exhaled, puffing my lips out like a fish. Elle was exhausting me.

"There are only so many places you can drop your resume off in town..." she trailed off, not really changing the subject at all, and winked.

I pulled up in front of her house, promising that I'd call her later if I changed my mind about the midway. Then I set to the boring task of handing out my resumes. It was the same at every stop I made: *we've already hired our summer staff but I'll put this at the top of the pile – just in case.*

I was never going to find a job at this rate; it was the curse of living in a small town that exploded with tourists every summer.

I was on the highway, just before the exit I would need to take to get to Brock's property. My hands gripped the steering wheel just a little too tightly. I was torn between what I desperately wanted to do and what I should do.

I made a split second decision to turn onto the off ramp that would take me to him. I drove up the road a little bit, pulling over to collect myself and organize my thoughts.

I wanted to go to him, to kiss him again. My body was practically vibrating with this need. But I shouldn't go to him; I should stay away from him. I should listen to the rules in place. Brock was nothing but trouble, and he'd never be welcome in our home.

But a part of me didn't care because I wanted him anyway. *He doesn't have to come over for dinner.* I told myself, chewing on my lip and staring at the road ahead like it would give me the correct answer.

I wanted to get to know him, and that was dangerous; that was against my rules, newly placed. Daydreaming about falling in love and actually falling in love were two different things.

Daydreaming was safe; it was an unattainable dream, a future goal. Daydreaming was an outlet, a way for me to pass the time. Falling in love was dangerous; it was the here and now, it was giving someone else complete control of my heart and I wasn't sure I knew how to do that.

He unlocked things within me. Things that I wanted to explore. He made me feel sexy and powerful and I wanted to embrace it. I wanted to bask in all of those feelings and sensations he coaxed out of me with a simple glance. I wanted to be the woman I knew he saw when he looked at me.

Only I couldn't promise myself that if I kept driving down this road, I wouldn't end up falling in love with Brock Miller. I wasn't prepared to do that, to fall in love, but thoughts of him occupied my waking moments and I felt like if I didn't do this... the not knowing would consume me.

If I was being completely honest with myself, I was hesitating out of fear. The fear of rejection, the fear of losing something I didn't even have. I played it safe because I was afraid of getting hurt.

But I was tired of playing it safe. I was tired of longing to feel something for someone, then running away at the first opportunity of that feeling growing into something more.

I had reached an impasse. Sighing, I shifted the truck from park to drive and took off down the road.

CHAPTER 8

rock

AFTER TOSSING and turning the rest of the night away, my mind restlessly spinning with thoughts of her, I finally drifted off to sleep around five in the morning.

I woke up several hours later to the sound of a truck pulling into my driveway and brakes protesting. Hunter's frantic bark was joined by someone pounding on my trailer door. I pulled on my jeans, crossing over from my bedroom to the door. I banged my head off the stupid light fixture, swearing lowly as I flung open the door.

Tessa Armstrong stood before me, looking sexy as sin in those tight jean shorts and that plaid, button up blouse. Her chest was rising and falling frantically, as if she'd run the entire way here. Her hair was still wavy and damp from a recent shower.

"Did you mean what you said last night?" she demanded. She didn't wait for me to invite her in; she just walked past me, the skin of her arm brushing against my naked chest. The muscles in my abdomen clenched with desire at the contact and my dick was definitely awake and wanting to greet her.

"What?" In that moment, I couldn't remember a goddamn thing I'd said the night before.

"All that stuff." Tessa frowned, turning to face me. Her eyes dropped down to my unbuttoned jeans, seeing the rather large tent I'd pitched for her.

I cleared my throat. I should lie to her; I should send her away. I should tell her that I wasn't interested in her. I should retract every word I said to her last night. "Yeah, I did, actually," I said instead, as if my tongue wasn't even linked to my mind. I ran a hand through my hair and turned away from her, but there wasn't much space to move in this God forsaken trailer.

When I turned back to face her, Tessa was unbuttoning her shirt. All sensibility and rational thought fell out of my brain like a bucket tipping over. My eyes widened as I took in the sight of her lacy white bra, the dark of her nipples acutely visible beneath the lacy material. I swallowed hard, struggling to find words.

"Well, Brock Miller. Its morning, I'm sober and I can pretty much guarantee that you aren't going to be something I regret," she said, her voice dipping sensually. She reached out, her hands tugging my jeans down enough for her hand to slip in. She cupped me through the thin material of my boxers.

"Jesus fucking Christ, Tessa," I hissed, my eyes practically rolling into the back of my head. How the fuck was I supposed to resist her when she was cupping and stroking me, half naked, standing in my goddamn trailer?

I didn't know what my problem was with Tessa. Yeah, I wanted her...more than anything. But I was resisting that urge to just take her in all the ways I wanted, because I wanted her in more ways than I'd ever wanted anyone else before.

That was it. That was the entire problem. I wanted to

romance her, she deserved that. She deserved flowers and dates and magic, but she was practically begging for me to fuck her and—I could still give her all that other shit she deserved, couldn't I?

I couldn't think when she was stroking me like that.

My lips crashed against hers fervently, my hands tangling in her hair, and I stopped fighting it. I embraced it; I lost myself in the taste and feel of her. I pressed my hardness against her belly, making her moan into my mouth. The sound of her whimpers of pleasure sent a jolt to my dick, and it jumped eagerly.

The door to my trailer was still open, and Hunter was whimpering under the table, the sudden increase of emotions confusing him.

"Give me a minute," I told her, kissing those lips once more before I tugged my jeans back up over my hips and whistled for Hunter. He darted outside and I closed the door behind him, turning around to find her standing exactly where I'd left her, her blouse and her shorts discarded on the floor. Her thong matched her lacy bra, and I felt my balls constricting.

She was a goddamn vision.

"I don't have much time," she said, explaining her rush to undress. I nodded, coming at her at the same time she came at me. Our lips met again, our tongues dancing a heated tango that made me acutely aware I wouldn't last long at all with her. I picked her up, my hands gripping her ass cheeks and grinding her against me. I walked her backwards, towards the end of the trailer where my bed was. I dropped her on it, taking a moment to admire her beautiful curves while I kicked off my jeans. I crawled back on top of her, leaving my boxers on, and went back to kissing those lips. I held myself up with my right arm, letting my free hand roam against the soft skin of her inner thigh. My fingers toyed with the lacy material of her panties, and I could feel her wetness through the barely there material.

"Fuck, Tessa," I groaned, the desire to taste her, be inside her and just consume her made me feel light headed. It'd never been like this for me before. I wanted to take my time with her, to explore every inch of her body, to taste her and please her to the point of her own destruction. But I also wanted to feel her immediately, to take her ruthlessly and frantically. I gently pulled her panties away, my fingers sliding against her wet skin and sinking into her. She arched beneath me, her lashes fluttering closed. She bit her lip as I pleasured her with my fingers.

I was enthralled with watching her, captivated by the soft whimpers that fell from her lips. "I need to taste you," I all but growled.

Tessa bit her lip harder, glancing at me while I positioned myself between her legs. "Um, what?"

"Um what, what?" I asked, my hands on her thighs.

She laughed nervously. "I've never..." She trailed off, her cheeks flushing. Now was not the time to demand to know who the fuck had been so stupid as to not lavish this remarkable body the way it was meant to be lavished.

I arched a brow instead, pulling her panties away, and took a tentative lick. She arched against me, her head dropping back against the mattress.

She tasted like salvation; her taste was the most sacramental thing to have ever passed my lips. I ate her like a starving man, like I hungered for her taste as much, if not more, than she hungered for the feel of my tongue against her clit. I was relentless, using tongue, lips and my fingers in time with one another to completely bring her over the edge, never stopping until I felt her hips buckle beneath me as she came undone.

"I need you in me, Brock," she whispered breathlessly. "Do you have a condom?"

"Fuck," I muttered, the mood suddenly halting when I realized that I did not have condoms on me, and the nearest store was a gas station ten goddamn minutes away. My dick throbbed painfully.

Tessa bit her lip, considering. "I'm on the pill," she told me. Those four words were both a blessing and a curse. It was a subtle way of her saying *please, take me anyway.* The goddamn thought of being inside without a latex barrier had me nearly seeing stars.

But I wasn't that kind of guy; I wasn't one to play with a loaded gun. I wasn't saying that I thought Tessa was lying about being on birth control, but that shit wasn't foolproof.

She said nothing, but I know she sensed my hesitation. Instead, her hand reached through the slit in my boxers and she gripped me, pumping me slightly. "It's alright, we'll take care of you anyway," she whispered coyly, slowly crawling over me. She forced me to lie down on my back, and then she took me in her mouth.

Her mouth was the sweetest sin. The way she worked me, taking as much of me as she could while pumping my base with her hand had me falling apart, shattering into millions of pieces. I couldn't think of anything outside of her; her lips, her mouth, and her body. It didn't take me long at all to explode in her mouth. She drank it all back, milking me for everything that I had.

"Jesus," I exhaled roughly, pulling her up on my chest. My heart was pounding frantically and my body was on a complete high.

"I never would have pegged you for a holy man," she joked, smiling almost shyly at me.

"Yeah, well. That was before you. What the hell did you do to me? Where did you learn how to do that?" Tessa opened her mouth, about to reply. I brought my finger up to her lips, the jealous anger rising like a current. "On second thought, don't answer that question."

I didn't want to think about where she'd learned her skills, not that I was complaining; it was the best goddamn head I'd ever gotten.

I watched as she crawled off me, searching for her discarded shorts and top. "Where are you going?" I asked.

"I told you I didn't have long," she reminded me, sending me a playful smirk over her shoulder.

The sinking sensation in my stomach told me that I didn't want to see her go. I stood up, crossing over to where she stood. I let her slip into her shorts again, and when she straightened, I kissed her. My hands framed her face, my lips and tongue coaxing a soft moan from her. I pulled away regretfully, keeping my hands on her face. "When can I see you again?"

"Soon," she promised, biting her bottom lip. "But next time I come over, you'd better have condoms," she added.

I pressed my hardness against her; yeah, I was primed and ready to go again. This girl was driving me wild. "That's a promise," I added, nipping her bottom lip gently.

I STOOD in front of my trailer, watching Tessa pull away. I watched until her truck disappeared into the trees, until I couldn't hear the sound of her tires on the freshly laid gravel anymore.

My phone started to ring, and I fished it out of my back pocket. "Hello?" I said, not even bothering to read the caller ID.

"Hey, Brock. It's Becky," my sister's voice came through the line, sounding exhausted and worn. "I have a tiny situation here…"

"What's wrong?" I demanded.

"Nothing." She sighed, the wariness evident in her voice. "My sitter bailed on me again, and I can't get a hold of Braden. I really need someone to watch Aiden today so I can go to work. I can't afford to miss any more time…"

I rubbed at my jaw with my fingertips, a heaviness pressing down on my chest. I wasn't ready to face things back home yet, but Becky wouldn't have asked if she wasn't absolutely stuck. Becky vehemently hated asking for help, all the Millers did.

"I can watch him. I'll be by soon," I finally said, disconnecting the call.

I grabbed my keys and got into my truck, whistling for Hunter. He hopped up into the cab and we set off.

I drove along highway seven, trying not to think about what I was about to do: see my dying mother for the first time since she called me with the news, and meet my nephew for the first time since seeing him in that incubator all those years before.

Instead of focusing on those heavy thoughts, I allowed my mind to drift to Tessa.

I had it bad for that girl, and there was no way in hell her family would let me within five feet of her. The look on Bill Armstrong's face last night when I simply dropped her off spelled that out clear as day, and he didn't know what had transpired between us minutes earlier.

Treating her the way she deserved to be treated, romancing her and taking her out places, was going to be next to impossible. I couldn't just pick her up for a date night on the town.

My thoughts stalled when I pulled into the driveway of the small bungalow I'd grown up in. Seeing it again was like a sucker punch to the heart.

The house was in disarray. The shutters were in desperate need of a coat of paint or two, and the roof needed new shingles. The yard was more weeds than grass and the gardens were overgrown.

When I lived there, the gardens were always pretty and free of weeds, the grass was always cut and the shutters weren't hanging on by a single hinge. The outward appearance of our house had been a façade, my mother's attempt at disguising the ugly that resided within, my father.

Brent Miller had always been an asshole. I don't know why my mother married him, or why she stayed. He was an abusive alcoholic and lazy. He couldn't hold down a job to save his life, and my mom was often left to work whatever double shifts she could get at the water treatment plant just to afford the basic necessities. Brent didn't lift a finger to help her, and his idea of parenting was beating us into submission when my mom wasn't there to stop it and direct his anger on her. Life carried on like that until I got big enough to fight back.

The day that Brent Miller drank himself stupid and drove his shitty car into the guardrail on a highway was the happiest day of my life. I know it's cruel to say that about the man who fathered you, but it was the truth. For years I prayed that my mother would kick him out; that we could live without his ugly shadow looming over us. His death was a blessing. His death released us all from the miserable spell he'd had on us. Or so... I'd thought.

My mom was relieved too, although she wouldn't admit it out loud. But with him gone, I was able to actually leave the house without fearing he'd take out his rage on one of my siblings. I was finally able to do stuff for myself; to leave this town. I started working out in Alberta, mining coal and sending any money I earned back home to my family. I did this for a couple years, only returning home for the occasional holiday.

Then, I got a phone call that changed my life.

My little brother was in hysterics. He told me that our sister, Becky, was in the hospital, in labor. The baby was coming early and I hadn't even known that she was pregnant. But it was far worse than that...it turned out that the father of Becky's baby had beaten her so badly that the trauma was what caused the preterm labor.

I hopped on a plane and came home to find my sister sitting at the side of her preterm son's incubator, praying he'd make it through another night. Her face was mangled, her right wrist was broken, and three of her ribs were bruised.

I'd never felt rage like that. That was a pivotal moment in my life; the turning point. I'd gone after the son-of-a-bitch that put my sister in the hospital and endangered not only her life, but the life of my tiny nephew. I found him at the shitty apartment he'd lived in with Becky, snorting coke on the coffee table beside a parenting magazine, of all things.

I snapped. I blacked out, and when I came to...I was standing over his body while he bled all over the carpet. Later, I would learn that I'd given him the same wounds he'd given my sister: a fractured cheek, bruised ribs and a broken wrist. I'd also broken his jaw for good measure.

I didn't regret it. I knew I probably should, but I wouldn't lie to myself and act like I did. In my eyes, it was justified. I guess in the judge's eyes, it was too. He'd given me the lightest sentence possible and allowed me to get out early on good behavior. My job in Alberta had been waiting for me, so I returned there.

I rolled up and parked in front of my mom's old Civic and beside my sister's little Accord. One of the tires on the Civic was flat, and I made a mental note to fill it before I left... before I realized that wasn't necessary. Mom wasn't driving her car anywhere these days.

I climbed out and held the door of my truck open, allowing my dog out of the cab. Hunter came everywhere with me, and had for the past two years. We'd rescued each other.

I'd only been back in Alberta for a couple of months. My freedom was still new, but I'd traded jail for a different kind of isolation. I worked insane hours and rarely got a day off. When I did, I always headed to the nearest town to do a little shopping at the general store. On one particular day, I stepped outside with my groceries and saw a group of local kids with a bat chasing a small pup. I dropped my bags and ran after them, getting to them just as one of the kids leveled a kick to the poor pup's ribs as he trembled against the wall between two garbage bins.

I managed to scare them off, and warily crossed over to him.

He was still trembling, his yellow eyes fixed on me with apprehension and hope. His fur was matted with mud and slush, and when I picked him up in my arms, I could feel that his ribs were protruding. He was starving, freezing, and terrified.

I took him to the local vet and was told that he was likely a little over a year old, and from the looks of it, he was a German shepherd wolf mix with some Husky. Once the mud was washed away from his beautiful agouti coat, his wolf traits were more noticeable and the vet insisted I put him down, expressly detailing all of the risks of owning a hybrid.

I couldn't do that. The way I saw it, all dogs could be dangerous without proper training, and this poor little pup hadn't lashed out once when cornered by a group of kids that were clearly trying to hurt him. He'd have sooner rolled over and taken a bat to the head than hurt any of them. I told the vet as much, and one hefty bill later, he was mine.

I wasn't ignorant regarding Hunter's breed though, and I started working with him immediately. He was an intelligent, loyal pup that was eager to learn and eager to please. Within a few months, I had him completely trained. His training didn't stop there and it still continued on to this day. A happy dog is an active dog, and Hunter was happiest when he was being challenged.

Hunter's thick head nudged my hand, as if he was thinking about the past too. I patted him once and then started walking up the gravel driveway. The porch felt soft beneath my boots, and I added that to my mental list of things to fix around here. I lifted my hand, about to knock. Before it made contact, the old door flew open. My sister, Becky, stood in the doorway with her hand on her hip, her crystal blue eyes boring a hole into me.

"I can't believe you didn't stop in here sooner," she huffed at me, crossing her arms and frowning deeply.

"Sorry, Becs." I sighed, swallowing hard. "How is she?"

Becky's gaze softened considerably. "She is as good as can be expected. Did you want to come in and say hi?"

I nodded stiffly and Becky took a step back to allow me in. Hunter trailed behind me obediently.

"Does it bite?" she asked warily. "Because I can't have it in here if it bites. Or if it doesn't like kids…"

"He won't leave my side, but Hunter is great with kids," I assured her. She nodded, accepting my answer. "Where is Aiden?" I asked, peering around the living room for my nephew.

"He's playing in his room," Becky replied. She brushed back a strand of her dark hair, repressing a sigh. "I really appreciate you doing this for me today. I can't believe Ashlynn bailed on me again. That's the third time this week."

"Don't mention it," I told her sincerely. "I've been meaning to get out here anyway and spend some time with the little guy. I just had to get set up on the property first."

Becky smiled tightly and nodded. She paused by the doorway to our parents' room, gently opening it. My chest constricted as I looked in at my mother's frail body, lost in the queen sized bed. She was skin and bones, her lids closed and fluttering against her cheeks. Her once lusciously dark hair seemed faded and wiry against her pillow.

"She's sleeping," Becky said, her voice full of apology as she gently closed the door. "She needs to rest, but when she wakes up…she'll want to see you. She's been asking about you a lot lately. I think she's been hanging on to see you."

I nodded, my throat tight with emotion. Becky hesitated for a moment before her slender hand reached out to grasp mine. She squeezed tightly before dropping it, gesturing down the hallway.

She led me down the hall to Aiden's room, my old room. The door was open and my little nephew was sitting on the car area rug in front of his bed, pushing a bunch of Hot Wheels around. He heard us in the hallway and looked up, his crystal blue eyes, so much like his mother's, staring at me blankly, without recognition.

One of my biggest regrets was not being around enough for Aiden to know who I was. Becky talked about me often, and I'd seen pictures of him and I was sure he had seen pictures of me too, but this was the first time I'd seen him since his early birth.

"Aiden, you remember your uncle Brock, don't you? He's going to hang out with you today," Becky said, crouching down so she was nearly level with him. Aiden nodded solemnly, looking from his mother to me. "You be good for uncle Brock, okay buddy? I'll be home after dinner, just in time to tuck you in," she added, hugging him goodbye. Aiden wrapped his arms around her and nestled his little head into the crook of her neck.

"Bye-bye Mom," he said sadly. Becky smiled at him and ran a hand through his dark hair before she stood up. She gestured to me to follow her out into the hall.

"Beth-Anne will be here in about an hour or so to take care of mom for the day, so you won't have to do much for her. Just…keep an ear out and check in on her every now and then. He'll have a peanut butter sandwich for lunch and there's a twenty on the refrigerator if you want to order pizza for dinner. There's a park down the street if you're bored and need to leave the house once Beth-Anne gets here and…"

"Becky, we'll be fine. I'm capable of taking care of other people, in case you've forgotten," I interrupted gently.

When Mom was working and Dad was passed out on the couch, it was me who took care of my younger siblings. I made sure they ate dinner, did their homework, took baths and got to bed on time. It was a lot of responsibility when I was just a kid myself, but I'd done it because I knew our old man wouldn't.

Becky's shoulders relaxed and she smiled at me. "Okay good," she said, walking down the hallway and grabbing her purse from a kitchen chair. I followed her, leaning against the wall as she slipped her work shoes on.

"Would you mind if I took him to the rodeo today?" I asked.

Becky's head snapped up at my question, surprise lining her features. "You'd want to take him to the rodeo?"

"Yeah, why not?" I shrugged, suddenly doubting my idea.

Becky chewed on her lip, considering me. "Are you sure that's a good idea?" She frowned, her gaze drifting down the hallway toward where Aiden was playing. "What if he gets lost?"

"He won't get lost; I'll make sure of it. I never lost you or Braden."

"Okay...you're right. Yeah that'd be great," she said, smiling. "I'll grab the car seat."

WAITING FOR THE HOSPICE NURSE, Beth-Anne, was difficult. As soon as Becky pulled out of the driveway, I felt the walls of our childhood home closing in, suffocating me. Seeing her once was like a bullet to the heart. I knew it was the medication, the pain killers she took, but seeing her like that only added to my internal panic. Hunter sensed this, and leaned his body against mine while he happily accepted a thousand pets and hugs from Aiden.

I'd put on a movie, turning the volume up just enough so that I'd be able to hear any sounds coming from down the hall. Part of me felt like I should go check on her to see if she was awake. The other part cautioned against this. I didn't need to fall to pieces right now, not when I was responsible for Aiden. Not when I'd already promised him a fun day at the rodeo.

Besides, I couldn't walk down the hall into her bedroom. I couldn't see her like that again, bed ridden and dying. I knew that made me a terrible son, but I just wasn't strong enough.

Not yet. I couldn't watch her sleep, knowing that she'd soon be taking her last breath.

My mother had endured so much in her life, and I didn't forgive her for some of it, like our dad. I resented her for not leaving him when we were kids. I don't think she understood the gravity that simple action of staying had on us, on her kids. Not until Becky was in an abusive relationship herself, not until Becky had almost lost her unborn child.

Instead of remaining apart, struggling with the individual burdens of our own lives, we came together for the first time ever as a united front. We stopped pushing each other away. I had their unwavering support when I went to jail. Mom did everything she could to afford a decent lawyer and get me a lighter sentence. Becky moved back home, and Mom and Braden helped her as best as they could with Aiden while I was behind bars. The second I got out, I went back to my job in Alberta, sending back everything I didn't need to lighten their financial burdens.

About three months ago, Mom was diagnosed with pancreatic cancer. It was too late for treatment and she'd opted out anyway. Now, according to Becky...she slept away most of her time, too exhausted to open her eyes. She was fading fast, and it was obvious that she didn't have much time left.

And I had a lifetime of things to say to her.

Hunter's bark alerted me to the black SUV pulling into the driveway, parking where Becky's car had been. I silenced him by lifting my hand and he sat down, waiting.

A jovial looking middle-aged woman pushed open the front door and strode inside. She was carrying a large paper bag with what looked like medical supplies. She paused when she saw Aiden and me sitting in the living room, her friendly face breaking out into a wide grin. "Hi there, I'm Beth-Anne. You must be Brock!" she said, approaching me with purpose and thrusting her free hand at me.

"Yes, ma'am. I am," I responded automatically, shaking her hand. "Can I help you with your bags?"

"These? Nah," Beth-Anne said, placing them on the dining room table. "Good afternoon, Aiden." Her voice was warm and affectionate and Aiden's solemn little face broke into a grin just as big as Beth-Anne's.

"Guess what! I'm going to the rodeo!" he declared with wide eyes.

"That's exciting! Is your uncle taking you?" Beth-Anne asked, keeping her eyes focused on him.

"Yup! Uncle Brock. I just met him today, but I like him. He has a dog and his dog is nice!" Aiden said, my heart warming at the seal of approval.

Beth-Anne's gaze went down to the dog at my heels and her smile wavered a little. "Is he now?"

"Don't worry; Hunter is friendly."

"He looks like a wolf," she commented, eying Hunter distrustfully. I chose not to respond. "Are you taking the dog with you to the rodeo?"

"No," I responded, knowing that it would be chaotic enough keeping track of my nephew. "I'm going to drop him off at my place before we go."

She nodded, her shoulders easing at my answer. "Well, have fun! Try to win me a prize, okay Aiden?"

"Okay, Beth-Anne." Aiden nodded with determination. "I'll win you the biggest bear there!"

Installing Aiden's car seat took little to no time. Within ten minutes, we were on the highway heading back to the property so I could drop off Hunter.

I hooked the long chain up to his collar and left him with a lot of water. Hunter preferred being outside, but he tended to wander when given the opportunity, especially when I wasn't around, and I didn't want anyone to mistake him for a wild wolf.

Hunter lay down beneath the large maple tree resting his head on his paws and gave me a narrow, unimpressed look as I drove away without him for the second time in two days.

"Do you like horses?" I asked Aiden, watching his face in the rear-view mirror.

"Yeah, they're okay. I prefer dragons though."

I chuckled. "Well, the rodeo doesn't have dragons unfortunately, but they do have horses and a petting zoo."

"That will do." Aiden sighed heavily, and I couldn't help but grin.

<hr />

THE FAIRGROUNDS WERE JUST as packed as they'd been earlier that weekend, but we made our way in easily enough. Aiden's tiny hand practically disappeared in my big one, but he didn't try to run away. If anything, the crowd made him move closer to me. He was intimidated by all the people. I didn't blame him, he was so small and everyone else probably seemed so huge to him.

One blue cotton candy stick later, we were making our way over to the petting zoo. Aiden loved the animals and they seemed to love his sticky hands. He giggled as they licked the cotton candy remains from his fingers.

When he grew bored of that, I took him over to the ride area. There was a section just for kids, and he tugged my hand the entire way there. He spotted the only roller-coaster, dragging me into the lineup. We waited our turn among the other little kids who were hopped up on sugar.

We waited a good ten minutes before it was finally our turn to board the miniature ride.

"I'm sorry, sir, but you're far too big to accompany him on these rides," the carnival worker said, stepping in front of me and blocking me from entering the tiny dragon rollercoaster that Aiden was hell-bent on riding. He was eyeing my build warily. I stood at just over six feet tall, and I had a lot of muscle from spending the majority of my free time working out.

Alberta had that in common with jail; there wasn't much to do in the entertainment department, and working out was the healthiest option. Other guys I'd worked with got into heavy drinking just for a bit of fun. Me, I needed to keep a clear head. I would never fall into addiction the way my father had.

I couldn't blame the carnival worker for his concern; I could probably snap the frame of that tiny little rollercoaster with my weight.

"Do you want to go alone?" I asked Aiden, crouching to meet his eyes.

He looked up at me fearfully, shaking his head.

"Sir, you're blocking the rest of the lineup..." I could tell the carnival worker was uncomfortable. Instead of giving him trouble, I gently led my nephew away from the front of the line. I scanned the crowd, looking for a suitable replacement to take Aiden on the dragon rollercoaster. Luckily, at that very moment, my brother and his girlfriend approached.

"There you are!" Braden grinned, his smile softening when he caught sight of our nephew. For all that he wasn't, Braden was a good uncle. He somehow managed to keep his arrogance at bay when Aiden was around. My mother too, for that matter. I had to respect him for all he'd done in my absence. He'd dealt with our sick mother, helped Becky out with Aiden, worked full-time and still managed to carry on a very active social life, from the looks of what I'd seen.

My eyes briefly darted to his girlfriend. She was thin and probably a good ninety pounds lighter than me. She was smaller than the mother I'd just witnessed climbing into a cart with her daughter.

"Elle, would you mind riding on the dragon roller-coaster with Aiden?" I asked, gesturing to the ride.

"Sure," she said, freeing her hand from Braden's. She crouched down, smiling at Aiden. "Do you want to ride with me?" she asked. Aiden nodded eagerly and reached for her hand. She smiled gently and led him back to the lineup.

"Guess you're too big?" Braden joked, smirking.

"Not like you'd have that problem." I snorted.

Braden frowned, his eyes narrowing. "Well fuck you too. I was going to invite you to go to the community bonfire tonight, but not after that douche comment." He smirked.

"Why would I want to go to that?" I asked.

"It's a good brother bonding experience." Braden shrugged, watching Elle and Aiden on the ride with a bored expression.

"Nice try, Braden. Cough up the truth."

"That is the truth," he responded, giving me an arrogant grin. "And Tessa will be there. Who knows, you might catch a little tail tonight if you're lucky."

At the mention of her name, my stomach did this weird little flip thing and I instantly thought back to this morning. Braden's next words sealed my fate.

"Besides, I already told Becky we were all going to take Aiden to the bonfire. She'll be meeting us there after she gets off work," he added as Elle and Aiden approached us, still holding hands. Aiden had the biggest grin on his face.

"Can we go again?" he pleaded, looking up at Elle for permission.

"Oh buddy, I'm sorry," Elle said, crouching down to look at Aiden with her expression full of apology. "We have to go now. We're going to watch the strongman competition."

"What's a strongman competition?" Aiden asked, his eyes going wide with astonishment.

"It's when a bunch of muscly guys show off how strong they are. Do you want to watch it, Aiden?" Braden answered with a troublesome grin.

"Okay!" Aiden nodded eagerly, before I could intervene.

"Are you sure Becky's going to be okay with this?" I demanded. Somehow, I couldn't see her comfortable with the idea—all of us at an event the entire town showed up for. I wasn't entirely sold on it, either.

Braden shrugged. "She'll get over it. Let's go."

It appeared my mind was made up for me as Aiden clung tightly to Elle's hand and followed her towards the show ring. Braden kept smirking at me, as if he knew I was pissed off about it. I had to take several deep calming breaths so I wouldn't get angry and say something I'd regret.

Elle shimmied her way into the stands, gently leading Aiden with her, while Braden and I followed behind them. She found us seats in the middle with a perfect view of the ring and pulled out her phone, quickly firing out a text.

The strongman competition was boring, but Aiden seemed enthralled with it.

"I want to go meet that guy!" he declared, pointing at one of the competitors.

"I'm sorry, bud. We can't go see the competitors. Let's go get some hot dogs and check out the tractors," I suggested. "Want to ride on my shoulders?"

"Alright." Aiden sighed deeply, as if he was doing me a favor. I couldn't help but laugh a little as I scooped him up.

"See you at the community bonfire." Braden grinned.

CHAPTER 9

essa

It was the final evening of the rodeo and the fairgrounds pulsed with bodies and energy. Tomorrow, they would start to take down all of the midway rides and pack up the rodeo for another year. The final events were the chili cook-off and community bonfire.

Both events were pretty huge; it was the last hurrah, so to speak. People came from far and wide for a taste of Sue Thompson's award-winning home cooked chili. When dusk fell, they would light the huge bonfire and set off fireworks. There was a wooden dance floor set up with a live DJ and there was plenty of booze for those who weren't underage.

I met Elle at the gates after the strongman competition. After going to Brock's trailer (and successfully having my mind completely blown to smithereens by him), I'd continued on my job hunt quest. I'd returned home with little to no promise of any leads, feeling defeated. Then, I changed into a pair of torn, dark denim jeans, a cream tank top and grabbed a sweater from my desk chair. It was supposed to get chilly tonight and I didn't want to freeze. Right now, even with the sun slowly setting, it was hot.

"Mom's already set up. She just needs us to help serve it. Braden's on dish duty," Elle explained as we walked through the fairgrounds.

"How'd you manage that?"

Elle smiled secretly. "I have my ways."

"Okay, ew." I rolled my eyes.

Elle's mom won the chili cook-off, again. No surprise there. Once the judging was over, we spent the next two hours ladling out and keeping up with the crowds that couldn't get enough of Sue's chili, all while I tried to keep my thoughts away from Brock Miller.

I filled the plastic bowl in my hand and looked up, passing it to the ridiculously large body builder in front of me; he was still wearing his competition number. He took the bowl and gave me a worn smile before leaving the lineup. When he left, the tall, dark and handsome object of my affection stepped forward.

Brock was smiling at me, his eyes roaming my body. His tongue darted out to sweep across his lips as if he was trying to taste something. With the hooded way he was looking at me, I could guess what he was thinking about. His stare was enough to unravel me and I nearly dropped the ladle into the chili pot.

"Tessa," he drawled, his eyes finally finding mine. I swallowed and gave him a small smile in response. "Could we get two bowls, please?"

"Of course," I murmured, my eyes finally dropping down to see that Brock was holding someone's hand; a little boy, who looked no more than three years old. He had dark hair and bright blue eyes.

"This is Becky's son, my nephew," Brock told me, sensing the unasked question. I flushed; I knew his sister had a kid, of course, but there's always that moment when you see the guy you like with a kid and you can't help but wonder…

I ladled a large serving into one bowl and a child's sized portion into another. I handed them both to Brock, then offered two buns to the little boy. "Here you go. It's a little hot."

"Thank you," the little boy said, smiling shyly at me.

"Will you be at the bonfire?" Brock's voice called my attention to him and I bit my lip when our gazes locked. It was funny that I'd thought he was so mysterious when I first saw him the other night. I supposed in a lot of ways, he was still mysterious. I didn't know a thing about him, I didn't know about his past or his plans for his future, but I could still understand him. His eyes were almost transparent. Right now, the need I felt within my core was echoing in those metallic eyes as he gazed at me.

"Yeah, I will," I answered. I could feel Elle's mom's eyes boring a hole into us. She was listening, watching our every movement.

"I'll see you there." he smiled as Sue started towards me. He nodded at her in acknowledgement before he led his nephew away to the picnic tables.

"Seems like someone has an admirer. Who was that handsome devil?" Sue asked, smiling in that motherly way she had.

"Just a guy," I muttered, dropping my eyes.

"That's Braden's older brother," Elle supplied helpfully.

"That's Brock? The same Brock that…" Sue let her sentence hang between the three of us. There wasn't a need to finish it; we all knew she was referring to the bush party where Ezra's cousin had attacked me.

"Yeah, the one and only." I sighed.

"Tessa's sad because her dad has forbidden her to be around him because of the whole 'jail' thing, but she really likes him. Like, a lot. She doesn't like anybody so, it's a big deal," Elle added, again supplying more information than I was comfortable with. I shot her a look, but she shrugged. This was how Elle was; she could talk to her mother about anything and she never left her in the dark.

"Elle, take this empty pot back to Braden for washing," Sue instructed, thrusting the pot at her daughter.

I waited until Elle had disappeared with the pot, worrying my lip. "Sue, you knew my mom. Do you think she'd agree with him? Do you think she wouldn't let me see Brock because of... well, that stuff?"

Sue was thoughtful, pondering my question. "It's hard to say, pumpkin. Your mom would have never wanted anything bad to happen to you, but your mom was also a huge believer in love. She was a lot like Elle in that regard. She believed in soul mates and eternal love and all that crap."

"What, you don't believe in it?" I questioned, taken aback by Sue's rather cynical answer.

"I believe in love, sure." Sue laughed lightly, her eyes crinkling when she smiled at me. "But I believe that there is all kinds of love out there and that it's possible to experience love more than once. Different kinds of love, mind you." She paused thoughtfully, her eyes regarding me. "I was the cautious one. Your mom, she was a genuine, loving person. She only saw the good in people and animals alike and she didn't believe love should be rationed or calculated. It's why she was so wonderful at rescuing broken horses... and people. Take your daddy for example."

"What about him?" I frowned, absently ladling some more chili into a bowl for another person. I barely looked up when I passed it to them.

"He was what she called a rebel soul." Sue smiled sadly. "He had been knocked around by life quite a bit. He was a troublemaker and as reckless as they come. But your mom...she saw past all that bad boy crap and saw the man underneath. The man he could be if given the opportunity, if he was given a little love."

"My dad was not a rebel." I rolled my eyes.

"Oh, you may not believe it now when you look at him; he's as still as the calm before a storm. But he used to be the storm, and the only thing that tamed him was your mom. Falling in love with a good woman will do that to a man," Sue added over her shoulder as she walked away, leaving me with my whirling thoughts.

I STAYED BEHIND to help Sue pack up, even after Braden and Elle had taken off. I was hoping she'd tell me more about my mom and dad, but she didn't. That was Sue, though. She'd give you a little bit to get you hooked, and then she'd fall silent, leaving you frothing for more details.

"Go on, get outta here. That boy isn't going to wait all night for you," Sue finally said as if she'd heard what direction my thoughts had taken. She smacked me with the towel she'd been using to dry off one of the huge pots that had housed her chili.

"Fine." I dropped my towel and walked away from her table, leaving her to carry her dishes to her truck.

Workers were about to start the bonfire and the crowd was growing. I spotted Elle and Braden sitting on a huge blanket on the grass. She was resting between his legs, her head against his chest, and he was whispering something to her that made her smile. I paused, watching them for a moment, and realized just how happy my best friend was when she was with him. She glowed. She sparkled from the inside out.

Braden tipped her chin up gently, bringing his lips to hers tenderly. They were completely lost to the world. Watching them made my heart ache a little.

I used to think that Elle's romantic heart was just finding love where it didn't exist, turning fairy tales into truth, but after watching the two of them together, it was obvious that she was living and breathing it. She was in love, and it was getting harder and harder to dislike Braden. He wasn't the same guy when he was with her; he was a changed man. I couldn't help but reflect upon the things that Sue had said about love.

Their quiet, stolen moment was interrupted by a little boy racing towards them. He dove onto Elle and she let out an audible gasp before they teamed up and started tickling him. He giggled, squirming around on the ground and pleading for them to stop.

"You're going to make him pee his pants!" a female's voice shouted from directly behind me, startling me. I turned, seeing Brock and Becky Miller approaching. She was dressed in jeans and a plain blue t-shirt, her dark hair pulled up into a messy ponytail. She looked exhausted. "Excuse me," she said, brushing past me to join Braden, Elle and her son on the blanket.

Braden and Elle stopped tickling the child, but he kept giggling in Elle's arms. She was laughing too and Braden was staring at her with a smile on his lips, like she was all he could see.

"Hey," Brock muttered, stepping closer. His breath was warm on my neck, prompting goosebumps to erupt on my skin, and I took a shuddering breath.

"Hi again." I smiled timidly. I didn't know how to act around Brock now that it wasn't just the two of us alone, especially after the talk I'd had with Sue.

"Shall we?" he asked, tilting his head in the direction of the others. I bit my lip and hesitated, looking around. There were a lot of people here tonight; a lot of people who knew my family, a lot of people who would eagerly start flapping their gums about the Armstrong girl hanging out with 'that Miller boy'.

I wanted tonight, and I didn't want the possibility of my brothers showing up to ruin it. "How about we go somewhere... more private?" I asked nervously. The fear of rejection was lurking just beneath the surface. I took a deep breath, trying to drown out that fear with oxygen.

Brock's eyes heated as he looked at me and then he nodded. "Alright, I know a place where we can still see the fireworks. Come with me for a moment."

I followed him to the blanket, and we came to a stop in front of it.

"Becky, you know Tessa, right?" Brock questioned.

"I've seen you around." Becky smiled warmly. "You're related to Tommy and Gordon, right? I went to school with them."

"Yep, I sure am," I said, trying to keep my tone friendly and light. I glanced around the fairgrounds, trying to see if any of my brothers were going to walk over and ruin the night with their terrible attitudes. At least I didn't have to worry about my dad finding me on a blanket with the Millers, he hadn't been to the community bonfire since before my mom died. It used to be their thing.

"Are they coming tonight?" Becky asked, still trying to make small talk. I could feel Brock's eyes on me, watching me, waiting for my response.

"Probably for the fireworks," I answered, shrugging.

"Is your car unlocked, Becky?" Brock asked, cutting her off before she could say anything else.

"Yeah…"

"Okay, I'm going to put Aiden's car seat in it."

"You guys aren't sticking around for the fireworks?" Becky asked, surprised.

"They'd rather set off their own," Braden joked, smirking.

Becky shot him a dirty look over her shoulder and turned to face us again. "Alright, that's fine. Thanks so much for watching him today, Brock."

"No problem," Brock said. "You should probably think about finding a more dependable sitter, though. I'm happy to help out whenever I can, but I'll be busy this week milling with Grady."

"I know." Becky sighed, her face falling momentarily. I went to ask her what kind of hours she needed a sitter for, after all, I was in the job market, but Brock grabbed my hand. It felt like an electric current pulsed through our skin at the contact, and I couldn't think about anything other than that feeling.

He led me away from them, weaving me through clusters of people until we reached the parking lot. Then he dropped my hand long enough to pull the car seat out of his truck and track down his sister's car. Once he'd secured the car seat in it, he turned to face me. Anticipation and desire danced across his features.

"You up for a drive?" he asked.

Always, I wanted to whisper. Instead, I smiled and nodded. He took my hand again and led me back to his truck.

I climbed into the cab, noticing for the first time how clean the interior was. Most guys liked to use their vehicles as portable garbage bins. Not Brock. "Where's your dog tonight?" I asked, remembering the yellow-eyed creature that had come to my rescue a few nights ago.

"He's at home," he answered, looking at me briefly before pulling out of his parking spot. He drove about five minutes down the road before turning onto another unmarked road. He drove up the steep incline, the four-wheel drive truck handling it with complete ease.

It took five more minutes, but the hill finally peaked. Brock gave me a lopsided grin, daring me with his eyes, his hand on the gear shift. I knew what he was thinking before he did it, and I grinned in response as he lowered the gear and stomped on the gas, doing a perfect donut. The wind from the open window blew my hair around my face, and I threw back my head and laughed. Dust blew all around us, and he did several loops before twisting the steering wheel and driving forward. He braked, parking so his truck bed was facing the north side of the hill.

He grinned at me again before climbing out from the cab. He opened the back door, grabbing a huge blanket from the floor. Shaking it off, he threw it into the bed of the truck. "Are you coming?"

I climbed out too, walking around to the back to join him. He was already standing in the truck bed. He held his hand out to me and I took it, settling onto the thick blanket he'd laid out for us.

We were high enough up that we could see over the treetops to the fairgrounds below. I watched the flames of the bonfire licking the dark sky, trying to reach upwards towards the stars.

"I missed this view," Brock remarked, settling beside me. His eyes never left the sky when he spoke.

"I bet Alberta has nice views," I said, brushing my tangled hair out of my eyes.

"Yeah, but it's got nothing on this one," he murmured, his eyes fixated on my face. The look we exchanged was heated, charged with intensity. The kind of sensation that evoked a smoldering desire in my lower abdomen.

Then, he was moving to me and I was moving to him. His hands found my face, framing it, and he kissed me with everything that he had. It was a searing kiss, full of heat and longing, that stoked the burning embers of desire.

I moaned, moving against him. He dropped his hand to hook beneath my thigh and tugged me up onto his lap. I could feel him, hard beneath me. His hands were roaming all over my body, exploring every last bit of me, touching me over my clothes—his hands lavishing me while he set me on fire using his lips and tongue.

He broke the kiss, moving his lips a fraction away from mine and smiled with his eyes closed. "Jesus, Tessa," he breathed. "What are you doing to me?"

"Basically, whatever you're doing to me," I muttered, just as breathless. In the background, in the silence of the night around us, I could hear the fireworks going off, cracking into the sky and illuminating the dark night with multiple colours. I couldn't drag my eyes away from his to watch and I didn't want to.

Brock smiled, his eyes still focused on mine. They seemed to peer straight into my soul and I couldn't help but wonder what he saw, what he was thinking.

"I'm thinking that I don't want this night to end," Brock said in a low voice and I blushed. I hadn't realized I'd asked him out loud.

"I'm thinking that I agree. I'm also thinking that we need to finish what we started this morning..." I whispered, feeling his cock move beneath my thigh as if it was struggling to free itself of the denim.

Brock's lips crashed against mine again and he kissed me deeply before pausing. His hands tangled in my hair and tugged it so that I had no choice but to turn my head and expose my neck to him. He sucked on it, kissing and tasting my skin, while I fumbled with his belt buckle.

"Woah," he laughed, his free hand stopping my quest. "I didn't exactly have time to go to the store yet...I wasn't planning on this..."

"I've got you covered." I grinned mischievously, pulling a condom out from the back pocket of my jeans. I'd grabbed a box from the gas station outside of town after leaving Brock's place.

"Thank God," he growled, taking it from me and flipping me onto my back. He held himself up with one arm while he kissed my neck, his hand roaming underneath my shirt. His fingertips left goosebumps in their wake.

My hands were just as greedy, tugging his shirt away so I could touch the defined muscles of his abdomen. They tensed beneath my fingers, and he took a shuddering breath as my hand traveled lower; his breath was hot on the sensitive skin of my neck. I slid my hand into his boxers, gripping his hard length.

I'd never wanted anyone more than I wanted him. I didn't care about the technicalities; I didn't care that we hadn't discussed anything aside from our desire for one another. I didn't care about tomorrow or about the heartbreaking fact that we couldn't exist in a world outside of our own.

My shirt was off and I could feel the heat from his naked chest against me as he kissed me, his hands roaming the thin material of my bra, teasing my nipples through it. He went at a lethargic pace, as if we had all the time in the world or like he wanted to commit every moment, every touch of his fingers on my skin to memory. I could barely breathe when he ran his hand along my abdomen, past the waistline of my jeans and panties and stroked against my core once, finding me slick and wet.

"Tess," he exhaled, his voice strained. It was as if he was pleading with me, as if he was desperately fighting for control. My need for him was consuming me; I was pulsing and vibrating, ready to come undone simply from the tantalizing way he kissed me and the subtle brush of his finger.

"I want you," I whispered, looking into those lustrous eyes. I bit my lip as I lifted my hips, drawing his finger a little deeper into my core.

He growled in response, deepening the kiss and changing the course from tender and slow to smoldering and passionate, heady with need. Our lips only broke long enough to peel off the rest of our clothes and for Brock to slide the condom onto his thick length. Then I was beneath him; he held himself up with his arms on either side of my head. His hands brushed my tangled hair out of my face and his eyes bore into mine. I felt him against my entrance, coating his head in my wetness. So many emotions rippled through me: sizzling desire, anticipation and things I couldn't even begin to pinpoint. Brock swallowed hard, his emotions echoing mine as he sank into me.

His breath escaped in a whoosh, and I closed my eyes against the sudden burning intrusion. It was uncomfortable; I had only ever slept with one person before, Ezra, and he hadn't been as large as Brock. But despite the sting, my body craved it—craved him.

Brock was watching my expressions carefully, reading me. He brought one hand down, his finger playing with my clit as he slowly dove in again and again, until I was arching with the desire to meet each of his thrusts, to have him fill me completely.

His eyes were dark with lust, and they only darkened as he brought me closer and closer to the edge with each slow, deep thrust. He stroked my clit and I trembled, coming undone around him.

He brought his hand back to hold himself up as he increased his pace, while I rode out my orgasm with each thrust until I felt another tiny tremor. His head dropped beside mine, and he thrust once more into me, hard and tense and breathing my name as he found his own release.

Our hearts pounded in sync, and Brock lifted his head to look at me, a huge grin lighting up his face. "Holy fuck," he exclaimed, his words echoing my thoughts. I smiled, biting my lip as he pulled out of me. I missed the sensation almost immediately.

He discarded the condom and fell back down beside me, completely spent. He pulled me closer to him and grabbed the sides of the blanket, wrapping it around us so we were covered. I lay with my head against his shoulder and my palm against his pulsing heart.

In the bed of his truck, we had a perfect view of the stars and the last few fireworks from the community bonfire.

"I think this is my favourite fireworks show," I remarked, biting my lip once the last of the words had fallen from my mouth. I looked up at him, waiting for him to freak out, but he was smiling in agreement.

"Yeah, hands down." He sighed, kissing the top of my head. His hand traced a gentle pattern against my shoulder, and his eyes never left my face. "What are you thinking?"

"I don't know," I answered honestly. "My mind is kind of blown, to be honest. I've never..." I trailed off, flushing. I'd never had an orgasm during sex before. I was vastly inexperienced and I had a feeling he wasn't, and that made me feel awkward and a little insecure.

Plus, I wanted more. More than just this mind blowing sex with him. I wanted to get to know the man, and I was afraid to admit that.

"Well, how about I tell you what I'm thinking?" Brock suggested, his eyes almost glowing in the light of the full moon. A slight smile tugged up the corner of his lips.

"Alright, what are you thinking?"

"I'm thinking that you are the best thing I've ever had the pleasure of being in. I'm thinking that you're my favourite flavor and my willing sin. I'm thinking that I want a hell of a lot more of this thing between us. I want to see where this goes. I want to be with you, Tessa."

His words made my heart clench and flip in my chest. "I'm thinking the same thing," I whispered. "I want more of this...I want to see where this goes. I just..." I sighed, biting desperately trying to figure out how I could make that possible. How could I sneak around my entire family and have a relationship with this incredible man without them finding out? It was a small town; everyone knew everyone else's business. Someone surely must have spotted Brock and me at the bonfire, and that would eventually get back to my brothers and ultimately, my dad.

"I know." His voice was strained as if it pained him to

acknowledge the huge elephant in the room. He cleared his throat. "I know that your family wouldn't approve of us, your dad especially. I guess if I was a parent, I wouldn't either."

I lifted my head so I could better look at him. "Could you tell me about it...about why?" my voice was full of hesitation. I was afraid to ask, afraid that he'd get angry at me for asking. But I felt like I needed to know.

He swallowed hard, his eyes searching mine for a moment. Whatever he saw there made him nod once and start speaking. "You probably remember that I went off and started working in Alberta, in the mines...right?" I nodded. "When I was gone...I guess things at home fell apart. More than usual, I mean. My sister shacked up with some guy who got her pregnant. He was a cokehead and he was abusive. I guess she was afraid to leave or tell anyone what was going on, so she pretended everything was fine. Then I got a phone call from my brother, saying Becky was in the hospital. He'd beaten her so badly that she went into preterm labor and nearly lost Aiden. I snapped."

"Oh my God," I muttered, my heart breaking for Becky. "I don't blame you for snapping, Brock. How come nobody knows the truth? Like, all of it?" I added, frowning. The rumor mill whispered nothing about Brock defending his sister and nephew; the rumors just said he'd snapped on some druggie and nearly killed him with his bare hands.

"My family has always been good at keeping secrets," he explained. "We know people like to talk about us and we don't like to add fuel to the fire."

"But if people knew the truth, they wouldn't blame you either," I argued, thinking about my dad and brothers. Given their fierce protectiveness over me, they would understand completely.

Brock smiled regretfully. "They don't need to know the truth, Tess. I don't give a rat's ass what this town thinks of me."

He brought his hand up to touch the side of my face. "The only opinion I care about is yours."

"Well, you don't have to worry about that. I think very highly of you, Brock Miller," I responded, smiling.

"I'll take it," he whispered, pulling me towards him so he could kiss me again.

CHAPTER 10

rock

WE LAY in the bed of my truck kissing and touching and talking for another hour before we dressed and I drove us back to the fairgrounds. I could have stayed there all night with her, but I knew she was anxious to get back. I knew she didn't want to get caught and I didn't want her to get caught either. I definitely didn't want to deal with her family right then, not when every-thing between us was so new and raw and potent. I wanted to enjoy it for a bit; I wanted to see where it would go, just like I'd told her.

The fireworks were over, but the party was still in full swing. Music, dancing and laughter surrounded us as we walked, our hands not touching but our arms occasionally brushing.

I wanted to hold her hand. I wanted to claim her as mine. It was the strangest fucking feeling, a desire I'd never had before. I'd only known her— seen her— like this for a few days, and I was in ruins. Part of me wanted to be cautious, to take a step back and regroup—to regain control of myself. But a bigger part was telling me this was natural and to it, to embrace her. I knew I could fall in love with her, that I was falling... if I hadn't already. With the way she looked at me and smiled, and with the way I'd felt when inside of her; I couldn't help but want to dive in head first.

"There you are!" Elle shouted, coming out of nowhere and tackling Tessa. "Your brothers are looking for you."

"What did you tell them?" Tessa's exquisite lips turned down in a subtle frown. Her eyes came to my face for a fraction of a moment before landing back on her friend's.

"I told them you went back with my mom for a bit to help her unpack. They didn't really buy it, but whatever." Elle shrugged, tossing her hair over her shoulders. "Unless you want to get caught with your hand in the cookie jar, maybe you guys could cool the lustful looks and all that shit? Brother coming in at two o'clock," she added, motioning with her eyes.

"Brock." Gordon's voice was dangerous. "What are you doing here?"

"It's a community bonfire," I responded dryly. "I figured that invitation was extended to me, by proxy."

Gordon laughed lightly, a small smile easing the hard look on his face. "Yeah, well. What are you doing near my sister?"

"Chill out, Gordon," Elle interrupted, scowling at him. "Brock was just asking us if we'd seen Braden."

"He's over by the beer tent." Gordon answered the question I hadn't asked. "I'm on my way there now. Come walk with me."

I didn't dare let myself look at Tessa again. I schooled my features to the mask of indifference the moment I'd seen Gordon approaching. I knew that she was nowhere near ready to tell her family and I wasn't ready to deal with that fallout either. I followed Gordon toward the beer tent, spotting my brother hanging out with a few of his friends. He raised a beer to me, but Gordon made no move to slow down. He kept walking over to where Grady and Travis were hanging.

"Two Bud Lights," Gordon ordered, nodding towards me. The bartender fetched two beers from the cooler and Gordon pulled out his wallet, raising his hand when I made a move to pay for mine. "I've got it."

I pursed my lips into a thin line and accepted the beer he handed me. It was strange how on the defense I was around the guy I'd once called my best friend. But I didn't trust his intentions, and I didn't feel like I knew him anymore.

"Cheers, to the dynamic four." Gordon smiled, lifting his beer. His eyes never left my face as we all raised our beers to the toast. I took a deep sip, never backing down on the challenge. I wasn't afraid of Gordon and I wasn't going to let him intimidate me.

"So when are you back on the road again?" Grady asked Travis, making small talk. Gordon and I both turned our attention to Travis for the answer.

"Took a couple weeks off," he replied, clearing his throat. "I needed a break and we don't have any shows until next month anyway."

"How does it feel to be a hot shot celebrity?" Gordon smirked, taking another heady sip of his beer.

"Pretty fantastic," Travis said, grinning and lifting his beer bottle again. He looked three sheets to the wind. "I get to bang hot chicks and have everyone scream my name. Plus the money doesn't hurt."

I wasn't paying attention to the conversation anymore. Movement by the flap of the beer tent caught my eye. I watched as Ezra Johnson walked up to Braden and his other friends, his DC decked cousin trailing behind him.

Braden's eyes, full of alarm and anger, found mine from across the tent. My blood was fucking boiling, after everything that disgusting worm had tried to do to Tessa.

Instantly, my mind conjured up the image of her terrified against that tree and I slammed my beer down on the table. Three sets of eyes went from the beer to my face, but I was already purposely moving towards the back of the tent where that slimy fucker was animatedly telling some story to the others. Braden stood up, about to intervene, but I already had DC guy's shirt fisted in my hands.

"What the fuck are you doing back here?" I demanded, my face inches away from his. He slunk back, his pupils dilating with fear, trying to get away from me.

"Relax, man!" Ezra demanded, grabbing at my arm. "Just because you want her doesn't mean you need to beat the fuck out of my cousin!"

"What the fuck?" Braden growled.

"I talked to Chris. He said Tessa wanted it and was eager for it, and this fucking jackass got all jealous about it. Fucking 'roid raging, crazy asshole!" Ezra spat.

"Are you that fucking dense?" Braden roared, spit flying from his mouth. "Tessa was beat the fuck up and you're gonna sit there and buy that piece of shit's excuses for what happened?"

Ezra paused, looking to his cousin for help. By now, Gordon, Travis, and Grady were flanking my sides.

"You can't hit me. You touch me, and you'll go straight back to jail, *convict*. Besides, I don't know why you're getting your fucking panties in a knot. Ezra said she wasn't a good fuck anyway," DC guy spat, his eyes darting back and forth between my face and the others staring at him.

"Don't, Brock." Braden jumped forward, placing his hand on my shoulder to keep me grounded after seeing the rage flickering in my eyes.

I took a calming breath, focusing on the feeling of Gordon vibrating with anger at my side, and I laughed darkly. "You must be all kinds of stupid," I said, shaking my head. I released my hold on his shirt, smoothing out the wrinkles and giving him a very dangerous smile. "I might not be able to hit you, but these guys? They sure can," I said lowly, threateningly. "And that one on my right? He just so happens to be Tessa's brother. And he doesn't take kindly to his sister being talked about like that, or what you tried to do to her."

DC guy's pupils were completely dilated now, the whites of his eyes showing.

"Better run." Gordon's lips barely moved when he spoke, but DC guy heard him clear as fucking day. He took off, stumbling out of the tent and running. Gordon finished the rest of the beer he was holding and wiped his lips with the back of his hand. He looked at me. "We're not done here, Brock. I respect what you did, but you and me? We need to have a chat."

I nodded, pursing my lips, and watched as Gordon took off, Travis and Grady following close behind, likely to keep an eye on him.

Gordon was a smart guy. Smart enough to chase him off public property and get him away from a crowd. Gordon wasn't deadly, but he was effective. With the other two with him, I didn't have to worry if he'd end up down the same path I'd gone.

I cracked my knuckles, exhaling deeply before I turned my gaze on Ezra. He almost seemed to wilt from the fire in my eyes. "I expected more from you, to be honest. You looked like a smart guy. Smart enough to know that when a girl emerges shaking, bloody and bruised from the woods, she wasn't a willing participant in whatever happened." I stepped closer to him. "And for the record, she's the perfect fuck. You just didn't know how to operate."

"OH SHIT!" Braden cackled, bowing over with laughter as I stomped out of the beer tent.

I was just reaching my truck when a hand reached out and clasped mine. I turned, seeing Tessa's mischievous smile as she pulled me towards her.

My body was still amped up on adrenaline and testosterone, and the way she was biting her lower lip was not helping. But losing control to Tessa was far better than losing control to rage. I looked around, finding the parking lot dark and empty, save for the parked cars. I grabbed her ass, pulling her against me as I walked her backwards to my truck. My lips found hers and I kissed her like she was water and I was a parched man. She kissed me back, sucking on my lower lip and I growled, thrusting against her and pinning her to the cold metal of the truck. My dick was impossibly hard again, like we hadn't just fucked a few hours before. My need for her was insatiable and I think she felt the same, if the way she grinded up against me was any indication. She pulled away, breathless.

"So, Elle has my truck keys," she whispered, biting her lip. "She's going to go find Braden and then they're leaving...in my truck...and I'm 'sleeping' over at her house. Take me home with you," she added, pressing her lips against mine again.

That was all I needed. I gripped her ass, picking her up and keeping her pinned against the side of the truck as I opened the door. I set her down on the bench seat without moving my lips from hers. Regretfully, I broke the kiss. If I didn't get her to my place soon, I was going to need to take her right there in that parking lot where anyone could see us.

I might have sped home—just a little bit. I might have completely ignored Hunter's excited barks, my own excitement taking precedence—along with the need to get her undressed.

But when I finally got her into my bed, I took my time with her, focusing all I had on bringing those soft moans to her lips. I basked in the feel of her, letting myself shut off every other thought and feeling but the ones she brought out in me.

Afterwards, my fingers twirled in the silk curls of her hair while she lay in my arms.

"I want to know everything about you. Is that crazy?" she asked, lifting her head up to look at me with a timid expression.

"No." I smiled. "I want to know everything about you, too."

"Alright." She exhaled. "Well, I like riding horses, jumping, fishing...basically any activity outdoors and I'm afraid of snakes. I'm going to college in the fall with Elle... who, as you know, is my best friend and has been my whole life. I want to be a veterinarian and open my own clinic and animal rescue one day, but that'll be a long time coming. Right now, I'm focusing on getting my veterinary technician diploma so I can work in a clinic and save up the money for vet school. Elle and I have a place lined up and everything. I'm excited to leave this town and get some space away from my family. I love them, but some-times when I'm around them, it's like..." she trailed off, thinking hard. "It's like that feeling you get when your shoes are too tight, and you just want to take them off and walk free for a little while."

"That was oddly poetic." I smiled, loving all these little facts she listed about herself. Now more than ever, it seemed she was conjured up just for me.

"Yeah well..." She blew a strand of her hair out of her eyes. "Your turn."

"Okay." I paused, thinking about my answer. My hand dropped to her shoulder, brushing against her soft flesh. "I like outdoor activities too. Fishing, camping, hiking, being outside. I like to work with my hands. I like to keep busy; I'm always moving, I guess. I'm restless. I like my solitude and I'd do anything for my family. I don't like people. I don't know, there's not much about me to tell." I figured it was obvious that I had a temper, not everyone serves time for beating the crap out of someone who crosses them, and I didn't feel like getting into my broken childhood, either. I didn't want to tell her the ugly things. I didn't want to taint this time we had together with my darkness.

"Tell me about your job," she urged, her toes brushing along my leg.

"My job?" She nodded. "Alright. I work in a coal mine in Alberta, driving a haul truck and a scoop. I don't mind it. It keeps me busy and it keeps my thoughts occupied. I don't notice the distance when I'm working because it's such a demanding job; there isn't much room outside of it. I took a leave of absence because my mom is dying."

She stiffened beside me, drawing in a deep breath. "I'm sorry."

I kissed the top of her head because I didn't know what else to say. It wasn't her fault that my mother was dying.

"Are you going to go back? To Alberta?" she asked, her voice a quiet whisper. The sound of crickets could be heard through the screen window over my bed.

"I'm not sure. That was the plan. I was going to build a cabin here, somewhere I could stay when I visit...but I was planning on keeping my job. The money is really good..." I hesitated.

"But what?" she muttered, her voice sounding tired.

I swallowed hard. "I don't know if I want to leave them," I answered, referring to Becky, Aiden and even Braden. I was only speaking half of the truth. The other half, the part that I couldn't tell her, was that I'd met a girl that I didn't want to leave 3,337.4 km away.

THE SOUND of tires on dirt and gravel and the low menacing rumble of Hunter's growling alerted me to the Ford pulling into my makeshift driveway early the next morning. Tessa was still sleeping in my bed, her hair strewn about on the pillow, her bare breasts rising and falling with every breath.

"Fuck," I muttered, diving out of bed and pulling on my jeans. I scooped up my t-shirt from the floor and pulled the blinds down in the kitchen while I tugged it over my head, watching as Gordon and Tommy Armstrong exited the cab of the truck, peering around the property.

I opened the door to my trailer, letting Hunter out. He followed me as I approached my unexpected guests. I knew this visit had very little to do with a social call and a whole lot to do with a certain blonde haired girl with amber eyes and a wicked grin.

A girl that was completely off limits, a girl that I couldn't stop thinking about despite the fact that I knew she was off limits, a girl that didn't seem to give a rat's ass that she was off limits, a girl that I hungered for, a girl that I'd give up everything for in the blink of an eye if she asked me.

A girl that was currently passed out, naked in my bed, a mere five feet away.

I raised my head, making eye contact with both Gordon and Tommy. I wasn't afraid of either of them. Gordon was every bit as burly and tall as he'd been in high school, but I had a least five inches on him, and I was in better shape. I knew I could take him, if need be. I just hoped that Gordon wasn't here to fight.

"So," Gordon drawled when he got close enough to us. His dark eyes assessed me, trying to decide just how much of a threat I really was. It was an intimidation tactic that went back to high school, one that I'd done too with Gordon and Grady alongside of me. His eyes met mine, hard and unyielding. "Looks like we've got to have a little chat, old friend."

If anything, his attempt at intimidation made me want to throw back my head and laugh. I'd fought bigger guys in jail, and I'd done worse things than Gordon Armstrong had ever done.

I clenched my jaw, not wanting to let the hint of a smile aggravate him. I knew how he reacted, and cocky arrogance was one thing that drove Gordon straight to fighting.

"I figured. You came here without a welcoming basket, after all," I said, casting a glance to Tommy. I didn't like how he was staring at me, like he knew things about me that I hadn't told anyone else. Things that pissed him off, like my staggering attraction to his sister, the things I'd done to her and would do to her again the first chance I got.

Gordon laughed lightly, scratching his beard and looking away. "Yeah, I guess we forgot the basket."

I stood calmly and watched as Gordon's eyes took in the area around us. His calculating gaze moved to the massive wood pile behind Grady's mill and the hole I'd excavated. The foundation was being laid tomorrow morning, and once it was completed, I could start building the shell of the cabin.

"We finally got that prick to fess up about what happened at that bush party," Tommy supplied. "Thanks for handling it, but we would have appreciated a call."

"I wasn't exactly focused on what you would have appreciated," I shot back, my voice clipped.

Gordon's attention snapped back on me like a rubber band. "Thank you for protecting her that night. But I still have to warn you. I need you to stay away from her."

I pursed my lips, nodding slowly and looking past them both. It wasn't a nod of *'yeah, sure bud. Whatever you say'* it was a nod of *'I hear you, and I disagree'*. Gordon knew it.

"Look man, you gotta understand where I'm coming from with this; you'd be livid if one of us got with your sister. Bros don't do that to each other."

"We are not 'bros'," I said, my tone a little harsher than I intended. "And frankly, not that it's any of your goddamn business, but Tessa is a grown woman. She can make her own decisions."

Gordon pursed his lips, nodding again. There was a lot of fucking nodding happening, like we were all bobble heads on someone's dashboard.

"Maybe you're right about that," he allowed, his dark eyes

fixed on mine. "But I still would hope that one of my old friends would keep the promise he made to me."

I clenched my jaw and remained silent. There was no need to tell Gordon that I'd already broken it on more than one occasion, or that it was fucking ridiculous to uphold a promise we had made when we were sixteen and horny, bagging chicks left, right, and center and promising each other our sisters were off limits because neither one of us could stand how we treated girls.

Times had changed; I wasn't going to hurt Tessa. I wasn't that stupid kid I was when I was sixteen.

"Alright, then. Now that we've got the uncomfortable chat out of the way, let's talk business." Gordon slapped his hands together, gesturing towards the wood pile. "What's your plan here?"

The last thing I wanted to do was talk business with Gordon right now. In fact, I was torn between punching him in the nose and kicking him off the property so I could go back to the pretty blonde in my bed. "Look," I sighed tiredly. "I have to be somewhere in an hour. Family stuff. But why don't we meet up at Flanigan's Pub Thursday night and I'll bring the blueprints?"

"Sounds fantastic." Gordon grinned, backing away towards his truck. He opened the door and looked through the open window at me. "Remember what I said about Tessa, though. I meant it."

I nodded, clenching my jaw tightly as I watched them drive away. I turned around, running my hands through my tangled hair as I stalked back to my trailer. I opened the door, surprised to see Tessa standing there with a sheet wrapped around her body.

"Morning," she said hesitantly, drawing the sheet tighter around herself. My cock hardened at the sight of her, straining against the denim of my jeans. Tessa's hair was a tangled mess, courtesy of me, and she had a red mark on her neck... also courtesy of me. I didn't know what in the hell got into me when I was with her. I hadn't given a girl a hickey since I was a dipshit teen, and that was an act of marking, not a moment of losing myself in the taste of her skin.

"Good morning," I muttered, stalking towards her. I cradled her face in my hands, brushing the hair out of her eyes before I kissed her slowly. "Are you hungry?"

"Elle's on her way," she said apologetically, shaking her head and biting down on her lower lip. "I have a lot of chores to do today. I have to exercise the horses."

"Ah." I nodded, remembering how hectic life at the Armstrong farm could get. One of my jobs when I had worked there was exercising a few of the horses by taking them out on the trail with Gordon.

"But..." Tessa grinned over her shoulder, dropping the sheet to the floor. My cock jumped as if it remembered exactly how it felt to be inside of her. "I might be able to steal away tomorrow afternoon."

It was difficult to think with her naked in front of me, but I somehow managed. I cleared my throat. "That'll be good...I should be free by then. I have some stuff to do in the morning, but..." I trailed off; thoughts about the foundation completely fell out of my mind when she bent over to grab her bra.

She shimmed into her jeans and turned around, slipping her bra on and reaching around to fasten it. "Okay, well, maybe we'll do something?" she asked, looking up at me as she pulled her tank top on.

All I could do was nod like an idiot. I wanted to make her stay, but she had things to do and I really needed to pay a visit to my mom.

She grabbed her phone off the kitchen table where she'd left it the night before. "What's your cell number?"

I told her and she typed quickly into her phone. A moment later, I heard mine buzzing from the back room.

"Now you have my number and I have yours." She smiled shyly, approaching me.

I wanted to make her feel our time apart the way I knew I was going to feel it, so I kissed her again. I backed her up against the bathroom door, breathing her in like fine wine. I felt her heartbeat beneath my palm as I gently kneaded her breast.

The sound of yet another set of tires pulling up my driveway was a sound I detested. Elle honked loudly, laying her palm against the horn long enough to wake the neighborhood, if I'd had any neighbors.

"See you soon," she promised, flying out my door.

CHAPTER 11

essa

"You won't believe who showed up this morning," I said, arching an eyebrow at Elle. She'd offered to help me exercise the horses, since she said she had nothing better to do. Exercising the horses was basically just code for 'Tessa and Elle spend the day talking and riding horses on the trails.'

I was on Spirit and Elle was riding one of the older females, Temptress. Chores felt a lot less like chores with her around.

"Let me take a wild guess…" Elle gave me a sarcastic look. "Tweedle Dee and Tweedle Dum."

"Yup. They wanted to have a chat with Brock." I sighed, the irritation I felt still swirling around within me. I'd heard Brock leave the trailer, and when I crept to the window over his sink, I saw the three-man showdown. Gordon and Tommy tried to tell Brock to stay away from me and Brock didn't promise them one way or another.

From where I stood, I could see that he was fighting to keep his emotions in check. He didn't want to cause trouble for me or my family, but he wasn't the kind of guy who was used to being told what to do.

"Well, that's surprising," Elle said dryly.

"I am so over the whole *'stay away from my sister, we're so tough'* bull crap."

"I don't blame you. I'm sick of it by proxy." She snorted, shaking her head.

"This has to change, right?" I added, my eyes wide and pleading as I stared at her. "When I go to college, it'll be better?"

Elle shifted on her saddle, avoiding looking directly at me. She brushed a strand of her long dark hair behind her ears. "I hope so." She sighed. "Do you think if you just told them all about him, they'd lay off a little?"

"Absolutely not," I deadpanned. "Besides, I don't even know what my feelings for him are."

My friend was quiet for a moment, lost in thought as we slowly made our way back to the farm. "Are you at least going to give yourself a chance to figure it out?" she asked, looking at me with wide, hopeful eyes.

"Yeah. I just want to do so without their interference complicating things, you know?" I said on exhale, biting my lip. I glanced around the expanse of the farm, making sure nobody lurked nearby. Rolling hills and pastures kissed golden by the setting sun with cattle grazing lazily, were the only things around. No brothers, no risk of being overheard. "I really like how he makes me feel. I want to...get to know him, see where it goes." Elle practically clapped, jumping up and down in the saddle. "Relax." I laughed, feeling embarrassed.

"I'm just excited for you." She couldn't hide her huge grin. "You've got the bug."

"Please don't say that." My lips stiffened, losing the carefree upward tilt. "It's way too early for you to be saying things like that."

"Why? There's no timeline on love, Tess," she told me, her eyes deadly serious. I sent her a scathing look and she sighed, smiling sadly. "You'll see," she declared, kicking her heels into Temptress's sides and lurching forward down the dirt road, towards the barn.

I sped up, digging my heels into Spirit's side, trying to catch Elle before she reached the gate.

By the time we finished putting away the gear and brushing the horses, it was dinner time.

Every Monday night, the entire Armstrong clan got together for dinner. My dad, all three of my brothers and Ben's wife Katie sat around the big oak table, enjoying the roast I had made. Elle stuck around too.

It was a regular scene, my best friend at our family gatherings. Nobody batted an eyelash and everybody treated her like she was part of the family. In a lot of ways, she was.

"So how many weeks are left, Katie?" Elle was asking, a whimsical look in her brown eyes as she smiled at Katie's round belly.

Katie rubbed it in a circular motion, looking at Ben with a demure smile. "Three weeks or so, but the baby could come at any time really," she answered.

"That's so exciting! Do you have any names picked out?"

"Not yet, we can't decide," Katie arched a brow at Ben, and he winked at her in response.

"Tessa, are you still looking for a job?" He asked, glancing at me from across the table. Ben looked identical to what my dad had looked like at twenty-seven. They shared a lot of the same mannerisms.

"Yeah, I am." I leaned back in my seat. "Basically nowhere in this town is hiring, not even any of the fast food places. All posts are full for the summer."

"You should have started looking earlier," Gordon supplied.

"Thanks, tips," I grumbled, rolling my eyes.

"Katie has a friend that needs a babysitter this summer," Ben continued, ignoring Gordon's jabs completely. Katie looked at me, her face lighting up a little.

"What friend?" I tilted my head, curious. I wasn't about to commit to watching just anybody for the money. If she was talking about the Peterson twins, they'd have to pay me a hell of a lot. Those kids were wired for sound.

"Becky," Katie answered, smiling softly. She glanced towards my father, as if testing the waters. If Dad knew that Katie was talking about Becky Miller, he didn't let on. He continued eating his dinner in silence, content to just be around us all without speaking. "She's got a little four-year-old boy. She just lost her full-time sitter and has been having a hell of a time finding anyone dependable."

"Are you talking about Becky Miller?" Gordon demanded, frowning.

"So what if she is?" Ben responded, sending a warning look to Gordon. Ben hated when anybody spoke to Katie rudely and he wouldn't tolerate any disrespect towards her.

Katie rested her hands on her swollen stomach. "I've known Becky for a while; she's a sweet girl, just trying to make ends meet. She works hard, harder than anyone I've ever known."

"Dad doesn't want Tessa anywhere near Brock," Tommy informed everyone. If I'd known what legs were his under the table, I'd have kicked him.

"Well, it's a good thing the job isn't to babysit him then," Elle responded, shooting Tommy a dirty look.

Dad cleared his throat, drawing everybody's attention to him at the head of the table. "What are the hours, Katie?"

"Sporadic, I'm afraid," Katie answered. "Sometimes its mornings and sometimes its afternoons, but it will definitely be full-time hours. She works at the grocery store my parents own, but she also goes to school full-time. I'm really not sure what her classes are like, but she'll let Tessa know all those details if she's interested."

Dad chewed over Katie's words for a bit, considering them. Then he looked at me. "What do you think, Tess? Is babysitting something you'd be interested in?"

"Well, I'm interested in making money so…" I shrugged. "I guess so?"

Dad nodded thoughtfully, pursing his lips. "I told you to stay away from Brock, not his sister. I'm not exactly worried about her getting you into any trouble."

"That means pregnant. He isn't worried about Becky getting you pregnant." Tommy smirked. Both Ben and Gordon, sitting on either side of Tommy, reached out and slapped him in the back of the head. "Ow," Tommy sulked, rubbing the back of his head and scowling at our older brothers.

"You deserved that," Dad remarked, anger flashing in his eyes. "You don't talk about your sister like that."

"Yes, sir." Tommy swallowed hard, looking ashamed.

"I'll call Becky this week, Tessa," Katie said, giving me a warm smile and barely giving a second glance to Tommy, Gordon or Ben. She was used to the antics of the Armstrong men.

I smiled tightly in response.

"Do you think I should take that job?" I asked Elle later as we hung out in my room, waiting for Braden to pick her up.

"I don't know," she responded, biting her lip. "It's kind of crazy there right now."

"Your cryptic half-answers aren't helping," I retorted. "I get that you want to keep all of Braden's secrets, but I'm not asking you to reveal the fact that he sleeps with a teddy bear or likes a finger shoved in his butthole. I'm asking if I should take the damn job."

Elle's head whipped around and she stared at me with her jaw dropped open in astonishment. Then she started laughing. "Oh my God, Tessa! That was the funniest thing I've ever heard you say, and I've heard you say a lot of funny shit!"

"Okay, great. Tessa is funny. Moving on, should I or should I not take the job?"

Her laughter faded and Elle considered me for a moment. "Becky lives at home still, and their mom is dying, Tessa. Babysitting Becky's kid would mean that you'd have to be around that every day."

"I know." I took a shaky breath, remembering the expression on Brock's face when he'd told me. This was exactly why I didn't know if I could, or should, take the job.

Mom stuff was like a swift kick to the gut for me. I was extremely empathetic, almost to a fault, towards anybody who lost their mom. When Levy Jefferson lost his mom in third grade, I'd cried for months long after even he had. I cried every time I saw him, thinking about how badly he must miss his mom.

It was one of those stupid quirks that came from being motherless. I mourned the loss of the woman I never got to know, of the relationship I never got to have. Then again, I'd been younger. I liked to think of myself as a little stronger now.

"But...that being said...Aiden is a great kid, you've met him. He's really easy and agreeable and a lot of fun. And their mom, Deanna, she's really nice too. I mean...if you're going to get involved with Brock, you're going to have to deal with that anyway."

I bit my tongue, thinking about Elle's response. She was right; if I did pursue whatever this was with Brock, as I intended on doing, I'd have to deal with it.

"Brock hasn't asked me to get involved with his family stuff," I pointed out just as headlights turned onto the driveway.

"And you didn't invite yourself anyway." Elle rolled her eyes. She paused, her hand on my bedroom door. "I think they need someone like you right now, if you can do it," she added, her eyes meeting mine. "I know Brock could use you. From what Braden's told me...he's never had anyone to lean on. He's always been the rock."

ELLE'S WORDS echoed through my mind the entire next morning while I went about my chores; *he's never had anyone to lean on. He's always been the rock.*

I couldn't help but long to be that person for him, to be there for him in any way that he needed.

"Tessa." My dad's voice startled me from my thoughts of Brock. I'd been about to run into the house for a shower before I took off.

"Yeah, Dad?"

"I need you to run to the co-op and pick up an order of feed." He sighed, scratching his beard. "Looks like the last rain we had leaked through the roof in the barn. Spoiled the bags we had."

"Oh no." I frowned, knowing that was an expense we could have done without. "What's happening with the room?"

"Gordon's fixing it now," Dad assured me. "I'm about to head over and help finish, but I need you to grab that feed."

"Of course." I nodded, my heart tightening with disappointment. I was going to be late getting to Brock's house after all. I forced a smile at my dad. It wasn't his fault and Brock could wait.

"Take my truck," Dad added, tossing his keys at me. He probably didn't want to make me waste what limited gas I had.

I drove to the co-op, picking up the order of feed from Mr.

Jefferson—Levy's great uncle. Two of his employees helped me load up the heavy bags into the bed of Dad's truck. Within the hour, I was heading back home to drop it off.

I parked near the barn and helped Dad and Gordon get the feed placed away in the newly repaired storage section of the barn. After the last bag had been shelved, I wiped my sweaty palms on my denim clad thighs and smiled at my dad.

"Okay, Elle's waiting for me," I told Dad, ignoring Gordon completely. I was still giving him the silent treatment, not that he knew why; he was completely unaware that I'd seen his display outside of Brock's trailer.

"What are you guys up to tonight?" Gordon asked, his hazel eyes studying me intently.

"I don't know. I don't exactly ask for an itinerary when she wants to hang out." I was growing aggravated.

"Have fun, honey," Dad said, his tone carrying a sense of finality that made Gordon stop his interrogation.

I started over to the house again, eager to shower and be on my way. Once I showered, I took time to blow dry my hair and use the curling wand that had barely been outside of its box. I didn't know what the game plan was for tonight, but I really wanted to look good. I coated my lips in a sheer, soft pink gloss, and stood back from the mirror.

"Well, aren't we all dressed up," Gordon remarked. He was leaning against my bedroom door, his arms folded across his chest. He looked conflicted, as if he had something to say but didn't exactly know how to word it.

"What do you want, Gordon?" I sighed, rolling my eyes as he invited himself into my room. He crossed over, sitting down on my bed. The entire time, he watched me with a slight frown on his face.

"I know about the bush party," he said, his tone almost soft and gentle, or at least as soft and gentle as Gordon was capable of.

163

I froze, turning slowly to face him. "What are you talking about?"

"Don't play dumb, Tessa." Gordon frowned, standing up and stepping towards me. He looked upset. "Why didn't you tell any of us?"

I took a steadying breath, trying to relax. "Because," I whispered, my brow furrowing as I looked towards my door, "it's none of your business."

"Yet somehow, it's Brock's business?" Gordon's voice was hard, his eyes angry and hurt. "Tessa, you're our sister, you're our family. You know you can count on us; why in the hell would you go to him?"

"I didn't," I shot back, my blood boiling with anger that I desperately fought to control. "He was there. His dog must have watched the guy follow me, or maybe it didn't trust him, or maybe it heard something. But Brock followed his dog and that's the only reason why it's his business. He was there, and he, and his dog, prevented anything from happening. It's not a dig at you guys, I just..." I trailed off, my voice weakening. I felt weak.

"You what?" Gordon demanded, expecting a better explanation than what I was giving him.

"I felt ashamed, okay?" I exclaimed. My eyes shot back to my door, to the hallway, but it remained silent. I took a steadying breath, trying to lower my voice and my temper. "I felt ashamed and embarrassed. I knew if you guys found out, you'd berate me for going off on my own, or for being a woman, or something equally as stupid and macho."

"We wouldn't have," he argued.

"You would have," I said levelly. "How did you find out, anyway?"

"The community bonfire," he answered, looking over my head and swallowing hard. "I guess the asshole had the nerve to come back and Brock reacted. I happened to be there."

The colour faded from my face. "What did he do?"

"He just threatened him a little; he left the rest up to me." Gordon shrugged. His eyes dropped down and he caught the horrified look on my face. "Don't worry, I didn't hurt him, much."

I took another calming breath, trying to center myself, and grabbed my phone from my desk, shoving it into the back pocket of my jeans.

"I love that you guys care, I do...but I can fight my own battles. I can take care of myself."

"Sounds like it," Gordon grumbled darkly.

"Okay fine," I shot back, scowling. "I made a mistake that night, but I'm not going to repeat it. I'm not an idiot. I'm not the one that had to touch the electrical fence three times to make sure it was really on!"

The dark frown on my brother's face lessened and he started to smile. "I never claimed to be the smartest one in the family," he argued. He paused, his smile fading as he became lost in his own thoughts.

"Earth to Gordon, is this conversation over yet? Can I go?" I waved my hands in front of his eyes, rousing him.

"Just promise me that you'll come to us next time."

"There won't be a next time," I growled, my eyes narrowing.

Gordon grinned, amused by my anger. He ruffled my hair that I'd spent so much time perfecting. "I'd hope not."

"Ugh, Gordon!" I glared at him, ducking away. My eyes dropped to the ground and I felt my anger rising again. "Seriously? You left your damn boots on in my room?"

He glanced down at his feet, a look of surprise crossing his face as if he hadn't even realized he'd left them on. "Sorry, I'll vacuum..."

"You'd better," I threatened, storming out of my room and down the stairs.

My thoughts were still swirling with the odd encounter as I

pulled up to Brock's trailer. I worried my lip, wondering if I should ask Brock about it. I put the truck in park, still undecided, and looked at the new addition to the right of his worn trailer. He'd gotten the foundation laid for the cabin.

I stepped out, hearing Hunter's deep barks from inside. A moment later, the door opened and he bolted out, running up toward me with his tail wagging in greeting.

"Hello, Hunter," I said, laughing when he jumped up on me. He put his two large front paws on either one of my shoulders, licking my face while his bottom half wiggled frantically from the movement of his long tail.

"Hunter, down," Brock instructed. Hunter licked my face once more before he obeyed and sat before my feet, peering up at me with his yellow eyes.

"You're such a good boy. I don't think I properly thanked you for...that night. Thank you, you are my furry little hero," I told him, my voice dripping with that affectionate tone most people's voices took with animals. I continued to scratch behind his ears. Hunter's tongue lolled and he pushed his head against my hand, leaning into the attention he was getting. "He's so well trained. How did you do it?"

"Magic," Brock joked, coming to a stop just before me. He watched me petting Hunter with a soft smile on his lips. "It didn't take much. He's always been a loyal, easy to please dog. Intelligent too. He was quick to learn."

"What's his breed?"

He hesitated for a moment. "German Shepherd Husky and Wolf mix," he finally answered, looking a little uncomfortable. It seemed by the defensive set of his shoulders that this was information that he didn't readily supply. It made me feel good to know that he'd told me.

"Wolf mix?" I repeated, glancing back down with interest. I'd never seen a wolf mix dog before. My hand was resting on the side of Hunter's huge face. He opened one eye lazily, as if wondering why I'd stopped rubbing. His coat was a mixture between cream and grey, with some darker tans through it. Now that Brock mentioned it, I couldn't believe I hadn't noticed before. "That's really cool, Brock," I added with a smile. My hands started moving again, massaging Hunter's silky ears. He let out a low, grumble-like moan and his eyes rolled to the back of his skull.

"I think he likes you," Brock remarked, humor in his voice. I looked back up at him, letting my hands fall away from Hunter's head.

"I think so." I smiled; the way that Brock was looking at me suddenly made me feel shy and uncertain. My hands fell away from his dog's face and I tucked a strand of hair behind my ear. "So..."

He shook his head as if clearing it and stepped towards me. Suddenly, his hands were on my hips and he was pulling me towards him. He kissed me languidly, making every thought in my head fall away. He left me breathless, almost panting before him when he finally broke the kiss.

"Are you ready?" he asked me, a delicious smirk on his lips, as if he was pleased with himself for my reaction.

"For what?"

He didn't answer. He just smiled and released me, walking over to the front of his trailer. He had a tackle box and two fishing rods propped up against it. He grabbed everything and walked back over to me. "Mind if we take your truck? That way if anyone drives up..." He arched a brow. He was referring to my brothers; we both knew it. Finding my truck in Brock's driveway would definitely not be a good thing, but finding Brock's truck there wouldn't mean much.

"Yeah, sure...where are we going?" I questioned, biting down on my lip. I wanted to go anywhere with him, but the reality of getting spotted made my stomach twist with anxiety. I couldn't help but worry. Each time we hung out, each time my truck was parked in Brock's driveway, we ran the risk of getting caught. I forced those thoughts back, not wanting them to taint whatever time we had together.

"Just a couple minutes away. Don't worry, we won't run into anybody," Brock said, dropping down my tailgate and slapping it once. Hunter jumped up gracefully, settling into a laying position. He closed the tailgate and walked over to the driver's side. "Do you mind if I drive?"

I could tell that he wanted to surprise me, so I went along with it. "Well, considering I don't know where we're going...I guess that'd be okay," I joked. I walked over and opened the door, climbing in and smiling hesitantly.

Brock grinned, twisting the key in the ignition to start the old girl up. He backed up slowly, conscious of his dog lying in the back, and drove back down his driveway. He turned right onto the paved road, driving for about two minutes minutes before he turned right onto another road. He drove for another minute before he turned onto a tiny access road, barely detectable by the eye unless you knew what to look for. He drove down the access road to a beach and parked the truck, his gaze sliding across the cab to rest on my face as my eyes drank it in.

"It's beautiful. How did I not know it was here?" I shook my head, astonished.

"There are a lot of small lakes all over Ontario." Brock shrugged, smiling. "Ours is pretty tiny."

"Yours?" I parroted, my eyes widening as I stared at him.

"Yeah." He grinned sheepishly, running a hand through his hair. "My grandpa owned a lot of land here. My siblings and I inherited it."

"How much of this is yours?" I asked, mystified as I looked at the area around me.

"One-hundred and sixty acres. Split three ways," Brock

answered, opening his door and stepping outside. "Are you coming?"

I joined him at the back of my truck. He dropped the tailgate for Hunter to jump out and grabbed the fishing gear, leading the way to a thin dock and a small, beat up tin motor boat. He lowered the tackle box and rods into it, then hopped in. The boat swayed beneath his weight, but he kept his balance, holding his hand out to me and nodding once as if he was urging me forward.

I arched a brow, ignoring his hand as I fluidly stepped in. "I've been in boats before...I've even driven a few." I smirked.

Brock chuckled, giving me half a grin. His eyes sparkled with humor and longing. "Oh, I know you're capable of doing it yourself. I just wanted another excuse to touch you."

"You have plenty of excuses to touch me," I remarked, sitting down on the middle bench facing him. His smile widened, his eyes promising that he'd make good on that later. He put two fingers in his mouth and whistled once.

Hunter, who'd been sniffing in the foliage, scampered up the dock. He dove into the boat, his huge paws clumsy on the tin floor. Once he was inside, directly in front of my feet, Brock set to untying the rope that anchored the boat to the dock.

"He comes fishing with you?" I asked, amused. We had a couple of dogs on the farm—two Kangal dogs that never came into the house and were essentially always working, guarding the cows and other livestock. Marley and Bob were affectionate, but more focused on the job my father had trained them to do.

"He comes almost everywhere with me," Brock answered. He dropped the motor into the water and pulled the cord, firing it up before he sat down on the bench across from me and started steering the boat away from the dock. Hunter's body leaned against my legs, tail thumping against the tin of the boat as Brock steered the boat out to the middle of the lake.

He took me on a grand tour, showing off what parts of the

lake were his. Then he drove to a small bend, where he assured me that the fish were almost always biting.

He turned the motor off. The calmness of the small lake enveloped us and I sighed contently as Brock handed me one of the rods. He had a container of fresh worms open and I dug my fingers in to grab one.

"Becky always hated that part," Brock remarked, chuckling at the sight of me shoving the worm through the fishing hook. I stood up, casting the line out and watching as my hook arched and dropped, the lure sinking.

"Well, not many things gross me out," I responded, looking over my shoulder at him. "It'd be pretty stupid if I got wigged out by worms and guts and stuff, considering I want to be a vet one day. I'll be dealing with grosser things than that."

"I guess that's true." He laughed, his eyes crinkling when he smiled at me. The expression on his face and the emotion in the depths of his eyes made my stomach drop pleasantly. I sat down and Brock stood to cast his own line out.

It was quiet on the lake, the peaceful silence only interrupted every now and then by a loon call. Neither one of us felt the need to fill the silence; we were content to just fish.

CHAPTER 12

rock

THE FISH WERE BITING TONIGHT, and between the two of us we caught enough pike to fry up for dinner.

I'd watched Tessa clean and gut the fish with a stupid grin on my face the whole time. Hell, I'd watched everything she'd done tonight with a stupid grin on my face... the whole time. It was hot, watching a girl who was fearless of things like fish guts and slime. She cleaned and gutted the fish better than I ever could. I knew that my grandpa would have gotten a hoot out of her.

We ate dinner in my trailer, sitting across from each other at the tiny kitchen table where I'd tended to Tessa's wounds. It felt like a lifetime ago, but it had barely been a week. My heart pounded at that realization. It had barely been a week, and already this girl was all I could think about, all that I craved.

"It's really good," she remarked, smiling at me. "Do many people know about your lake?"

"Not many, no," I replied. "My great grandma was of

Mi'kmaq decent. She shared her culture with her children and grandchildren, and Grandpa passed those lessons on to us as best he could. The land had always been extremely important to him and I think he worried that they wouldn't respect the land or the balance. If everyone found out about our lake, the fish would decline because people just don't know when to stop."

He worked hard to instill those values in his kids and grand-kids. He hadn't exactly succeeded with my dad, but I thought he did pretty well with my siblings and me.

It brought me great comfort to know that he would have liked Tessa simply from the way she loved the land around her. She didn't harm it and she wasn't afraid of it. She bloomed in it, or maybe it bloomed around her.

Tessa's eyes lit up as if she was pleased I was sharing bits of myself with her. "I didn't know you were part native," she said thoughtfully, tilting her head.

"Didn't you?" I said dryly, thinking about my dad. I wasn't blind to the cruel things people had said about him, that his alcoholic tendencies came from his native blood. I couldn't say if that was true or not. I'd never seen a single drop of liquid pass my grandpa's lips, but then again...there was so much about the man I hadn't known.

One memory flooded back to me. It was after my dad died, at his funeral. I caught my grandpa staring at his freshly dug grave with a look of complete remorse and defeat across his strong features. He didn't know I had approached, and I paused when I heard his deep voice.

"I haven't got many regrets, my son," Grandpa said, staring down at the dark soil. His eyes were watery. "Except you. You are my regret. I failed you, and for that...I am sorry."

I didn't know what he meant; I didn't know why he believed he'd failed my father, but seeing my grandfather that broken up over my dad's death stung. I knew they hadn't gotten along when he was alive, but then again…my dad hadn't gotten along with anyone. He wasn't a very likeable man.

Tessa stood, rousing me from my impromptu trip down memory lane. She'd finished her dinner, and was walking around the table, her eyes focused on me. I turned my body so she could straddle my legs. "Thank you for today, for sharing this with me," she whispered, her lips inches away from mine.

"You're welcome," I told her, my voice sounding deeper even to my ears. I had told Tessa more about myself and my family than I'd told anyone else, ever. That alone should have terrified me, but instead…it was comforting.

My hands roamed along her back, exploring her body over her clothes. She exhaled softly before she lowered her mouth to mine, kissing me as she moved her hips against me. My dick hardened, stirred to life by her lips and her tongue and the feeling of her body grinding against mine.

Her hands dropped from around my neck to the waistband of my jeans. She ran them beneath my shirt, against the hard muscles of my stomach. I drew in air sharply, my abdomen tightening against the subtle brush of her fingers.

There was no taking it slow with Tessa, not when she touched me like she was now, not when she kissed me like she was now.

I lost myself in the sensation of her. Her fragrance, her taste, the feel of her. I had no regrets about it either.

I stood up, bringing her with me, carrying her over to where my bed was on the other side of the trailer. I undressed her slowly, my lips only leaving hers so I could pull her top off and let my gaze linger on her beautiful curves. My hand snaked around to her back, unclipping her bra in a fluid motion. I pulled it away, letting it fall on the floor without a second glance. My eyes were too busy taking in the sight before me.

"You're beautiful," I told her, my voice husky with wanton desire as I cupped her breast. She arched, offering herself to me, her lashes fluttering against her cheeks and her chest rising and falling with bated breath. I brought my lips to her neck, kissing her soft flesh as I gently kneaded her breasts with my hands. I teased her until her nipples were hard against my palms.

Tessa whimpered in protest when my mouth finally found her nipple. I teased her with my tongue and lips, making her writhe against me. She fought back, stroking my length through my jeans. Her fingers made short work of my zipper, then she tugged my jeans down my hips before I could draw my mouth away and tell her to slow down. My eyes fluttered closed when her hands started to slowly pump.

She took advantage of the moment, leaning forward and drawing my hardness into her mouth. I let out a hiss as she bobbed against me, taking my length in as far as it would go. "Jesus, Tessa. I won't be able to last at that rate."

She pulled her mouth away from my cock and I ached at the absence of her warm mouth. "We've got all night," she said sinfully, giving me a sinister smile.

AFTERWARDS, we lay in my bed together. The gentle rise and fall of Tessa's chest against me had me believing she'd fallen asleep in my arms.

I couldn't sleep. I couldn't stop thinking about her, about how good it felt to hold her like this in my arms…in my bed or about how it was all I never knew I wanted and needed.

I was in deep shit.

What did you expect? I thought, frowning. *You knew there was something different about this girl. You knew there was a very real possibility you'd develop feelings for her.*

But I hadn't counted on it happening so quickly, or to this degree. I hadn't counted on her brother wanting to pick up where our friendship had left off. I also hadn't counted on him trying to hold me to some stupid promise we'd made to each other years ago.

I'd always known that Tessa's family would pose a challenge, but I still thought we could have had what we had without letting anyone know. Now, I realized how wrong I was. I wanted everyone to know she was mine. I wanted to take her out around town without worrying about the shit-storm that would ensue. I wanted everyone who came anywhere near her to know she was with me. I wanted her to know I'd defend her and protect her.

"Does it intimidate you?" Tessa's quiet voice startled me from my thoughts. For a fraction of a second, I worried that I'd spoken aloud.

"Does what intimidate me?" I asked, not catching her meaning.

She lifted her head and looked at me, drawing her bottom lip in and trapping it with her teeth. "Us. This...thing." She gestured to the two of us. "Do you think things between us are moving too quickly?"

I moved my fingers against the small of her back, tracing a small pattern as I thought. "Yes and no."

"That's not really an answer." She arched a brow, vulnerability crossing her features. The smile I gave her made that vulnerability vanish.

"We're adults, Tessa. Adults have consensual sex. The fact that I'm deeply attracted to you and want to have lots of consensual sex with you doesn't mean things are moving too quickly," I told her, shrugging. "This does intimidate me, yes, because I've never had it this bad before. I've never wanted to give someone the 'girlfriend' label; I've never wanted them to spend the night just so I could hold them in my arms..." I let my voice fall into silence. I couldn't tell her the rest of it; that I wasn't sure if I could keep us a secret, or for how long. The kind of chemistry between us was intense and obvious. I'd have to be very careful around her. Hell, even the mention of her had me in a tailspin.

"Same." She exhaled and was silent for a few more seconds, her warm breath fluttering across the skin across my rib cage. "So…what happens when I go to college?"

"You go to college." I smiled, kissing her head. "I'll visit you whenever. Hell, it might be easier to keep it a secret then. We could actually go out in public and not worry about running into any of your family members with loaded shotguns."

Tessa laughed, her shoulders shaking as the rest of her unease disappeared. "That's true," she said, yawning.

"Get some sleep," I said, holding her closer. I fell asleep shortly after her, escaping into dreams that were just as sweet as the small slice of reality I'd made with her.

THE NEXT MORNING came before I wanted it to. I knew the arrival of a new day would mean Tessa would have to leave. That didn't stop me from taking her again, with her hair still a tangled mess from the night before. It didn't stop me from kissing her hard against her truck before I finally let her climb in and go, either.

I couldn't get enough of this girl. She could be my downfall and I'd be perfectly okay with that.

I had a lot of things on my to-do list and none of them were at the cabin. I was in limbo now; I had a meeting with Gordon tonight to discuss me possibly hiring him. In the meantime, there wasn't anything else I could do.

But there was plenty of stuff for me to do at the family house.

I loaded up Hunter and made a quick stop at the local hardware store for supplies. I bought outdoor wood paint and ordered a bunch of shingles to be delivered and installed next week.

When I got to the house, I set to work immediately. I found the lawn mower and weed whacker in the shed where they'd always been. Despite the lack of use, they worked just fine. I started on the yard, moving all of Aiden's toys before cutting the grass.

Then I set up a work bench in front of the garage and took off the shutters so I could put on a fresh coat of paint. Once the first coat was drying, I went to pull weeds from the front gardens. I wasn't a gardener, but the weeds had overtaken everything. I pulled them all, shoving them into the brown bags I'd picked up.

I'd long since abandoned my shirt, and sweat was dripping down my spine. I was hot and day dreaming of diving into the lake.

"BROCK!" I looked up, seeing Becky standing on the front porch with her hands on her hips. "Did you not hear me calling you?"

"No, obviously, or I would have responded," I answered, my eyes narrowed. "What's up?"

The annoyance faded from Becky's face. "I've made lunch. Come in for a minute, eat something. Hydrate. You've been at it for six hours now."

"Six hours?" My brow furrowed and I swallowed hard. I hadn't even realized time had passed that quickly.

"Yeah, six hours. Aiden's been watching, waiting for you to come in and say hi." Becky tilted her head, concerned. I ignored her worry and walked over to the lawn mower. I'd draped my sweaty shirt over the handles to dry it out a little.

"Are you sure he's waiting for me?" I joked, looking back at Hunter. He was sleeping beneath the shade of the old oak tree. As if he knew we were talking about him, he opened his eyes and lazily raised his head. I clicked my tongue at him and he slowly got up, stretching his limbs before he pranced over to us.

"Okay, so he wanted to see Hunter. Don't be jealous." Becky smiled, leading the way into the cool house. The air conditioning was welcome against my hot skin. "We set a bowl of water out for Hunter," she added, gesturing towards the kitchen. But Hunter had already found it and was greedily lapping it up.

"Uncle Brock!" Aiden's little voice hit my ears just as his arms wrapped around my legs. "We made sandwiches! My favourite kind, ham and cheese!"

"That's my favourite kind too," I told him, ruffling his hair.

"Can I go pet Hunter now?" he asked eagerly, his blue eyes lighting up.

"Just wait until after lunch, okay? You don't want to have to wash your hands again," Becky interjected before I could reply. "Come on, let's eat."

"Where's Braden today?" I asked, sitting down. "And how come he hasn't been keeping up the outside of this place?"

"He works a lot," Becky explained. "At the mechanic's. When he's not working, he's usually with Elle."

"Hmm..." I frowned.

"He's still a kid, Brock. Go easy on him. He hasn't taken this well at all," Becky lectured, her eyes drifting to the hallway where the bedrooms were, where our mom was slowly fading away. "Kind of like someone else I know?"

"I get it, I do," I managed. "But cutting the grass a little more often isn't asking much."

Becky looked at me pointedly, but said nothing. She turned her attention to Aiden. He'd been trying to sneak pieces of his sandwich to Hunter, but Hunter was trained not to take any food unless given instruction and Aiden was caught red-handed with a guilty look on his face. "He looks hungry, Mama!"

"I'm sure he isn't," Becky argued, arching a brow at me.

"Nope, he had his breakfast this morning. Hunter eats in the morning and in the evening. Dogs perpetually look hungry though, because they'd eat anything you'll give them."

"Why didn't Hunter eat the sandwich?" Aiden asked, sounding disappointed. "Does he not like ham?"

"Oh no, he likes ham a lot. But he's trained to not touch it unless I tell him he can." I felt a little guilty that my nephew was taking this as a personal slight. I looked at Becky pleadingly.

"Fine, just the crust," she said, rolling her eyes.

THE LAST THING I wanted to do was meet up with Gordon, especially after the night before and the morning I'd had with Tessa. But I'd promised him and I knew if I didn't follow through, he'd come to me. I couldn't risk him showing up when Tessa was there.

Begrudgingly, I made my way to Flanigan's bar.

Flanigan's had been around for about eighty-eight years now, always run by someone in the Flanigan clan. It was aged with dingy lighting and old, dirty hardwood floors that were perpetually sticky from spilled beverages and blood-stained from the infamous bar fights that had occurred over the years.

I wasn't surprised to see that it was still open. The bar had been around since 1925, and although it had seen limited upgrades and updates since then, the kitchen and bathrooms were always spotless and up-to-date. Countless bars and clubs attempted to open in Parry Sound, but none of them stuck. Flanigan's offered cheaper drinks, pool tables that didn't cost per game, and darts. Not to mention it was a piece of history. This had been the local watering hole for almost a century. Plus, Flanigan's had the best wings in town.

I spent a lot of time in this bar as a kid. My dad would take me out supposedly for a "father and son day" and our first stop was always Flanigan's so the old man could "whet his whistle".

It was often our only stop.

While the bar itself held no good memories for me, Mick Flanigan had never been anything but kind. He'd slip me food under the guise that the kitchen had cooked too much and he kept an eye on me. I knew Mick didn't like my dad, but not many people in this town did. Mick was stuck between a rock and a hard place: you didn't meddle with other people's business around here and my old man was one of his best customers.

I hadn't set foot in Flanigan's since I was ten years old. That was the last time my dad bothered with the excuses and the weak attempts at hiding his drinking problem. That was the year that he stopped being just a drunk and started being abusive as well.

Squaring my shoulders, I walked into the old bar. Mick was still behind the old oak bar, his dark hair now completely gray and his rough face wrinkled and worn. His bright eyes still sparkled. They were always a contradiction, light and happy while the rest of him was as tough as an Irish bartender could be.

I nodded at him in greeting and peered around, searching for Gordon. Flanigan's wasn't exploding with bodies, but it was crowded for a Tuesday night. I found him sitting at one of the old, worn booths. He had a mug of beer in his hand and an empty pitcher before him. Grady and Travis sat with him, nursing their beers.

Suppressing a sigh, I walked over. My work boots thudded heavily against the old floor, announcing my arrival. The three guys from my youth looked up, each of them grinning.

"Brock! Buddy! It's about time you showed up!"

"Yeah, sorry," I said, sliding in beside Grady. I sent Gordon a curious look. "I thought we were going to talk business?"

"We will," Gordon replied, waving his hand dismissively.

"That won't take long at all. Figured we'd get together while we were at it, just like old times."

I nodded and tried to relax my stiff posture. It wasn't like Gordon was a mind reader or a bloodhound. He didn't know I'd been spending a lot of time with Tessa lately, or that I intended on continuing to spend time with her.

Gordon turned around, facing the bar. "Yo! Flanigan! Can we get another round of beer?" he shouted. Mick raised his hand in acknowledgment and went about filling another pitcher. He grabbed a cold mug from the freezer and brought both over on a tray. He walked with a limp, barely bending his left leg at the knee. Despite his gait, he didn't spill a droplet of beer.

"Brock," he said gruffly, nodding at me. "How are you doing these days?" he asked, concern lining those light eyes as he cleared away the empty pitcher on the table. He was probably the only one in this goddamn town that didn't completely hate me.

"I'm good," I replied honestly, giving him a warm smile. "How are you doing?" I added, looking down at his leg.

"Oh, I'm alright." Mick laughed roughly. He had the laugh of a man who'd spent the greater half of his life smoking. "Just getting old is all. A little stiff leg never hurt nobody. Need anything else, fellas?"

"How about some of those wings?" I asked, my stomach rumbling. I hadn't eaten much in the last twenty-four hours.

"Of course." Mick nodded, his eyes twinkling. "I'll send some right over," he added before turning around and hobbling towards the kitchen to alert his cook.

Forty-odd minutes later, our table had demolished forty of Flanigan's hottest wings. We cooled the burning sensation in our throats with beer, making short work of the entire pitcher. Mick brought over a fresh one without any prompting from Gordon.

Conversation around the table flowed easily, mostly led by the others. I kept to the background, smiling and nodding on occasion each time they brought up a funny story about the past. It was nice to sit with my old friends again, to pretend for a fraction of a minute that my life wasn't as fucked up and out of control as it was. It was nice to escape for a little while, in what limited good memories I had of my past.

"So, let's talk business," Gordon declared half an hour later, leaning back against the booth and fixing me with a serious gaze. Travis and Grady took the cue to leave us, hedging that they were going to play a few games of pool. "Can I take a look at the blueprints?"

I shoved them over to him and picked up my mug, taking a slow sip while I watched his face.

"It's a pretty simple design. Two bedrooms, a living room and kitchen..." he trailed off, nodding in approval. His brow furrowed and he looked up from the blueprints. "You just want one bathroom? Are you sure about that? We could make an ensuite."

"What would I need an ensuite for?" I countered.

"You won't always live alone," Gordon pointed out, smirking. "And even if you do, when you eventually go to sell the place, an ensuite amps up the price."

"It's a cabin in the forest near a lake on 60 acres. The price will be outrageous as is." I massaged my temples, trying to control my irritation. "Besides, the concrete is already poured for the current square footage."

"Alright." Gordon raised his hands in defeat. His eyes twinkled with mischief. "But you could always lay down more concrete. Why don't you just let me show you what I have in mind?"

He didn't bother waiting for me to reply. He just pulled out a notebook and started drawing. He changed the flow of the rooms, drawing the kitchen and living room with an open concept and hanging the bedrooms to the east, unlike my original plans. "Don't worry, it'll all fit onto the concrete you've already laid out. You won't even need to change your permit," he said, showing me what he'd done.

I had to admit, it was a lot better than my original plan. "Fine, whatever. That works."

"Don't sound so excited." Gordon looked put out.

"Sorry, man." I sighed, scratching the stubble on my jaw. "Just going through some shit."

"How's your mom doing?" he asked.

"Hanging in there for now," I replied, looking away. My jaw clenched in aggravation. I didn't want to talk about my mom right now.

"I heard Tessa is going to start babysitting for Becky soon." My gaze flitted back to his face and I quickly tried to mask my surprise.

"What?"

"Yeah," Gordon said, carefully watching me. "I guess Ben's wife is tight with your sister, and told Tessa about the babysitting job. Tessa's been talking to Becky and she's supposed to start soon."

"Huh," I said, keeping my expression and tone natural. Inside, I was twisted with complicated emotions that I couldn't even name. Why hadn't she told me this herself?

"I worry about her." Gordon leaned forward, his eyes intense. "I worry that this will hit her hard. She's never had a job like this before, working around someone whose...well, you know."

"Yeah, I know," I muttered, my brow furrowing. It was unsurprising that Gordon would be worried about his sister when my mom was dying, but I understood too. I was worried, but for different reasons. I didn't want Tessa to witness this. I didn't want her to see what happened behind closed doors. I didn't want her to see that part of me. It was as if I was afraid that my past would be etched on those walls and she'd be able to see it all simply by being there.

"What I said earlier still stands," Gordon reminded me, arching a brow. "Even if she's going to be helping Becky out."

"Right, well…" I stood up, grabbing the blueprints off the table. Gordon's hand shot out, stopping me.

"Look, man, I'm sorry. That was a dick thing to say. All of it was. But you know me."

"No offense, Gordon, but I don't feel like working with someone who is going to be cautioning me to stay away from his sister every five minutes. I don't need that kind of bullshit drama. I just want to build the fucking cabin."

Building the cabin had become an obsession. I hated half-finished projects, probably because that was all I'd known growing up, all my old man had been capable of. I couldn't think until this cabin was built. I felt like it was just something I needed to do. It was how I needed to focus my energy so I didn't fall completely apart regarding everything that was happening back home.

"I know." Gordon stood up. "And I promise I'll stop with the warnings and reminders. Hell, I won't even talk about her at all. It'll just be work."

I stared at him, contemplating. I did need the help. I wasn't clueless, but I wasn't exactly a carpenter.

"Fine. When can you start?"

"Monday, actually." Gordon grinned. "I'll give you a deal, too."

"Alright, fine. See you Monday." I sighed, grabbing the blueprints.

CHAPTER 13

BECKY MILLER CALLED me when I was doing chores and left a voicemail, asking me to call her. I paced my bedroom, staring at the number. I had meant to talk to Brock when I was over at his house the other day, but our evening had distracted me. Actually, I'd meant to talk to him about a lot of things, about Gordon knowing what happened that night with Ezra's cousin and about this babysitting opportunity.

I wasn't sure if Brock would want me to babysit his nephew. He'd only just started opening up about his past to me, and even then, it wasn't like he'd given me the whole history. I could tell he was still holding back a lot.

I peered out the window for Gordon's truck in our driveway, just to double check. He and his crew had started working on Brock's cabin this week, which meant I was going to have to be extra careful about planning my visits. It was parked in its usual spot and I let out a sigh of relief, firing out a quick text to Brock.

Feel like company?

He responded a couple of minutes later. *Of course!*

With that, I turned on my heel and headed out of my room. Gordon, Tommy, and my dad were sitting around in the living room, watching some kind of documentary on the History Channel.

"Where are you off to at this hour, Tessa?" Dad asked, peering up from the TV to address me.

"I need to go to the store," I answered, crossing my arms and leaning against the doorframe.

"What for?" Gordon asked, as per usual, weaseling his way into the conversation.

"To get female supplies. You know, tampons and stuff?"

"Okay, ew. Didn't need to know that." He grimaced and turned his attention back to the TV.

"That's what you get for being nosy." I shrugged, smirking to myself.

The drive to Brock's house didn't take very long. I pulled up to see him grilling on his barbeque with Hunter lying at his side. No matter where he was, his dog wasn't far. I thought it was endearing, the bond he had with that dog. It reminded me of my bond with Spirit.

My thoughts danced back to our trail ride today. Elle had been busy and unable to accompany me, and I'd saved Spirit for last. I'd ridden him through the wooded trails my mother had made, thinking about the woman I only knew from the memories of others. These trails were another way for me to know her, or at least a small part of her. She could have chosen any pathway through the woods, yet she'd chosen to make this route her trail. I couldn't help but wonder why.

I shook my head, clearing the memories as I stepped out of

my truck and walked towards the barbeque. I supposed Hunter had long since gotten used to the sound of my truck; he barely moved an inch when I pulled up. "What are you cooking?" I asked Brock, coming to a stop beside him.

"Steak," he answered, grinning. "And baked potatoes."

"What, no vegetables?" I joked, petting Hunter behind the ears.

"Didn't know I was having company." Brock shrugged, closing the lid of the barbeque. He turned to face me and an unreadable look crossed his features. It was as if he had things to say, but was stuck on how to phrase them.

I stepped towards him and his arms lifted to embrace me. He pulled me against him and I sighed, the familiar scent of him calming all of my frazzled nerves and easing the worries that chewed at me.

"I've already eaten, so don't worry about feeding me. I just came here to see you…and to talk," I said, my voice muffled by his chest.

"About?" Brock released me and I pulled myself onto the wooden picnic table he'd gotten sometime during the last few days.

"Nice table," I remarked, arching a brow.

"Yeah, I figured it'd be good to have with the crew around. Somewhere to sit down for breaks."

"Makes sense," I hedged. I took a moment to draw in a calming breath. "So my brother, Ben? He's married to Katie, whose parents, as you probably know, own the grocery store that Becky works at. Anyway, she told me that Becky needs a sitter and then told me she'd give her my number."

"I know," Brock said simply, the right corner of his lip lifting in half a smile.

"Oh, really?" I exhaled the breath I'd been holding, my brows furrowing.

"Yeah. Gordon mentioned it the other night."

"Oh, right. So…you'd be okay with that?" I couldn't help but worry.

Brock looked up at me, those steel eyes locking with mine. "Why wouldn't I be okay with that?"

"I don't know. Maybe because we haven't really talked about that whole thing yet," I babbled nervously. Those intense eyes were making me unravel and lose my train of thought. I tried to break away, but I couldn't. They captivated me, keeping me grounded.

"What whole thing?" He gave me another half-smile and stalked towards me, his eyes never leaving mine.

"The meet the family one…"

"You've already met my family," he said simply, coming to a stop before me. He stood between my knees and placed each of his hands on my thighs. "At the community bonfire," he added, reminding me.

"Oh, right. I just meant…" I faltered, trying to grasp my ability to speak. The words seemed to evaporate on my tongue, melted by the glare of heat radiating from Brock's eyes.

He gave me a gentle smile and brought his lips closer to mine. "I know what you meant," he muttered, his breath warm against my face. I squirmed, the heat pooling between my legs. "And don't worry. If you're fine with it, I'm fine with it," he added before his lips pressed against mine.

I responded to the pleasant onslaught, giving myself over to him completely. My body arched against his, desperate for his touch. His hands went to unbutton my shorts. The action brought me back to the now and I broke the kiss. I was breathless, trying to control my reaction to him. "I can't," I said, smiling apologetically. I was surprised that Brock didn't immediately ask why not, or pout about it. He just looked at me through heavy lidded eyes, the desire evident not only from his expression but the huge bulge pressed against my inner thigh. "Not this week, anyway."

"Gotcha." He winked. He sniffed at the air and frowned. "Shit," he added, leaving me quickly to return to the barbeque. He flipped the lid over and used the spatula to turn the steaks.

"Did you burn them?" I chuckled, shaking my head at him. At least he was as equally affected by me as I was him.

"Nope, they're good." He grinned at me from over his shoulder.

I sighed regretfully, standing up. "Well, I have to go."

Disappointment lined Brock's features, but he nodded with understanding. "When will I see you again?"

"I'm not going to be much fun this week," I pointed out, a small frown touching my lips.

His expression changed again and he stalked over to me. "I'm not only focused on that, Tessa...although I won't lie, the feeling of your tight pussy around my cock is one of the greatest feelings in the world. I want to spend time with you; I don't care what we're doing."

I inhaled sharply, my heart jolting in my chest. Brock's delivery was the perfect amount of sexed up sweetness that could easily sweep a girl off her feet. "Well then, I guess I'll see you tomorrow."

WHEN I GOT HOME that night, it was too late to talk to Becky; I had to wait until the following morning to return her call. Even though I'd met her, my heart still pounded frantically in my chest when I dialed her number. Each ring, while I waited for her to pick up, was like an exclamation point.

Aside from working on the farm, I'd never had a job before. Not an official one, anyway. Even if it was only babysitting, at least it was steady work outside of the farm. It was still nerve wracking, especially knowing all that I knew about Becky and her history, and knowing what the Millers were going through now.

"I'm running low on time, so I'll cut to the chase. Katie has nothing but good things to say about you and I know my brothers like you too. Elle swears you're dependable and responsible. Since we've already met each other at the bonfire, I don't really feel the need to do that awkward *'come over and meet the kid'*. If you're comfortable with just starting, you're more than welcome to do that." Becky's voice was strong and sure, direct and purposeful. I knew she was young, but the authority and wisdom in her voice made her seem older.

"Yeah, I'm totally fine with that," I responded, sitting down on the edge of my bed.

"Awesome," Becky said on an exhale, the relief palpable. "Is there any chance that you could be here at ten? I work until eight tonight. Go figure, the sitter you'll be replacing... bailed again."

"I could swing that," I answered. Becky rattled off an address, and I scribbled it onto the back of the old envelope from Georgian College that had contained my acceptance letter. I shoved it in my back pocket and hung up my phone.

I had just enough time to prepare dinner before I left. I tossed a seasoned roast in the crock pot and chopped up some carrots and onions. Dad walked in when I was putting the lid on the pot.

"Where are you off to in such a hurry?" he asked.

"I start my new babysitting job today," I told him. "I need to be there at ten."

"What time will you be home?" he questioned, grabbing a mug from the cupboard to pour himself coffee.

"She said she works until 8, but I'm not sure how long it

takes her to get home...or if she runs errands or anything..." I trailed off, worrying my lip.

"That's alright. I think we'll survive at dinner," Dad remarked.

I glanced towards the crock pot and laughed. "When I go off to college, you're all going to have to learn how to cook."

"Can't be that hard," Dad argued, a smile softening the hard edges of his face. He went to speak again, but I cut him off.

"And barbequing everything doesn't count."

Dad chuckled, shaking his head. "Have a good day," he told me. His eyes searched mine, his brow furrowing slightly. I knew he wanted to lecture me, likely about staying away from the oldest Miller boy and was warring with himself. After all, he'd promised that he would ease up on the protective father routine. He knew I was growing up; he knew I needed to make my own decisions, but he also knew I needed this job and that I wanted it.

I leaned forward and gave him a quick kiss on the cheek, not giving him the opportunity to talk. "Thanks, you too!" I said over my shoulder, exiting through the side door.

I drove to the Miller's house, pulling into the driveway behind an old tan car. The smell of freshly mowed grass and paint greeted me when I stepped outside. All of the weeds had been cleared from the front gardens, a limited selection of freshly planted flowers scattered haphazardly about. The shutters that had hung off at odd angles were fixed and had a new coat of black paint. Even the old wooden door had a face lift; it now matched the shutters for the first time ever.

I'd driven past the Miller house a few times the last few years, dropping Elle off or picking her up. It hadn't been this well-tended to in all that time. I had a feeling Brock had something to do with the new improvements.

I walked up the front steps and knocked against the freshly

painted wooden door. Becky opened up, dressed in her grocery store uniform. She smiled at me with relief. "Tessa! I'm so glad you could start today. Come in! Aiden's just watching some cartoons and having a snack." She stood aside, allowing me entrance to the tiny bungalow. "Aiden, do you remember Tessa from the bonfire?" Becky asked, directing her question to her dark-haired son.

Aiden looked up from the television, his blue eyes landing on me. "Is that Uncle Brock's girlfriend?"

Becky laughed, shaking her head. "Sorry about that. Kids say the darndest things," she said to me before turning back to him. "They're just friends, Aiden."

"She gave us chili and Uncle Brock said she was hot," Aiden said matter-of-factly.

"He probably said the chili was hot," I corrected, my face flushing. Becky didn't seem bothered by it though. She sent me an amused look and shrugged.

"Well, come on. I have just enough time to give you a quick tour," she said, leading me in to the worn kitchen. "Aiden will probably want chicken nuggets and French fries for lunch. You can find both in the freezer. I'm sure you know how to use an oven, so I won't bother you with instructions. He can have juice, but only if it's watered down… otherwise you'll have a kid with way too much energy on your hands," she explained, rolling her eyes. The smile on her face was full of love for her child. "He doesn't nap, unfortunately, but he'll watch a movie and have some quiet time after lunch. I've made a casserole for dinner; all you need to do is heat it up. After dinner, he has a bath and goes to bed at seven."

I nodded, absorbing this information. "Okay, that sounds easy enough."

Becky nodded, moving from the kitchen and down the hall. She stopped in front of a child's bedroom. "This is Aiden's room. He knows where to find his pajamas and anything else he needs. There's a park around the corner if you get bored of the backyard, and all of the emergency contact numbers are listed on the refrigerator." Becky turned, walking back down the hallway. She paused at a partially closed door and peered inside. "Oh! Mom...I didn't know you were up!" she exclaimed, pushing open the door and walking all the way inside. She motioned for me to come in. My heart was pounding in my chest, but I obeyed her, slowly walking the rest of the way into the room.

The air smelled stale and sterile, like that of a hospital. It made a swell of panic rise in the pit of my stomach. I swallowed hard, trying to breathe through my mouth and not my nose.

"Hi, dear." The voice that answered her was fragile and wispy, almost undetectable to my ears. Had I still been in the hallway, I likely wouldn't have heard her at all. "Who's this?"

"This is Tessa Armstrong," Becky explained. "She's going to babysit Aiden while I'm working today."

Mrs. Miller was every bit as frail as her voice. She gave me an exhausted, pained smile. "Don't worry, I'm not much trouble."

I smiled shyly, not knowing what to say or how to act. Picking up on my discomfort, Becky took charge. "Do you need anything before I go?" she asked.

Mrs. Miller shook her head in response. "I'm just going to close my eyes for a bit," she whispered, her lids fluttering.

Becky and I left the bedroom and she slowly closed the door before turning to me. "The nurse, Beth-Anne, will be here in half an hour anyway," she explained. "She won't need anything in the meantime, but if...if she does, just call Beth-Anne and she'll hurry over. Okay?"

"Okay." I nodded, trying to remain calm. Becky gave me a tiny smile and turned around, heading back down the hallway to the kitchen. She picked up her purse and disappeared in the living room to kiss her son goodbye.

"I'll sneak in and give you kisses when I get home," I heard her saying as I joined them in the living room.

Aiden nodded solemnly, his little arms around his mother's neck. "Bye, Mommy," he said.

She straightened up and ruffled his hair. "Alright, off I go. Remember, the numbers are on the refrigerator if you need them," Becky told me, her eyes fixed on mine as if she was drilling this information into my brain.

THE DAY PASSED QUICKLY. After Beth-Anne arrived, we headed outside to play in the backyard until lunch time. I made chicken nuggets and French fries, and he ate everything on his plate. Then we curled up on the couch to watch a movie together. After quiet time, Aiden asked if we could go to the park. We stayed there until four o'clock then I lured him back home so I could toss the casserole in the oven.

Beth-Anne was nice, but she mostly stayed in the bedroom with Mrs. Miller. She knitted or read her novel whenever Mrs. Miller slept, which was a lot. Any time she woke up coughing or gasping for air, Beth-Anne was at her side to administer pain medication and offer her water.

Dinner was ready and cooling on the stovetop when I hesitantly approached the bedroom and knocked. Beth-Anne looked up from her chair and gave me a warm smile. "Yes, dear?"

"Dinner is ready...I wasn't sure if you guys wanted any?" I said, glancing towards Mrs. Miller. She was awake, her tired eyes watching me curiously.

"I don't suppose you feel like a small plate, huh Deanna?" Beth-Anne smiled hopefully at Mrs. Miller.

"I'll pass. Becky never did really learn how to cook," Deanna joked. She started to cough lightly, as if her throat was raw from talking.

I gave her a small smile, my heart aching a little. I didn't know this woman, but she was clearly in pain and suffering and she was Brock's mom.

Beth-Anne chuckled. "Oh, Deanna, that's not very nice. She tries," she scolded. "I'll have a plate," Beth-Anne added, glancing at me with warmth.

I was dishing the casserole out onto three plates when the front door opened and Aiden let out an excited squeal from the living room. I peered up, my brow creased in a frown until I saw who Aiden was so excited for.

The little boy had his arms wrapped around Hunter's thick neck. Brock was standing in the foyer, a grin on his lips as he watched his nephew with his dog. His hair was wet from the shower, and he was dressed in his usual uniform of jeans and a t-shirt. This time, his t-shirt was a dark gray that made his eyes appear even more smoky and dark.

"I figured I'd come hang out, see how your first day went," Brock explained, seeing the questioning look on my face.

"Oh. I thought Gordon was at your place."

"The crew left an hour ago." Brock shrugged. He glanced down the hallway, towards the bedroom where his mom was.

"Did you want to take this plate to Beth-Anne for me?" I offered, biting my lip. "She's in the bedroom."

"Yeah, sure." He stepped forward, taking the plate and fork I offered him, and disappeared down the hall. I could hear their quiet voices drift down the hall. From the sounds of it, Brock's mom had fallen asleep again.

Five minutes later, he returned. I had set one more place at the table; Aiden and I were already sitting down.

It was strange sitting around a table with Brock and his nephew, eating a meal. It wasn't a bad strange...just a surreal strange. He was very good with Aiden, paying full attention to him when the little boy spoke about our day.

I cleaned up after dinner, listening to the sound of the two of them playing in the living room. Aiden had pulled out one of his favourite games, Hungry Hungry Hippos, and was intent on showing Brock how to play.

I joined them once the rest of the dishes were cleaned, and watched as they played. Strange emotions came over me as I watched the large man before me lose horrendously to a four-year-old. I couldn't tell if he was throwing the game purposely, or if Aiden was just that talented. Either way, my heart swelled at the sight.

"Okay, Aiden, we need to start getting ready for bed now," I said, checking the time. It was nearly seven, and I still needed to run him a bath. He'd gotten pretty dirty at the park.

"Alright." Aiden sighed heavily and began to clean up his game. I arched an eyebrow, impressed. Elle used to do a lot of babysitting for her neighbors, and the kids were never as cooperative as Aiden.

After he was clean from his bath and dressed in his pajamas, Aiden looked up at me with his bright blue eyes. "I always curl up in Grammy's bed for a visit. She used to read my bedtime story too, but she can't anymore. She can still cuddle me though."

"Oh," I faltered, blinking quickly. "Um, let me see if she's awake?" I suggested, looking to Brock for help. He shrugged, looking just as surprised as me. I padded out of Aiden's room down the hallway and paused by the open door.

Deanna was awake again, conversing with the hospice nurse in her raspy voice. Beth-Anne was standing near the head of the bed, supporting the dying woman's upper body with one arm while she propped up the pillows so Deanna could sit up more. They both glanced up, catching my movement by the door.

"Is Aiden ready for bed?" The amount of effort it took

Deanna to say those five words tugged at my heart strings. I could tell she was exhausted, but this ritual was something she was clinging to, something they were both clinging to.

I nodded, trying to speak. I had to clear my throat before the words would come. "Yes, he's ready," I said, glancing down the hallway. Aiden was standing by his door, holding a stuffed animal to his chest and waiting patiently. Brock stood beside him, leaning against the doorframe of Aiden's bedroom. Many emotions were rolling through his stormy eyes.

"Come on in," Beth-Anne said, speaking on behalf of Deanna. Aiden's face lit up and he raced down the hallway, slowing when he got to the doorway of his grandmother's bedroom. He carefully crawled into her bed, taking great care to not hurt her. "It's alright, dear. I'll bring him out when they're done visiting," Beth-Anne assured me, her warm brown eyes catching me still standing awkwardly by the door.

I nodded, closing the door a little more to allow them some privacy. My gaze flitted back to where I'd last seen Brock, but he wasn't there anymore. I padded softly down the hallway, peering back into Aiden's room. Brock was sitting on the twin sized bed, his head buried in his hands.

"Are you okay?" I asked, instantly regretting the words the moment they tumbled past my lips. His shoulders stiffened and I cringed, wishing I could take those words back. "I'm sorry, that's a stupid thing to ask."

"No, it's not." Brock sighed, finally raising his head to look at me. His eyes were dark, the pain and despair he felt rolling around within their depths, and his strong features were pinched as if he was forcing that stoic mask he'd worn the night I met him back into place.

I walked towards him, keeping my gaze locked on his eyes. I knelt in front of him, placing my hands on his knees. "I want you to know I'm here, okay? And I get it. I don't remember my mom's death, but I still mourn the loss of her. This isn't easy for you, and..." I tried to reorganize my thoughts. Everything Elle had said about Brock came rushing back to me. "I get the impression that you're used to carrying everyone's problems and grief so...let me carry yours, or at least help you."

Brock raised a hand to gently cup my cheek. He swallowed hard, absorbing my words as his eyes searched mine. "Thank you," he finally said, giving me the tiniest of smiles. He looked as if he had more to say, but thought the better of it. Instead, he slowly brought his lips to mine and kissed me tenderly.

CHAPTER 14

rock

I WANTED to tell her that she had no idea what kind of comfort she provided me, because she didn't. She didn't realize that she made me a better man, a better person.

She made me a better man, but I was still a coward. I was still avoiding my mother. So far, I'd been lucky. Each time I had stopped by, she'd been sleeping. Right now, she was awake. I knew I should go in and say something, but I didn't want to interrupt her time with Aiden. From what Becky had told me, Aiden had a special bond with our mother.

"Alright, Aiden, off to bed you go." Beth-Anne's voice drifted down the hallway and into my nephew's room. I stood up, pulling Tessa up with me just as Aiden rounded the corner. His eyes were bright with emotion, and his bottom lip jutted out. I could tell by the way he was walking that he was putting on a brave face. His chest was puffed up and his shoulders were drawn back as if he could steel himself from the emotions he was feeling. It was the exact act I'd performed most of my life. Hell, I still did.

"Do you mind if I tuck him in?" I asked, arching a brow at Tessa.

"Of course not." She smiled, sensing we both needed this. She crouched down, smiling at Aiden. "I had a lot of fun with you today, Aiden. I can't wait to hang out again tomorrow. Maybe we'll go somewhere fun, like the lake. What do you say?"

Aiden nodded and slowly raised his eyes to meet Tessa's. They were still watery, but he gave her a smile. "I had fun too. See you tomorrow, Tessa," he answered, giving her the famous Miller man nod. Tessa grinned and I could tell from the look on her face that she saw the similarities between Aiden, Braden and me.

"Goodnight," she added, disappearing down the hall.

Aiden sighed heavily and shuffled over to his bed, his shoulders slumping slightly with defeat. He looked like a child that carried the weight of the world on his shoulders. I pulled back the blankets and he crawled in.

"Do you want to talk about it?" I asked, nodding my head in the direction of my mom's bedroom.

Aiden's eyes welled up with the tears he'd been trying to repress, his bottom lip trembling slightly. "I'm just really going to miss Grammy when she goes to Heaven. I wish I could visit her, but Mommy says I can't visit people in Heaven."

"No, you can't visit her," I confirmed, my heart clenching painfully in my chest. "But you can talk to her whenever you want."

"Will she talk back?" he whispered, his eyes wide.

"Not in words." I smiled sadly and sat down on the bottom of his bed. Aiden's face folded into confusion as he tried to work out the meaning. "When my grandpa died, I would talk to him and I would hear his replies in my heart."

"Oh," Aiden said softly, his frown lessening. "It's not the same, though."

"No, it's not," I told him. "But Grammy loves you very much, and she'll watch over you always."

"Why does she have to leave us?" More tears streamed down Aiden's face.

I swallowed hard, trying to keep my own heartache and emotions at bay. "You know that she doesn't want to go, right? She doesn't want to leave you, buddy. She doesn't want to leave any of us. But we don't often get a choice."

Aiden's chest heaved with the breaths he fought to draw in. Without thinking, I scooped him up in my arms and held him close, stroking his thick dark hair and rocking him back and forth. His heartbreak was killing me.

I didn't know the first thing about raising a child, let alone raising one going through something like this. Part of me wanted to suggest that Becky stop with this nightly routine; it looked like it was breaking him. Then and again, one day he wouldn't be able to curl up beside her and talk to her at all, and preventing him from doing that now might only make things worse.

Still, when I'd heard the news, I'd desperately hoped that Aiden would still be unaware, that he wouldn't know that she was dying. I hoped that he could keep the childlike wonder and innocence a while longer. Death ages a child, similar to the way that abuse does. The last thing I wanted was for my nephew to grow up faster than he was supposed to.

I continued rocking him until his sobbing ebbed and his chest started to fall in slow and gentle patterns. He'd cried himself to sleep in my arms. I held him for a while longer before I gently stood up and placed him in his bed. I tucked him in, watching him for a moment. Then I sighed and left his room, closing the door quietly behind me.

I paused by my mother's door, conflicted. Part of me wanted

to go in there and see if she was still awake, but another part of me cautioned that I'd had enough emotional shit to deal with tonight. My anxiety was rolling; my rage was lurking beneath the surface. I clenched my fists, the desire to punch something strong. I was angry at her; angry at her for dying and leaving this mess behind. But I knew that wasn't rational. It wasn't like she was intentionally dying.

I found Tessa sitting at the kitchen table with two cups of steaming tea in front of her. She pushed one towards me without saying a word. Her eyes were red rimmed. I wasn't sure how much of our conversation she had overheard.

"I'm sorry," I said. I brought my hand up to scratch at the back of my neck.

"Don't be." She waved my apology away, not meeting my eyes. "It's nobody's fault. It's just...life."

"Yeah," I said on an exhale. I pulled the chair out and sat down across from Tessa, staring into the mug. "You made tea?" I asked, looking up at her. The corners of my lips twitched with a small smile at the domestic gesture.

She shrugged, finally meeting my eyes and fighting a smile of her own. "I don't know. It seemed like a good idea at the time."

"Do you even drink tea?" I asked, arching a brow.

"No," she muttered, her tentative smile finally breaking free. "Do you?"

"No." I laughed lightly, shaking my head. I was a black coffee kind of guy. I'd never had a sip of tea in my life, but I appreciated her attempt at comfort.

Tessa's eyes floated to the clock over the stove, her smile fading slightly. "Beth-Anne left ten minutes ago, and I guess Becky should be here soon," she said, looking back at me. She sounded uncertain, as if she wasn't sure that I should be here when Becky got home.

"Becky probably knows," I told her, shrugging. I didn't care what Becky thought about me being with Tessa. I picked up the tea, taking a small sip just to do something with my hands. It wasn't that bad, but I still preferred the strong kick of coffee. "You don't have to worry about my family ratting us out to anyone."

"That's not what I'm worried about," Tessa argued, her eyes flashing a little. "I just didn't want her to think I invited my boyfriend over to hook up with when I'm supposed to be watching her kid."

"But you didn't." I grinned, amused. It was startling how Tessa could change the way I felt. When I'd left Aiden's room, I'd been an emotional wreck on the verge of exploding or punching a wall. Now I was smiling and bantering with her. Now I felt almost happy, simply from being around her. "I showed up, remember? Besides, I'm her brother and I technically live here."

"Still," she muttered, her eyes lowering as she fought another smile. She was amused with the situation and her reaction to it too.

I opened my mouth, about to say something else, when the front door opened and Becky walked in. She didn't seem surprised at all to see me sitting at the table across from Tessa. Then again, she had probably seen my truck parked out front. "Hey, guys." She sounded cautious and she looked exhausted. Worry lines creased her forehead as she came into the kitchen and eyed the tea mistrustfully.

Tessa sat up straighter, a sheepish look on her face. "I made tea, but neither one of us like tea, apparently. You can have mine."

Becky inhaled slowly, as if preparing herself. Her eyes narrowed while she studied our faces. "So, what happened?" she asked, squaring her shoulders. "I mean, if you made tea and nobody wanted any...something happened, didn't it? How is Aiden?" She sounded borderline panicked, but she fought to keep it under control. She was clinging to what little strength she had left.

"Relax," I instructed firmly. "He just got a little emotional after he cuddled with Mom."

"Oh." Becky exhaled, her brow furrowing. "I'm sorry, Tessa. I completely forgot to give you the heads up about that," she added guiltily, chewing on her lip. "He doesn't get emotional every night, but I guess he knows that she's getting sicker."

"He knows." I cleared my throat, about to fill her in on what Aiden had said.

Tessa picked at the old vinyl on the table. "I should go. This is probably a conversation for you two to have alone," she said, standing up. "I'll call you later, Brock. And I'll see you tomorrow, Becky...same time?"

"Yeah, same time." Becky swallowed, nodding at Tessa and giving her a small smile.

I wanted to ask her to stay, but I could tell by the look on her face that she needed out. We watched as Tessa gathered her things and left, her head bowed slightly. When the door clanged shut behind her, Becky fixed me with a piercing stare.

"So tell me. What happened?"

I swallowed hard, steeling myself before I launched into the recount of what Aiden had said. Becky's eyes welled with tears as she listened and her shoulders slumped in utter defeat. When I finished talking, she buried her head in her arms on the table and sobbed.

I stood up, about to put my arms around her and comfort her. Becky raised her hand, stopping me. "I'm fine," she said, lifting her head with great effort. Her eyes were watery. "This is just...it's hard. Not only am I losing Mom, but I..." She bit down on her lip in an attempt to keep her emotion at bay.

"I know it's hard," I said, that ball of emotion stuck in my throat. Seeing my sister fall to pieces was tough, almost as tough as seeing Aiden fall to pieces. I'd protected this girl since the day she was born. I took a steadying breath, trying to keep my emotions at bay so I could get through this conversation without exploding. I couldn't break down in front of Becky, and I wouldn't. She needed me to be strong.

"I didn't think sheltering him would be a good idea, but now I'm not so sure."

"Becky." I sighed, the emotion and exhaustion cutting into me. "There's no right answer here; you have to see that. There's no way that you can ensure he won't come out unscathed...you can't control the outcome of this. It's obvious he has a close bond with Mom, and it's obvious that even if you sheltered him from all this, he'd still miss her greatly. You're doing the best you can with the hand you've been dealt. You're a fantastic mom and Aiden is a fantastic kid."

Fresh tears poured down her cheeks at my words and she forced a smile. "Thanks, Brock," she said, swallowing hard. "I'm really glad you're back," she added. "I don't know what I'd do without you."

THE NEXT WEEK passed in a blur. I was busy framing with Gordon and his crew, and didn't have time to go to the house again. I didn't end up speaking to my mom that night I was there; she remained sleeping and I hadn't wanted to wake her.

I saw Tessa almost every night, though. She'd stop in after she finished babysitting to hang out for a bit. I knew we were pushing our luck; she knew it too, but she didn't seem to care. She seemed every bit as captivated by me as I was by her.

On Saturday morning, at the crack of dawn, I went outside to the sound of her truck rumbling up the driveway. She'd texted me forty minutes prior, asking if I was up. I'd told her to come straight over.

"Wow." She whistled, stepping out of her truck and peering

up at the skeleton of the cabin with wide eyes. It was all framed in and the roof was finally completed. Next week we were going to start sheathing the walls. "It's going up faster than I thought it would," she remarked, walking into my arms.

"Yeah." I smiled against her hair, enjoying the scent of her as I held her to me for a moment longer than necessary. I loved the feel of Tessa in my arms. "The crew works fast."

"No kidding," she said dryly, peering up at me with a smile. "So...I missed you, I guess," she added, her smile turning a little sinister as her eyes roamed over my face. The carnal need in her eyes made my dick harden.

"Did you, now?" I arched a brow, my hands dropping to her ass. I pulled her tighter to me, pushing my pelvis against hers. Even though I'd seen her almost every night that week, we hadn't had a chance to be intimate; she'd been on her period. Instead, we spent our nights fishing on the lake and just... talking.

It was the oddest goddamn thing. I'd never felt the urge to get to know someone like this before, to want to know how their mind ticked and what their deepest desires were. I craved her mind, body and soul.

Today, we both had the day off and it was assumed that we'd be spending it together. Her lips met mine and I kissed her deeply, conveying all of the emotion I felt for her in that kiss. She practically melted in my arms.

"I need you," she whispered breathlessly, trying to push me back towards the trailer. I followed her lead, hoisting her up effortlessly in my arms and carrying her the remainder of the way. I couldn't wait for the cabin to be finished, to have more secure places to take her on and more space.

Tessa didn't seem to care, though. She ripped off my shirt and tackled my zipper with fervor. I peeled her tank top and her tight shorts off of her, throwing them over my shoulder.

I teased her to the point of frustration, almost laughing at the impatient set of her lips before I finally slid a condom on and positioned myself over top of her. Her amber eyes swirled with desire and she bit her plump lower lip lightly with her teeth, knowing what was to come. I drove home, diving into her like she was made for me and God, it felt like she was. Every time I entered her, I had to pause and collect myself. She fit around me like she'd been sculpted to do just that. It was enough to drive even the most controlled man completely wild.

Afterwards, we lay in my bed in a breathless, sweaty heap of tangled arms and legs. Tessa let out a deep sigh of contentment, a satisfied smile playing on her swollen lips. I couldn't even find the energy to talk. We fell asleep that way, snoozing on and off for an hour until the sound of an engine coming up the long driveway and Hunter's alarmed bark woke us.

Startled, I practically jumped out of bed, shoving my legs into jeans. My heart was pounding from the adrenaline of the sudden jarring wake up. Tessa was sitting up in bed, frantically peering around for her clothes. I opened the trailer door, letting Hunter escape before me as Gordon's black truck pulled to a stop behind Tessa's.

The look of utter and complete rage and disbelief on his face as he climbed out of the cab made my stomach feel sick. "Gordon –" I started, my voice carrying warning.

"You know, I didn't want to believe it." He spoke calmly, cutting me off. His voice was dangerous and he wore a formidable smile on his face. He was almost laughing, but not with humor. His hazel eyes were dark with anger. "Guess I really shouldn't be surprised, huh?" he growled, his fists tensing at his sides.

"It's not what it looks like," I argued, frowning deeply.

"Well, fucktard. It looks like you're screwing my sister, you no good piece of shit," Gordon scathed, stepping menacingly toward me. I held my ground, my own hands clenching into fists so tightly that they cracked with the strain.

"I'm not just screwing her, Gordon. I'm *with* her," I said, my voice thick with tension. I wouldn't back down. I hadn't backed down ever before, and I wasn't about to start with Gordon Armstrong.

"Call it what you fucking will. You broke a promise. I told you to stay away from her," he replied narrowly.

"We made that promise when we were kids, Gordon!" I shot back, my voice rising a little with anger. "I'm not the same person I was back then."

"Tessa! Get the fuck out here now!" he roared, ignoring me and looking past me to the trailer.

The trailer door slammed open and Tessa stomped outside, pulling her hair out from under her tank top. Her eyes flashed dangerously. "You have no fucking right," she snarled at him.

"Tessa, you don't understand. You're a child, you –"

"I am not a fucking child, Gordon!" she yelled, brushing past me and shoving her finger into her brother's chest. "I'm going to college in the fall and I am more than capable of making my own decisions."

"You're eighteen!" he exploded, spit flying out of his mouth with rage. "You don't know what's good for you and if you did, you wouldn't be wasting your time on this ex-convict!"

"How can you say that?" she asked, her voice so low it was almost a whisper. "He's your friend."

"Was my friend," Gordon corrected, glaring at me. "Years ago. He's dangerous, Tess. Let's go home, I won't mention this to Dad – "

"I am not going home," Tessa said firmly, crossing her arms while staring him down. "You are in the wrong here. Brock isn't dangerous, and you need to pull your head out of your ass. When are you going to realize you can't control me? None of you do! I'm my own person, Gordon."

"It's not about control," Gordon argued, his eyes flashing.

"Save it," Tessa responded coldly. "I'll see you later, when I decide I'm ready to go home, not when you decide."

The entire time this exchange was happening, Hunter was poised at my feet, staring at Gordon with an unnerving stillness. When Gordon went to grab Tessa's arm, Hunter let out a low, threatening growl to warn him. He finally took notice of the huge dog staring him down. His eyes narrowed at me as if he took it as a personal threat.

Tessa heard too. She turned around, tossing a smug smile at her brother. "He won't attack you unless he feels that you're putting Brock, or me, in danger. Grabbing me and dragging me into your truck against my will would definitely get him to attack you, so I'd rethink that plan of yours and head on home. See you later," she told him while he stared at her in disbelief.

"This is a fucking joke," Gordon growled, stomping back to his truck. "Don't think for a moment that this is over, Brock," he added before slamming the door. We watched as he peeled back up my driveway, gunning it towards the road.

When the sound of his truck had disappeared, Tessa's shoulders fell. "I'm sorry about that, Brock." She sighed, biting her lip as her eyes met mine. She looked hopeless, at a loss for what to do. Her gaze flitted back to the driveway and I knew she was thinking about leaving.

"Hey," I said gently, stepping toward her. I framed her face with my hands, brushing her messy hair away. I looked into her eyes, giving her a small smile as my heart stuttered in my chest. I cared about this girl, a lot. I cared about her so much that the thought of having her family talk sense into her, of having her see me the way that everyone else in this town saw me, completely gutted me. I realized, as I looked into her beautiful amber eyes, that I was terrified of losing her. "Whatever happens, Tess, this means a lot to me. You mean a lot to me." I kissed her quickly, passionately, as if it was our last kiss and there was a time limit. "God, Tessa, I think I'm falling in love with you," I told her, pressing her forehead to mine.

She smiled, her eyes wet with unshed tears. "I think I'm falling in love with you too," she whispered, her eyes meeting mine with open vulnerability. My lips crashed against hers again, her words unleashing raw need in me. A need to possess her, to consume her so I was all she could think about until she was absolutely positive she was in love with me, because I'd lied to her.

I knew I was already in love with her and had known it the moment she'd been in danger, the second I'd gotten close enough to her to feel that burning chemistry between us. It linked me to her, tethered me to her, but I'd been too afraid to voice my thoughts.

CHAPTER 15

 essa

THE SCREEN DOOR clanged opened as I raced inside. My cheeks were flushed from anger and from Brock's confession and the way he'd looked at me when he had told me that he thought he was falling in love with me. I wanted to stay there with him and forget about everything, all of my problems and the shit-storm that was waiting for me back home.

And the shit-storm was definitely waiting for me, in the form of all three of my brothers and my very angry father, as they gathered around the huge oak table in the kitchen. My dad sat at the head of the table, fixing me with a piercing stare that made me feel as if all my sins were etched clear as day on my face.

It was obvious by the formidable look of disappointment in his eyes and the family intervention, for that matter... that he knew about me and Brock and he wasn't happy about it.

Gordon sat in his usual place at the table, completely

avoiding my eyes. Tommy sat beside him, and even Ben was there.

"Seriously?" I narrowed my eyes, my blood roaring with anger.

"Seriously," my father agreed darkly, standing up. He towered over me, and I knew he was using his size to intimidate me. It had, after all, worked a billion times before when I was in trouble.

It wouldn't work now. My mind was made up and I wasn't going to let my family attempt to change it by bullying me into "seeing reason", which actually really wasn't reason at all.

"I thought I told you to stay away from that Miller boy." He frowned at me as if I'd truly broken his heart by disobeying his order.

"And I thought I told you that I was capable of making my own decisions," I responded, straightening my spine and matching my father's angry look with one of my own.

"He's dangerous, Tessa," Gordon interjected, standing up too. His eyes pleaded with me.

"How can you even sit there and say that?" I demanded, shaking my head with disgust. "He's no more dangerous than any of you are. You have no right to act all superior, Gordon. You either, Tommy. You act like a bunch of brainless cavemen!"

"What are you talking about?" Gordon demanded.

"Oh, let's see here," I said, pretending to think about it. "Corbin, Ezra, to name a few."

"That's nowhere near the same thing!" he argued back.

"YES IT IS!" I bellowed. "Do you even know what actually happened that night that he was arrested?" I demanded, stomping towards Gordon and getting in his face.

"He lost his shit." My brother shrugged, his eyes narrowing at me. "The reason doesn't matter. He's got a criminal record, Tessa."

"The reason does matter!" I laughed darkly, rolling my eyes

with exasperation. "Brock was defending his sister, something you're probably telling yourself you're doing right now. Something you have done, only Brock had every right to rearrange that asshole's face. He beat Becky so badly, she ended up in the hospital and she almost lost her baby because of it! You, on the other hand, have no right to scare off any and every guy that's ever come within five feet of me."

Silence followed my angry outburst as my family absorbed my words. My father's brow creased. "Even if that's true, Tessa...he's still six years older than you," he said diplomatically. "What business does he have being with you?" he added, looking me straight in the eyes. It was as if he thought Brock was interested in one thing and one thing only.

But they didn't know Brock, and they didn't know who I was when I was with him. They didn't know who we were together. They didn't know how he made me feel: safe, cherished, desired, protected and yet equal. They didn't see the looks he stole when he thought I wasn't paying attention. They didn't see the way he'd come to my rescue, the way he hadn't judged me or made me feel stupid about it. They just saw an ex-convict, a guy that wasn't and would never be worthy in their eyes.

I arched a brow defiantly. "Really? You're going to play the age card on me?" I asked, gesturing to Ben. "Ben's four years older than Katie, but that's okay because it's Ben. You were older than Mom, but that's okay because it's you. Age only seems to matter when it involves me."

"That's not true," Dad argued, his brow furrowing even more.

Ben cleared his throat, drawing attention to himself. We all turned to look at him, our eyes flashing dangerously. "It is true," he said, nodding at me. His eyes were full of apology. Out of everyone in the room, Ben seemed to be the only one willing to hear me out, the only one not judging me or making assumptions. "We've always been overprotective of Tessa, almost to a fault. It's because she's the youngest, the only girl. We've all felt a need to shelter her from everything."

"Bullshit," Tommy argued, siding with Gordon and my dad.

"Any time we've ever interfered was when it was needed," Gordon remarked, scowling.

"So I guess Corbin deserved a broken nose for dancing with me and I guess Ezra deserved a black eye for...taking me to the movies," I amended, my face turning red underneath my dad's never wavering gaze.

"Technically, I didn't mean to break his nose," Tommy corrected, his eyes almost sparkling with humor. "He moved at the last minute, so that's on him. He was talking shit though, and it was about more than that. He was doing it to get underneath my skin. And Ezra deserved a black eye because you don't disrespect someone we care about like that."

"None of those guys were worthy of you, Tess. And neither is Brock Miller," Gordon added with disgust.

"You really ought to be ashamed of yourself," I told him, my eyes narrowing as an angry tear escaped down my cheeks. "For someone who claims to once have been his friend, you really never knew him at all."

I turned on my heel, storming up to my bedroom. I packed my overnight bag quickly, more angry tears escaping down my cheeks. Ten minutes later, I was packed. I fired out a text message before I flew down the stairs, my eyes on the front door.

"Where are you going?" Dad asked. Usually, I'd stop to address my father properly. I was raised to give my full attention to someone who was speaking to me, but today I couldn't care less about being respectful of my elders. I was severely disappointed and hurt by my family's actions.

"I'm going to Elle's," I responded, not even bothering to look over my shoulder to see if that was okay. I didn't care if it was okay or not; I was sick of this testosterone-filled, hell-hole. At least at Elle's house, I'd be surrounded by rational thinking women, women who supported me and could understand where I was coming from.

"Let her go," I heard Ben say as the screen door slammed shut behind me. I ran out to my truck, wiping the moisture from my eyes with the back of my hand before I pulled open the door.

It didn't take me long to rip up Elle's driveway. She was waiting for me on her front porch, alerted of my arrival from the frantic text I'd sent her. She watched me approach with a sad and wary look on her face and when I got close enough, she opened her arms and hugged me silently, letting me cry into her shoulder.

"Tessa." Sue Thompson's smoky voice was gentle. I looked up at my best friend's mom. Her kind eyes were full of moisture at the sight of my tears. Elle stood back, letting me go to her mom. Sue's arms wrapped around me protectively, and she ran a hand through my hair to provide comfort. "It's alright honey. It's okay."

"No, it's not," I hiccupped. I couldn't even form words to express what I was feeling. This was about more than Brock, more than me falling for someone my family dubbed as "not good enough". I was angry, hurt and fed up. The hypocrisy within the walls of the Armstrong house was outrageous.

"Come inside," Sue urged, as she and Elle gently guided me into the Thompson's worn kitchen. Elle sat down at the table beside me, rubbing my back in circular motions while I tried to pull myself back together.

I'd never fought with my family like that. I had disagreed with them and stomped my feet in anger, sure. I'd even slammed my fair share of doors in my dad's and my brothers' faces. Somehow, they always got the last word. Somehow, they always got their way, because I usually backed down.

But this fight...this fight was different. For starters, I hadn't

backed down, not even in the slightest. This fight was prom-
inent. It came from years of being treated like a child, years of
having my brothers and my father meddling in my business to
the point where I felt like I couldn't even make a single decision
myself without first seeking approval.

While I was lost in my thoughts, Sue had made three cups of
hot chocolate. She placed two steaming mugs, overflowing with
marshmallows, down on the table in front of Elle and me. She
carried hers to the other side of the table and sat down, taking a
slow sip while her brown eyes studied me.

"I've been warning your daddy for years now." She sighed,
shaking her head regretfully.

"Warning him about what?" I asked, raising my eyes from my
mug to meet hers.

"That he needs to let you grow up a little. He needs to let you
do the things that you desire doing. I thought I'd reached him
when we talked about the whole college thing –"

"Wait…what college thing?" I interrupted.

"He didn't want you to go so far away. He didn't like the idea
of you not having your brothers around. You knew that,
though," Sue answered patiently, smiling. "Hell, if there was a
decent school locally that would allow you a proper education
in that field, I'm sure he would have insisted on that."

I exhaled, knowing she was right. He would have. Sue fell
silent, lost in her own thoughts.

"Some fathers are just never ready for their daughters to
grow up." She finally looked back at me and said, "He'll come
around though."

"I don't think so." I frowned. "I really let him down. You
should have seen the look of disappointment on his face. All
because he found out I was hanging out with Brock Miller. He
doesn't even know that I…" I clamped my mouth shut tightly.

"That you what?" Elle pressed, gently nudging me.

"No need to make the girl say it," Sue scolded her daughter, a slight frown on her face. Then she turned her head and gave me a small smile.

"It doesn't matter. Dad will never let me be with him and neither will my brothers." I sighed sadly.

"They're angry now and they'll probably be angry for a bit," Sue cautioned me. "But they'll come to see reason soon enough."

"What makes you so confident?" I sniffled.

"You're a grown woman now, Tessa." Sue smiled at me wisely. "They'll end up accepting whoever you love simply because you love them."

A FEW HOURS LATER, I sat on Elle's porch swing with a large blanket wrapped around the two of us. We were looking up at the stars as they shone brightly in the night sky. It was something we'd been doing together since before either of us could remember. Our sleepovers always included stargazing and daydreaming.

Tonight, Elle was oddly silent. I almost expected her to attack me the moment her mother let us be, but she didn't. She was content to sit there quietly.

"You know," she said, finally breaking her silence, "I'm glad you're letting yourself fall for him. Even if your family are all being jerks about it." She nudged me with her shoulder and gave me a small smile. "Mom's right, they'll get over it."

"Maybe." I sighed heavily, lifting my chin and resting my head against the back of the swing. "It's just...not how I wanted this summer to go. I definitely didn't want to end it on this note. I don't like fighting with my family."

"I know," she whispered. "Nobody likes fighting with their family."

"You and your mom never fight," I pointed out, concerned by the ominous edge to Elle's tone.

"Oh, it's not us fighting…" she trailed off, biting her lip. She was keeping something from me. I could tell by the way she avoided meeting my eyes.

"What is it, Elle?"

She finally brought her eyes to mine and I startled to see the pain reflecting in their dark depths. "Things aren't going so good between Braden and me right now."

"What do you mean?" my frown increased. "You guys spend every possible minute together. I saw you at the bonfire; you both seemed incredibly happy."

Elle looked away, staring down the driveway. "I just feel like there's a wall between us and I can't penetrate it. I can't get past it; I can't reach him. He's…he's not the same person that he was, even a few days ago. It's like the wall gets thicker and taller every day."

I was silent, mulling over my best friend's concerns. "Well, their mom is getting sicker; maybe that has something to do with it?"

"Probably," Elle said dejectedly. "I just wish he'd let me help him."

"Knowing that you're there and willing to listen is probably helping him enough," I told her, giving her a small smile. "He'll come around."

"I hope you're right." She sighed, wiping away the tear that had escaped. She looked at me, forcing a smile.

I WASN'T REALLY ready to go home and face the music, but I knew I couldn't hide out at Elle's forever, even though both she and Sue insisted it was fine. Hiding out really wasn't my style. I preferred to face my problems head on, even if they came in the form of an angrily disappointed father and two brothers. I wasn't really sure where I stood with Ben; he'd stood up for me a little, but I wasn't about to count him on my side yet.

I gave myself one night, one night to calm down and contemplate my situation in a clear head. I didn't want my dad to think I was acting rashly based on hormones or enticement. This had a lot to do with Brock, yes, but it was also about me.

I was distractedly rehearsing what I wanted to say as I drove up the long driveway. I almost didn't see Sue's car parked beside the front of the house.

It wasn't uncommon for Sue to visit our place. She usually came with Elle (who I knew was with Braden) and a bunch of delicious foods. I hopped out of my truck and walked up the creaky front porch, letting the screen door clang behind me loudly. I walked around the main floor, finding it empty. Nobody was in the living room or the kitchen. There weren't any heaping dishes of casseroles or bowls of chili on the counter either, so Sue's visit hadn't been to bring food.

Frowning, I went out through the side door. I had chores I needed to do, chores that I'd put off enough already. I headed towards the barn, intent on tending to the horses. The sound of voices made me still outside the door. I cautiously peered around, seeing both my dad and Sue standing in the aisle with Temptress. The old horse was tethered and my dad was slowly grooming her, a scowl on his face as he spoke.

"Sue, you know I appreciate all that you've done for us over the years, all that you've done for Tessa, but I don't think your opinion is needed here."

"Wait just one minute, Bill Armstrong." I couldn't see her very well, but I knew from the sound of her voice that Sue was livid. "I'm the closest thing to a mother that girl has ever known. I have every right to voice my very accurate opinion when it's needed, and I know Alice would have agreed with that! Alice believed in love, Bill. She believed in chances and goodness. She would have welcomed any boy into her home with open arms if Tessa loved him."

The hand that was holding the brush stilled mid stroke, and I watched as my dad took in a jagged breath. "Alice isn't here, and you can't use her as a weapon in this conversation. Tessa lives under my roof and she needs to follow my rules. That's the end of it. I don't want her getting tangled up with that Miller boy and jeopardizing her future."

Sadness crept in at the sound of my dad's voice. I'd been hoping that he had cooled off enough to maybe see how unfair he was being. Apparently not. The disdain he felt for Brock was still very detectable in his voice.

"Do you even listen to yourself, Bill? You sound ridiculous and you know it. It wasn't long ago when you took 'that Miller boy' under your wing because you saw something in that boy. You saw potential," Sue argued.

"That was before," Dad replied, his voice low with warning.

"Before what? Before he went after the guy who put his pregnant sister in the hospital and endangered the life of his nephew?" she shot back. My heart rate increased with adrenaline. I hadn't known that Sue knew this about Brock. "Tell me you wouldn't have done the same thing. Tell me that Ben, Gordon, and Tommy wouldn't do that for Tessa."

My dad was silent for several moments. I could hear the sound of the wire brush against the horse's fur as he mechanically resumed his task.

"That's not the point," he finally said on a sigh. "What kind of life could he give Tessa? He's got a record."

"Record be damned," Sue replied, her voice gentle. "He could give Tessa things that money can't buy. Besides, the boy has a job, Bill. I doubt his record affects him as much as the people in this town do, reminding him how unworthy he is every chance they get."

My heart clenched at Sue's words. It was true. Brock had a

job, he'd worked since his release. It was everyone around us that constantly made him feel like a criminal.

I wordlessly walked away from the barn and back up to the house, my thoughts tumbling continuously with what I'd overheard. I saw my truck and I veered left instead of going into the house. I didn't want to have it out with my dad, after all.

The engine roared to life and I reversed. I shifted into drive and tromped on the gas, watching both my dad and Sue standing in the doorway of the barn from my rear view mirror, staring at me as I took off down the dusty driveway.

Fifteen minutes later, I was pulling to a stop in front of Brock's place. He was inside the skeleton of his cabin, using a saw to cut plywood. He'd already started sheathing the outer walls. The left side of the outer wall that faced the driveway was already sheathed.

Brock hadn't heard me pull up; the saw had covered the sound of my truck's tires on the gravel. I climbed out of the cab, adjusting the knee high white sun dress I was wearing, and crouched down on my knees to pet Hunter. He'd been lying beneath a huge tree, but watched me pull up. After he got a few pats, he headed back to his resting spot while I went inside.

I leaned against the freshly sheathed wall and watched Brock quietly while he worked. He had no shirt on and his muscles rippled while he slowly ran the wood beneath the saw, cutting with perfect precision. His skin was coated in a light sheen of sweat. I waited until he'd finished cutting the plywood and turned off the saw before I spoke.

"You look like you could use a break," I told him, smirking.

He turned around at the sound of my voice, a smile playing on those sensual lips. "Well, I figure I'll probably run behind schedule now. Not too sure I have a team anymore, so I figured I'd get started."

"You haven't heard from Gordon yet?" I arched a brow, feeling guilty.

Brock shrugged, pulling the safety glasses off his face and setting them down on the workbench. He wiped his damp hands against his Wrangler jeans. "Not yet."

I sighed, biting my lip. "I'm really sorry. I hope I didn't cost you your crew," I said, trying to urge the tears back. I didn't need to cry around him. I wasn't that kind of girl; I didn't turn into a sobbing mess every time something didn't go my way. But even still, my heart hurt as I remembered Sue's words about how Brock was treated around here, and not just by my family. It disgusted me that my family was a part of it, though. "I'd like to tell you that my family will come around, but..." I shrugged apologetically, my shoulders slumping in defeat. I didn't know if they would come around.

"Hey, it's not your fault," Brock told me, crossing the distance between us. He cupped my face in his hands, looking deep into my eyes. I felt like he could read everything there, plain as day. "Besides, I'd rather have you than the crew," he added, the left corner of his lip perking up in half of a smile. The wave of emotions that overcame me was staggering. My heart sped up in my chest, my stomach clenched with desire and I felt an incredible, overwhelming surge of love for this man standing before me.

It unnerved me, not because I should fear him like everyone else thought, but because I'd never felt this way about anybody before. There was a tiny voice inside of me that proclaimed it was too soon for declarations of love.

Brock seemed to sense what I was thinking and feeling, or maybe he felt it too. His eyes were swirling with adoration and desire; he seemed to be in some sort of trance. "Sometimes, when love happens, it happens fast," he muttered.

"You sound like Elle," I said on exhale, smiling. I closed my eyes for a moment, leaning into his touch. His thumb gently rubbed against my cheek, and I could hear the smile in his voice before I saw it on his face when I opened my eyes again.

"I love you, Tessa Armstrong. I'm in love with you, and I've been in love with you since that bush party, when you looked at me with those amber eyes."

"I'm in love with you too," I whispered, tears falling without restraint down my cheeks. Brock patiently brushed them away with the pad of his thumb, a gentle smile playing on his lips.

"Don't be afraid to love me, Tess," he said, swallowing hard. "I won't hurt you."

"How do you know you won't hurt me?" I asked, my brow furrowing as I looked into those steel coloured eyes, searching for some kind of assurance. I had a bad tendency of saying whatever was on my mind. "People hurt people all the time. It's what they do."

Brock considered my question, his eyes never breaking from mine. I expected him to feel angry that I'd ruined our moment, the first time we actually said those words aloud; but instead, he was reflective, as if he was truly considering an answer. "I guess I don't know that for sure, but I can promise you, Tessa...I would never willingly hurt you. I will protect you with everything that I have. I would never let you fall and be unprepared to catch you."

"So you're prepared to catch me?" I smiled, my heart rate speeding completely out of control.

"Always," he said, bringing his lips to mine.

CHAPTER 16

rock

THERE WAS a weight pressing down on my shoulders and the moment I told Tessa how I truly felt about her, that weight lifted, relieving some of the pressure. She ran her hands through my hair, tugging it gently while she lit me up with her inflamed responses.

"Jesus," I exclaimed, pulling my lips away from hers for a moment to collect myself. I pressed my forehead to hers, shaking it slightly.

"What?" She asked, her brow furrowing.

"You make me lose control every time you touch me," I told her.

"I see nothing wrong with that." Tessa grinned mischievously. Her eyes dropped down to the straining evidence of my arousal and her hands tugged on my jeans, pulling me tighter to her. She stroked me through the denim and my eyes practically rolled into the back of my head. I heard the sound of the zipper opening, and then felt her warm hand releasing me. She pumped slowly and I let out a low hiss. "Let's break in your new house," she whispered. Her eyes were aglow with desire.

I couldn't say no; I didn't want to say no. Tessa was wearing a sinfully short dress and cowboy boots; no hot-blooded male would be able to resist that. We could talk about everything later; we would talk about everything later.

She took control, kissing me with fervor. I picked her up, using the frame of the house to balance her and my hands to support her weight. The lust surged in my veins when I felt her bare thighs squeeze around my hips. The only thought in my head was a prayer to God for the creation of short dresses and Tessa. I let out a low growl as I deepened the kiss, pressing my body against hers. I pushed aside her thong with my hand before I drove into her in one fluid moment. She gasped, arching her back and bringing me deeper into her core.

It didn't take us long to both come undone.

"You're amazing," she said breathlessly against my shoulder. It was a miracle I was still able to support her weight afterwards.

"You're amazing," I corrected, kissing her forehead before I finally set her down. She fixed her dress and tried to run her hands through her hair to detangle it. "Are you hungry?"

"A little," she admitted, giving me a small smile.

"Let's go get some food," I told her, leading the way to my trailer.

At the mention of food, Hunter slowly got up from under the tree where he'd been laying and stretched before ambling over to us. I didn't have much in my tiny refrigerator; just a sip left of orange juice and some eggs that had expired the week before. I pursed my lips, looking over my shoulder at Tessa with a lopsided grin. "Are you against going out to eat? I mean, if we're still hiding...I could just bring us back something from McDonalds."

She wrinkled her nose, thinking. "No, we're not still hiding. I mean, my family knows now." She sighed heavily, like this wasn't good news.

"Does their opinion bother you that much?" I asked as I closed the refrigerator door and turned to face her. There was a tiny seed of doubt seeping into my heart. I understood the reasons why Tessa had wanted to keep our relationship from her family, but I couldn't help but worry that now that they knew... they'd change her mind.

I didn't want her to change her mind about us. I'd meant every word I said to her.

"It's not that," she assured me, looking up with her wide eyes full of honesty. She bit her lip. "They can't forbid me from being with you. They don't have that kind of control over me. I'm just worried that they'll do something to you."

"They won't," I said with confidence. "For one, it'd be too obvious. Your brothers may be hotheaded, but they don't let their tempers run their lives." Not like I had, I added in my head. "Now come on, let's go. I'm starving." I smiled, holding my hand out to her.

After I gave Hunter water and chained him up, I drove Tessa to one of my favourite breakfast spots in Parry Sound. My grandpa used to take Becky, Braden and me there once a month and I hadn't been back since I'd been home. I hoped they still had the best breakfast in town.

It was Sunday morning and it was crowded. Even still, we didn't see anybody that we really knew. We were in the thick of the tourism season, and most of the people in the restaurant were cottagers.

Tessa eased when she realized this and chose the first empty booth we came across. She sat down, grinning at me as I slid onto the bench across from her. Her face shone with excitement.

"I guess this could count as our first official date," she remarked, concealing a smile.

"I guess so." I chuckled.

"So," she sat up straighter in her seat and picked up the menu, "what do you feel like ordering?"

"Everything on the menu. I really worked up an appetite," I answered.

She looked at me from over the top of the menu, her eyes dancing. "Well, maybe you should stop trying to put up walls by yourself. I could help with that, you know."

"In a dress?" I challenged, arching a brow.

"I bet I could," she shot back with a grin, lowering the menu. "But I do really like this dress, so maybe you could loan me something else?"

I let my eyes roam her body. She was smaller than me; none of my clothes would stay on her, not that I'd complain about that, but it would provide a distraction around power tools and that probably wasn't the safest thing for either of us. "No can do. I've got nothing that'll fit you. Besides, I've decided to take the rest of the day off."

"Can I get you guys anything to drink?" The jaded tone full of irritation interrupted our playful banter. I looked up, my smile wavering slightly at the sight of Melanie Clayton.

"Black coffee," I ordered, taken aback by the jealousy emanating from her.

"And what does 'Little Miss gets whatever she wants' want today?" Melanie sneered, turning her glare on Tessa.

"That's uncalled for." I said.

Tessa didn't seem surprised by Melanie's hostile attitude though. "I'll take a coffee too, with some creamers and sugar on the side. Oh, and a new waitress, preferably one that's less of a bitch." She smiled sweetly and I couldn't help but laugh at her smooth delivery.

Melanie stalked off, her red hair bouncing against her back with every angry step. "I really do hope she brings us a new waitress," Tessa said, frowning a little.

"I'm sure she will. She didn't seem to want to deal with us any more than we wanted to deal with her," I remarked, my fingers rubbing against the stubble on my jaw.

"What's up with her, anyway?" she asked, looking into my eyes as if searching out the answer.

I shrugged, leaning back in the booth, debating on how honest I needed to be.

"Oh, I see." Tessa pursed her lips, nodding as she looked away from me. "You too, eh? Well, that's the entire town."

"Basically, huh?" I chuckled. "I was young and stupid."

Tessa huffed with agreement and picked up her menu again, her eyes scanning it. "If we could change the topic now so I don't completely lose my appetite, that'd be great."

I didn't need to ask her if she was jealous, I could see that she was. I fought a smile as I picked up my own menu, thinking about how Melanie Clayton would never come close to Tessa Armstrong. I couldn't even remember my night with Melanie, but each and every moment with Tessa stood out clearly in my mind.

Much to my relief, a new waitress approached the table with our cups of coffee and a bowl of various creamer packets. She was a middle aged woman with a gentle smile that she willingly gave Tessa. "Here you go, Tessa! It's been forever since I've seen you around! How are you doing, honey? How are your dad and brothers?"

"We're all good, thanks, Heather," she responded with a small smile.

"You're off to college in the fall! I bet your daddy isn't too happy about that, huh?" the waitress, Heather, chuckled. Her eyes slid over to me, seeming to notice me for the first time. "And who's this handsome gentleman?"

"This is Brock," Tessa answered, her smile growing as she regarded me warmly. I noticed the pinched edge Heather's smile took on almost immediately.

"Oh, Brock Miller? You've certainly changed since the last time I saw you," the waitress said. I looked at her, trying to place her. Although she seemed vaguely familiar, nothing came to memory. Heather's smile slid completely away. "I used to volunteer for school trips when my boys were younger."

"The Andersons," Tessa supplied helpfully.

"Oh right, Owen and Ethan. How are they doing?" I said, their faces finally coming to mind. Owen had been in my grade in public school and Ethan was a year younger. I could now easily recall each school trip that Mrs. Anderson had come on. She'd never seemed to like me much back then. Judging by the disapproval she wore on her face when she looked from Tessa to me, I could take a wild guess on what her opinion of me was now.

"Just lovely, thank you. They really made something of themselves. Owen is in law school and Ethan is a dentist." There was an odd emphasis in her words, one that neither Tessa nor I missed.

I cleared my throat awkwardly. "That's great to hear," I said, forcing my smile to stay in place.

"I think we're ready to order," Tessa said quickly. "I'll have eggs Benedict," she added, folding her menu and sliding it towards the waitress with a tight smile.

"I'll have the omelet supreme special with bacon and a side of sausage," I said, handing over my menu as well.

"Sounds great," Heather said soundly as she finished writing our orders out. She picked up the menus and gave us another rigid smile. "I'll be back soon with your food."

I watched as Tessa poured three creamers into her coffee

and then dumped a heavy helping of sugar. The expression on her face was one of aggravation. Her brow was furrowed and her lips were pursed, like she had tasted something she wasn't quite so fond of. She was extremely focused on the task at hand. She didn't notice me staring until she'd finally fixed her coffee to her preference.

"How do you deal with it?" she asked, seeing my questioning gaze.

"I'm used to it," I replied honestly. It had been like this for as long as I could remember, even before the arrest. People in this town just didn't like my family, or me. I'd long since learned not to take it personally.

"Well, it's not right," she huffed, her gaze focusing on the four waitresses gathered near the kitchen window. Melanie was talking and Heather and the others were shaking their heads solemnly and glancing back at us every now and then. It was obvious what the topic was.

"Tessa," I said. She looked back at me, a smile playing on her lips. I leaned forward, taking her hands in mine. "Your opinion is worth more than every other person in this town put together. If you think I'm worthwhile, that's all I need."

"Good, because I definitely think you're more than worthwhile," she whispered.

AFTER BREAKFAST, we headed back to my place to grab Hunter, my ATV and the fishing gear. We spent almost the whole day on the lake, fishing. We brought in the late afternoon by sitting on the end of the dock, hanging our feet off into the cool water.

The sun was beginning to set over the lake and Tessa let out a soft sigh. "This is beautiful," she said, looking at the setting sun.

"It is," I remarked, my eyes on only her. She turned her head to look at me, a small smile on those kiss-me lips.

"Can I ask you something?"

"You just did," I joked, leaning back on my arms.

"This is serious," she said, nudging me gently with her shoulder. I smiled and arched a brow, urging her to continue on with her question. "How come you don't go see your mom often?"

I looked at her quietly for several long seconds. Her question had caught me off guard. I swallowed, forcing my gaze out over the lake. "I don't know what to say to her."

"Who says you have to say anything?" she said softly. She reached out her hand to cover mine.

"I have a complicated relationship with my mom," I admitted, looking back at her wistfully. "I have a lot of resentment towards her."

"Why?"

"Because," I shifted uncomfortably. I'd never talked about this with anybody before, but I found myself wanting to tell her. I sighed heavily. "My dad was a drunk, which you probably know, because everyone else in town knows. But he was also abusive, not just towards her, but us too. I couldn't understand why she stayed with him or why she let him continue to control her every move and destroy us."

"You were the oldest," Tessa said knowledgeably. "You probably remember better than they do what it was like before."

"I know they remember." I sighed. I didn't tell her that I took the brunt of the beatings so they wouldn't have to feel the pain. Even though I'd tried to shelter them, they weren't unscathed. It was painful enough to watch someone you cared about get beat. I forced my thoughts away from there, though. "Our relationship did change after he died. She blossomed without him there kicking her down. She did a lot for me, and I know she's done a lot for Becky and Aiden, and for Braden."

Tessa was silent, absorbing what I'd said, and what I hadn't, with a sad look on her face. "I guess I'm just wondering...would you be able to forgive yourself for not seeing her in her final days?" she questioned gently, her eyes landing on mine.

I exhaled deeply. I knew she was right; she was just saying everything I'd said to myself. "Yeah, you're right." She bit her lip, looking like she had more to say. "What are you thinking?" I asked, cocking my head to the side. I brought my hand to her face, brushing back her long, wayward hair from her eyes.

"I need to go home," she replied, looking at me as if going home was the last thing she wanted to do.

"Well, whenever you want to come back...you know where I am," I said before I kissed her softly.

I drove her back to my place with her hands around my abdomen. I went faster than the first time and I could feel her laughing against my back. That short ATV rip back to my trailer was over too soon, and before I knew it...I was watching her tailgates disappear.

CHAPTER 17

rock

MY PHONE RANG SHRILLY beside my head. It was nearly three in the morning. My hand fumbled across the pillow, searching for it. Clasping the cold plastic in my hand, I answered it on the second ring. It was Becky, calling to tell me that it was time and I needed to go home.

I threw off the blanket and jumped out of bed. Twenty minutes later, I walked into the house I'd grown up in, Hunter hot on my heels. I felt numb.

Both of my siblings were sitting in the living room with Beth-Ann. My eyes locked with Becky's for a moment and the sadness behind them nearly ripped me in half.

But I was the oldest; I had to keep it together for my siblings. If I broke down, they'd break down. I could tell Braden was inches from falling apart. His eyes were tormented and panicked and he looked at me as if pleading with me to fix this.

"Am I too late?" I kept the emotion out of my voice to the best of my ability. My voice sounded cold and detached.

"No." Becky shook her head, her eyes welling again. "But soon. I think she's waiting for you."

Hearing that was like a kick to the goddamn heart. Our mother lay dying down the hall, and I'd put off talking to her because I was a selfish coward.

I was supposed to be here to help lessen the burden on Becky and I hadn't done that. For the first time, I felt like I truly failed them... and myself.

My feet weighed a thousand pounds as I walked down the hallway and entered my mother's room. She was awake and alert, her eyes wide open. She was staring ahead, her gaze faraway and almost dazed. She turned her head slightly, wincing at the movement when she heard the door open.

My heart felt like it was caught in my throat. "Mom..." My voice broke.

She smiled. "Brock...I'm so glad you're home," she said, her voice raspy and raw.

All the things I wanted to be angry with her for over the years, melted on the tip of my tongue. I couldn't say anything I'd rehearsed in my head. I couldn't ask her why she stayed with my dad or why she allowed him to abuse not only her, but us too. I couldn't ask her any of this because she was dying. She was dying and her words wouldn't and couldn't change the past. She smiled and I reluctantly walked over to her bedside, falling heavily into the chair someone had placed there.

Her frail hand crept towards the end of the bed, reaching for mine. I reached too, intertwining our fingers.

"I'm sorry I haven't –"

"Never mind that," she said, dismissing my excuses. Looking into her eyes, I knew she didn't have much time left. They were glassy, transparent. I felt as if I could see her soul, and it was torn between here and the hereafter. "There are a lot of things I need to tell you," she added, her voice scratchy. She cleared her throat, focusing on me. It was as if she could read my mind. "I'm sorry he hurt you. I'm sorry I didn't protect you when I should have. I thought..." Her voice broke again, the tears pooling in the corners of her eyes. "I thought I was the only one he hurt. I should have left. I failed to protect my children and I have lived with that regret all these years."

I inhaled deeply, forcing my heart not to shatter in my chest at her words. My fingers gently rubbed against her papery skin, trying to comfort her. "You should have left when he started hurting you, Ma. You deserved better than that."

"You're a good man, Brock," she stuttered, tripping over her words. She took a deep breath, resolving to finish whatever it was she had to say. "I'm proud of you. I know you'll do great things; you'll all do great things. I just wish I could be here for it all. I wish I could meet the girl you finally give your heart to. I wish I could see you on your wedding day. I wish I could hold more grandbabies in my arms. I wish I had a thousand more days to tell you each how much I love you and to tell you how proud I am of you. But I'm not scared of dying, and I know I'll see it all from above. I'm not afraid to leave with you home. I know you'll watch out for your siblings. You always have."

"Of course I will," I promised, trying to ignore the moisture that was building up in the corners of my eyes. I wish I could tell her that she'd already met the girl I'd given my heart to, that I wished she could get to know her too and see all those milestones she'd talked about wanting to see...but there wasn't enough time. "I love you, Mom," I added, my voice catching on the realization that this was the last time I'd be able to tell her that.

"I love you, Brock," Mom said, the volume in her voice lowering as if the act of dying was slowly turning the dial. "I love you all."

Her head fell back against the pillow, her eyes fluttering

closed. She was too spent after her speech. I stayed like that, holding her hand until her lungs gave her last breath. I sat there, numb until Becky's strangled cry roused me. She rushed to the bedside, Braden and the hospice nurse following quickly behind her. Beth-Ann checked for a pulse, and finding nothing, announced the time of death with a hollow finality.

THE CORONER ARRIVED to remove Mom's body an hour later, after my siblings and I had stood solemnly in her room, unable to speak our goodbyes to a body that no longer housed our mother. When Aiden woke up and padded down the hall, he peered into Mom's empty room before walking into the kitchen, where Becky and I sat at the table with cold cups of coffee. Braden had wordlessly exploded out of the house the second the coroner left with the body bag. His eyes were red rimmed, his anger palpable.

"Is Grammy better now?" Aiden asked, his blue eyes wide and hopeful as he looked from Becky to me.

Tears welled up in Becky's eyes and she blinked them away as she stood up. Crouching down so she was on his level, Becky broke the news to him. Aiden accepted it with a quivering jaw, his eyes lifting to meet mine briefly. I nodded at him, giving him the only smile I could muster.

"Remember what I said, buddy; she'll be with you always," I told him, thankful that my voice hadn't choked up at all. It was the first time I'd spoken since the last words I'd said to Mom. When I told her I loved her.

Becky called Tessa to come and pick up Aiden for the day. When she pulled up, I watched as Becky gave her the keys to her car and tried to pass her a couple hundred dollars to keep Aiden entertained. Tessa softly closed Becky's hand, shaking her head.

"Becky, keep your money. I've got this, okay? It's the least I can do right now."

While Becky strapped Aiden in his car seat, Tessa walked over to me. She put her arms around my waist, pulling me against her and resting her head on my chest. "I'm sorry, Brock," she murmured, her voice vibrating against my skin.

I brought my arms up to hold her closer, stroking the back of her head as I swallowed the emotion. "Thanks," I told her, squeezing her hand before she walked over to the car.

Becky and I spent the entire day finalizing the funeral details and arranging the wake and ceremony times. Just after her dire diagnosis, Mom picked out her casket and got her affairs in order. She hadn't wanted us to have the burden of trying to figure all that out.

The wake would be in two days' time, and the ceremony would take place the next afternoon. The notice was printed in the newspaper and the flowers were ordered.

"Have you heard from Braden at all?" Becky asked, looking up from her phone as we exited the flower store. She'd been checking it obsessively for the last ten hours.

"No." I answered. "But I know where he is. I'll drop you off at home then go get him."

Becky nodded with a sigh, biting her lip as she looked at me. "I'm really glad you're here, Brock. I couldn't do this without you." The pain of loss etched in Becky's eyes was acute. She'd been the closest to our mother, especially after Aiden's birth. They'd lived with her and Mom had really helped out with Aiden before she got sick, so Becky could work and go to school part time. She was supposed to graduate from her personal support worker course at the college this fall and I knew she had plans to go on and pursue a degree in practical nursing.

I wrapped my arm around my sister, hugging her as we walked to the truck. "It'll be okay, Becs," I told her, needing to believe it myself. While the death of our father had been a blessing, the death of our grandfather was harder to take. He'd been more of a father than the man who'd created us. It had been a tough time, but we survived.

After I dropped Becky off at the house, I pulled out of the driveway and drove to Flanigan's. I could see Braden's old beat up Chevy parked out front; I parked behind him in and walked inside.

Braden was putting his legal age to good use. He was blitzed, sitting at the bar, hammering back a glass of whiskey. Mick looked up when I walked in, relief soothing the lines of concern on his weathered face. I nodded at him as I walked up to Braden and pulled out a stool.

"What are you doing here?" Braden slurred, scowling as he squinted at me.

I arched a brow. "Whiskey, Mick. On the rocks," I told the bartender, not breaking eye contact with my brother. Braden's shoulders eased at my words, the defensive walls dropping just a bit now that he thought I was there to drink my problems away too.

I wasn't. I'd long since learned not to turn to booze to ease pain. Still, I knew ordering a drink would relax Braden enough to maybe talk to me. He was so drunk that it'd be either a fist fight or an explosion of pent up hurt and desperation.

I took a sip of the whiskey, letting it burn my throat. Millers and drinking was a dangerous combination. Addiction ran in our blood.

"Funeral details are handled," I said, not looking at him. "The wake is in two days, the funeral the next day."

"Whoopty shit," Braden grumbled, tossing back another heavy sip while scowling at me. "It's not like she'll notice if I'm not there."

"Aiden will," I pointed out.

Braden's shoulders slumped further, as if he hadn't considered that. "Fine, I'll be there. But I ain't sticking around for that shitty party afterwards," he told me, referring to the receptions that usually occurred after funerals. I nodded with understanding. I couldn't blame him. Becky was the one that insisted on doing it, just having coffee and cake for the guests afterwards. I wasn't entirely sure anyone would even show up.

Mom hadn't been very popular in town either. She'd been judged by everyone for scum she'd married, for loving him. She'd been taunted from behind. She hadn't had any real, true friends... except for maybe Beth-Ann, who she befriended after her diagnosis. Mom mostly kept to herself, focusing on her family and her job.

We stayed at the bar for another half hour until Braden's eyes were too heavy to remain open. He didn't even noticed that I'd barely touched my tumbler of whiskey. I threw some bills down on the counter before I hoisted up my brother, tossing his arm around my shoulders. I tugged him upright, heading to the door that Mick held open for me. I nodded my thanks, moving towards my truck. My steps were slowed by my brother's obliterated state. I made it to the truck and had one hand on the door handle.

"Should have known I'd find you at the bar." I turned my head at the sound of the voice, watching warily as Gordon and Tommy Armstrong approached.

Tommy cracked his knuckles and Gordon looked every bit as pissed off as he'd been the day he found Tessa at my place.

"I don't have time for this right now," I said through bared teeth. I opened the passenger side door, shoving Braden in.

"Sorry, bud, but we can't have this chat on your schedule. That's not exactly how this kind of thing works." Gordon laughed darkly, shaking his head.

Rage bubbled just beneath the surface, threatening to consume me. I clenched my knuckles so tightly that they turned white and protested the strain. I fought to draw in each breath slowly, accenting my anger without speaking.

"You need to back off, man," I warned.

Tommy stepped forward, his eyes flashing with anger. "Is that a threat?" he challenged. Almost every muscle in my body was tense with the need to unleash the anger I felt at these two idiots. I wanted to knock the smug look off Tommy's face. I knew I could easily take both of them. But I also knew that if I so much as lifted a finger, I'd be back in jail and I didn't want to risk my freedom over their prejudice.

"No, I'm not threatening you," I said with disgust. "I'm telling you to back off. If Tessa wants to be with me and I want to be with her, nothing you say or do is going to change that. You're just going to push her further away. Do you want that? Do you want her to end up hating you guys? Because she's close, man. She's close." I said this last part to Gordon, looking at him to drive home my words.

He watched me as I spoke, his lips pressed into a thin line. Tommy took my words as an insult and attempted to lunge at me. Gordon's arm shot out, stopping his brother. His brows furrowed and he shook his head.

I relaxed, exhaling the breath I'd been holding.

"If you're serious about Tessa, you need to prove your worth," Gordon said, looking back at me.

"I know that," I replied, scowling. "And I plan on doing just that. But like I said, now is not a good time." I walked around the front of my truck, opening the door.

WE ARRIVED EARLY at the funeral home for the wake. Becky thought it was important that we all get a little time alone with her before it began.

Mom was lying in a beautiful, mahogany open casket. Originally, she'd picked out the most basic one, the cheapest. The first thing I'd done upon seeing it was ask the funeral home if it was too late to upgrade. They'd willingly taken my money, of course.

Someone had done her hair and makeup, giving false colour to her face, and they'd somehow managed to make her hair appear healthy and shiny. She looked almost like she had the last time I'd seen her, before the judge sentenced me and before she'd gotten sick.

I couldn't help but think that she looked a lot like a figure from a wax museum.

A warm, slender hand found its way into mine and I turned, catching Tessa's solemn eyes looking back at me. She didn't say anything; she didn't need to. The fact that she was here was enough.

The wake passed in a blur. We stood near the front of the room, forming a receiving line to greet guests. Tessa was at the end of the line, holding my right hand. Becky stood beside me, with Aiden between us. Aiden grasped tightly to his mother's hand as he solemnly watched the events around him with wide eyes. Braden stood beside Becky, sending dark, reproachful looks at everyone, likely feeling the same anger I felt, while Elle quietly stood beside him with her right arm linked in his.

This was the part I hated. I hated talking to people I didn't know, acting like they cared. Maybe they did, but none of my mother's co-workers were there when she was sick, or even before. I doubted she had any meaningful relationships with any of them, and their words of practiced condolences pissed me off. I couldn't help but feel like they were there to get the afternoon off work, as harsh as it was.

My theory was hard to debunk as they sat on the couches in clusters, showing absolutely no remorse as they gossiped. Braden's jaw was clenched tightly and he occasionally glowered at them, his blue eyes dark with rage. I knew he was hanging onto his temper by a sliver and likely the only thing stopping him from going overboard was Elle. I was thankful she was here, thankful that my brother had someone to lean on. He needed it. Out of all of us, he'd taken Mom's death the hardest.

Tessa still stood by my side, mostly because I hadn't let go of her hand the entire time. Her hand grounded me. Her hand kept me from focusing on the complicated emotions roaring through my mind, from the anger that surged over the amount of face-less people proclaiming to be sorry for our loss.

"Are you okay?" Tessa whispered, squeezing my hand gently.

I looked down at her, forcing a smile. "I'm fine," I said, and I found it was true when I looked into those amber eyes. She gave me a small smile.

"Becky, I'm so sorry for your loss," a woman's voice said, drawing both of our attention to the left where my sister stood. Becky hugged the speaker, a massively pregnant woman with blonde hair and sad, gentle brown eyes. The woman stood beside a tall man that I immediately recognized as Tessa's oldest brother, Ben. He'd changed a lot since the last time I'd seen him, but it was still obvious that he was an Armstrong.

"Thanks, Katie," Becky said, releasing the woman. Her eyes drifted down to her pregnant belly. "May I?" she asked with a smile.

"Of course!" Katie said, gently taking Becky's hand and placing it on her swollen stomach. Becky closed her eyes, the smallest of smiles lifting her lips upwards. When she opened them again, they were watery with unshed tears.

"Thank you," she whispered, drawing in a shaky breath. "It's so nice to have this reminder of new life." She swallowed hard. "Congratulations. You two will be remarkable parents."

"Thank you." Katie smiled, moving on to me, Ben trailing alongside of her after shaking Becky's hand briefly. Katie's eyes drifted to Tessa's hand in mine before she raised them again. "Brock, I'm sorry to be meeting you under such circumstances," she said before she reached out and hugged me too.

I'd never hugged a pregnant woman before. It was rather

awkward and I was completely shocked that she even made the move. When she released me, all I could do was blink at her while Tessa smiled gently at my side. "I'm sorry for your loss," Katie told me with a sad smile. "But I hope you'll come around soon for dinner. You're welcome at our home any time." She looked at her husband.

Ben nodded, extending a large hand to me. "Good seeing you again, Brock. Treat her good," he added as I shook his hand, bewildered.

"Of course," I said, my brows slightly furrowing at their reaction.

Katie and Ben moved on to hug Tessa and exchange words with Braden and Elle before they left. I loved that they didn't linger. They paid their respects and they left to allow room for others to do the same.

I thought that would be the most surprising event of the night, but I was corrected several moments later when Gordon, Tommy, Grady and Travis walked in through the doors. They made their way over to us, solemn looks on their faces.

The younger Armstrong brothers didn't have a flicker of the anger and contempt their expressions held two nights ago outside of Flanigan's. In fact, they looked apologetic and ashamed.

Gordon extended his hand to me and then pulled me to him for a hug, causing Tessa's hand to fall free of mine. He clapped my back and pulled away. "I'm sorry about your loss, man. I wish you'd told me..."

"It's fine," I brushed off his apology, not wanting to make a scene or have Tessa realize what had almost transpired outside of the local bar. Grady, Tommy, and Travis all shook my hand and gave me what Becky had affectionately nicknamed "bro hugs". It was the same gesture that Gordon had done; the handshake turned hug with a firm clap on the back.

"Feel like coming out for drinks tonight?" Gordon asked, his eyes drifting to Tessa briefly as I reached for her hand again. He looked at Becky and Braden, nodding to extend his invitation to them too.

"I'm game," Braden said, earning a pinched look from Elle, which he promptly ignored. I knew I'd be going now regardless to keep an eye on my self-destructive brother.

Travis was eyeing Becky appreciatively as if he really wanted her to say yes, earning a narrow glare from me. He grinned, raising his hands in apology. My sister seemed oblivious to his attention, though. "I can't," she said, glancing down at Aiden, who was peering out around her leg at the people gathered around him. The charming smile fell from Travis's lips and a look of disappointment crossed his features.

"I'll watch him if you want to go, Becky," Tessa offered, smiling gently. "You need to get out of the house for a bit."

I squeezed her hand, thanking her silently for her offer. She was right, Becky did need to get out of the house. Since I'd been back, I hadn't seen her leave the house once for fun. Any time she was gone, it was to work or attend a class. The last few days had been hard on her. She'd been dealing with Aiden's emotions over losing his grandma as well as her own grief. She could use a break.

"I don't know." Becky frowned, uncertain.

"No need to decide now," Gordon assured her. "We'll be at Flanigan's at nine. If we see you, we see you. If not, we get it."

"THIS IS A BAD IDEA," Becky murmured later on that night as we walked into Flanigan's pub. It was crowded, full of familiar faces. I spotted Gordon, Grady, and Travis hanging out at the bar along with Tommy, Ezra, and Peter. Braden made a beeline for his friends without a single glance at either of us. Becky's brow furrowed with concern as she watched him go. "I'm worried about him," she told me, nodding at our younger brother.

I watched as Braden ordered a beer, a small bubble of relief blossoming to see that he hadn't headed straight for the hard liquor. "I'll keep an eye on him."

Becky sent me a disbelieving glance. "I'm worried about you too."

"Don't." I frowned. My friends caught sight of us and waved. Gordon and Travis walked up to meet us in the middle of the room.

"Glad you could make it." Gordon said, his words sincere.

"What's your poison?" Travis spoke to both of us, but his eyes were mostly focused on Becky. He gave her his classic flirtatious smile, the same one I'd seen him wearing when he was dancing with Tessa a few weeks back.

"Oh, I don't know…" Becky blushed, looking away. "I haven't had anything to drink in a long time."

"You look like a Sex on the Beach kind of girl." Travis grinned. I shot him a dirty look and he laughed. "I'm just saying, something fruity and tasty. I didn't name the damn drink," he added, shrugging at me apologetically.

Becky gave me a warning look before she turned her attention back to Travis. "That sounds good actually. I'd love to have Sex on the Beach," she said, driving her point home as she accepted his outstretched arm. He led her over to the bar so they could order her drink.

"Not so fun when your buddy hits on your sister, huh?" Gordon joked, seeing the look on my face.

"Considering that buddy was all up on Tessa a couple weeks ago, yeah. Not so fun," I replied with a frown. "Becky doesn't need a player right now."

"Don't worry about it." Gordon waved away my concern with a tight smile. "You never know, he might be good for her."

"This coming from you?" I arched a brow pointedly, referring to his dislike over me being with Tessa.

"Hey, at least he's a loaded country singer." Gordon winked and shoved my shoulder to show he was joking. "I'm sorry, man. I was just looking out for Tessa."

"I know." I said, relating to Gordon more than I cared to admit as I watched Travis hit on Becky.

"How about that drink, then? Looks like your brother's already started the fun," he remarked, looking back at the bar where Braden was currently doing shots with two girls I recognized as friends of Elle and Tessa, who were both back at the house, babysitting Aiden.

I got the sense that Becky was right; this was a bad idea.

"Fine." I sighed, heading to the bar.

I nursed my first beer for the next three hours, keeping a wary eye on my siblings. Becky was busy talking to Travis in a booth. She sat across from him and he never made a move on her aside from giving her his full attention, so I let it be, my eyes focused mainly on my younger brother. Braden had taken so many shots that I'd lost count. He was hitting on the blonde girl, playing with a strand of her hair with one hand while the other rested on her upper thigh. She bit her lip, looking at him through thick lashes as she said something.

I frowned, thinking about Elle and wondering what in the hell my brother was thinking. I set my beer down just as his lips grazed against hers. By the time I reached them, they were heavily making out. I yanked on Braden's arm, pulling him away from the girl. "Alright, you've had enough. Time to go," I told him sternly.

Braden looked at me with disgust, red lipstick on his lips. "What the fuck are you talking about? I'm not ready to go. 'Least not with you," he slurred, glancing back at the girl. "Hey, Joanna, wanna go back to your place?"

"How about you go home to your girlfriend, Braden?" I suggested. The girl, Joanna, ducked her head shamefully.

"I ain't married to her," Braden spat, angry. "I'll do what I want."

Becky had watched the altercation happening by the bar. Judging by the pissed off look on her face when she approached, she'd seen Braden's antics with the blonde girl. "Brock is right. We're going. Now." She grabbed one of Braden's arms and tried to tug him away.

Braden shoved her hard and she stumbled, almost falling. She would have landed on the floor if Travis didn't catch her. "I'm not a kid. You can't fucking tell me what to do," he spat.

Mick Flanigan limped around the bar. "Hit the road, Miller. You're cut off," he said gruffly, speaking to Braden.

"Oh, you know how to cut people off, huh? Coulda fooled me," Braden shot back. "Maybe you should have tried cutting my old man off so he wouldn't come home and beat his family. But then how would your shitty bar stay open without his wallet, eh?"

"Braden, you're making no sense. Let's just go," Becky pleaded, sending an apologetic and embarrassed look to Mick. I didn't wait for my brother to reply; I grabbed him by his shirt collar and dragged him out. I let him go once we were on the street.

"Get in the fucking truck," I growled when he went to argue with me. Although he was completely blitzed, Braden recognized something dangerous in my expression. I was livid and he knew not to push. Obediently, he crawled into the back seat of the cab. "And wipe the goddamn lipstick off your face," I added once I climbed into the truck. I slammed the door hard. Becky climbed into the front passenger seat, shaking her head. She tossed me a look that said, *I told you so.* I said nothing as I stomped on the gas and tore down the street.

CHAPTER 18

essa

"Why didn't you just go with them?" I asked Elle. "You have a fake ID." We were sitting on the couch watching some romantic comedy on television. Aiden had been sleeping for the past three hours; even Hunter was curled up at my feet fast asleep. There wasn't any need for Elle to remain here, yet she did.

She gave me a smile that didn't quite reach her eyes. "I figured you'd want some company," she answered, bumping her shoulder into mine gently. "Besides, it seemed like something the three of them needed to do alone."

My eyebrows rose in disbelief. There was more to it; there were things that Elle wasn't sharing. She stared at the television screen, avoiding meeting my eyes.

"Elle..." I said, about to push her a little more. Hunter sat up abruptly, staring at the door. The sound of footfall on the front porch made his ears turn back. A moment later, the door swung open and Becky walked in, holding it for Brock. He was half-carrying Braden.

Elle and I stood up, making room so Brock could dump Braden's almost unconscious body on the sofa.

"Rough night?" Elle joked weakly, her shoulders slumping at the sight of him.

Braden opened one eye and stared at her. "The fuck you doing here?" he slurred.

"Is that...lipstick?" Elle leaned forward, spotting the smear of red against Braden's lips. He brought his hand up, wiping his lips in a half assed attempt at removing the proof. I looked towards Brock and Becky for an explanation. The matching dismal expressions on their faces said it all. Elle saw too and tears welled up in her eyes. She took a shaky breath.

The heartbreak was etched onto her face. Becky took a step towards her, but Elle backed away. "I'm just...I'm just going to go," she said, her voice wavering with broken emotion. She wordlessly left, her eyes downcast and her shoulders trembling.

"I'm going to go too," I said, nodding to Elle's retreating back. Brock nodded with understanding. His hand gripped mine as I passed and he gave it a gentle squeeze. The expression in his eyes was heavy with apology.

"He's hurting right now," he said lowly. "It doesn't make it right and I'm not saying it does. Elle deserves better than that," he added, catching the furious look that passed across my face. It was clear that Brock didn't agree with his brother's actions either.

"I know." I sighed, biting my lip. "I'll see you guys tomorrow, at the funeral."

Brock nodded and gently pressed his lips against my forehead, then he released my hand so I could follow my broken-hearted friend.

Elle was leaning against the passenger door of my truck, her face buried in her hands. I wrapped my arms around her tightly, letting her cry for several long minutes. Finally, she pulled away. "Let's just get out of here," she croaked, glaring back at the house.

We drove back to her house in silence. Sue was already in bed, so we went straight up and got changed, crawling into Elle's bed. She cried herself to sleep.

THE NEXT MORNING, it seemed her tears had run out. She didn't want to talk about Braden, about the lipstick on his mouth, or about how he'd crushed her heart. She had a stoic expression on her face while we went about getting ready for the funeral.

Sue kept sending her worried glances. "You really don't have to go, honey."

"I'm fine, Mom," Elle snapped, her cool disposition wavering. "I've been a part of the Millers' lives for two years. I knew Deanna. I'm friends with Becky. I'm not going to bail out on the funeral because Braden..." She swallowed hard, gathering every last bit of her strength. "Let's just get this over with."

We took Sue's car over to the church. Finding parking was surprisingly difficult. The church was full of people; it was as if the entire town had shown up for Deanna Miller's funeral. I even spotted my dad and all of my brothers sitting at a pew towards the middle of the room. There was just enough space for Sue, Elle and me.

"I'll be right back," I told them, spotting Brock near the front of the church with Becky, Braden and Aiden. Braden looked like shit. I couldn't tell if it was grief, the fact that he was nursing a massive hangover, or that he'd broken Elle's heart. Maybe it was all of the above. He wouldn't even meet my eyes when I approached.

Brock took me in his arms and I pressed my cheek against his chest and squeezed him as hard as I could. His eyes were full of sadness, but the smile he gave me when he released me was authentic.

"I'm sitting with my family," I said, gesturing towards the back of the room. He looked up, tensing when he saw my father.

"I appreciate them coming out," Brock replied automatically.

Pastor Bruce joined us, putting a hand on Brock's arm. "Are you ready?" he asked with his gentle, commanding voice. This was the same man that had baptized me and every one of my brothers; the same man who'd married my parents and Ben and Katie.

"Yes." Brock nodded. He was still holding my hand in his. I gave him a tiny smile, releasing it so that we could both return to our seats.

Pastor Bruce stepped up to the altar, clearing his throat to capture the attention of the church.

I slid into the pew beside Elle, feeling the intensity of my father's gaze. He said nothing as the services began.

Pastor Bruce's voice rang out loudly and clearly. "Jesus said, 'Blessed are those who mourn, for they shall be comforted...'" He paused, his eyes peering out at the full pews. He started speaking again, lecturing the room at large about how Christians ought to not fear death.

I tuned out, unable to focus. It was the first time I'd really been in a church since Ben and Katie got married, and I was distracted, my thoughts pulling me in several different directions. I ached for Brock and his siblings. I thought about my best friend sitting beside me, who I knew was hurting deeply over Braden's careless actions, even if she wouldn't say as much. She was focused intently on Pastor Bruce, her eyes unblinking and her back rigid.

"Deanna asked me to read this for her children," the minister was saying. His voice drew my attention to the front again. "Peace I leave with you; my peace I give you. I do not give to you as the world gives. Do not let your hearts be troubled and do not be afraid." The room was silent, absorbing the scripture. "Now, Becky Miller, Deanna's only daughter, has some words she'd like to share."

Becky stood up, soothing the creases of her black funeral dress. She walked on steady legs towards the altar. She adjusted the microphone, her watery blue eyes taking in how many people were there. "Wow. There's a lot of people here," she said, her voice trembling. A few people laughed awkwardly. She gave a tight smile and drew in a shaky breath, readying herself.

"My mom lived with a lot of regrets, but she always told us that we weren't one of them. We were the driving force behind everything that she did." She was silent for a moment, collecting her thoughts. She had a piece of paper in her hand, but I noticed her eyes barely glanced at it. "My mom wasn't good at letting people in. She learned not to trust them at a young age. People judge. People throw stones. She was never good at accepting help. She bowed her head and dealt with things herself. *My strength comes from within,* she always said when I asked her if she was lonely. It wasn't until she got sick that she started opening up more to me. She told me it was okay to trust, that she hoped I would again. She told me that it's okay to lean on people, to cry when it hurts, to speak up when someone isn't treating you right. She said these were things she wished she'd known back then, but that it was better to learn them later than never at all."

The church was silent, each person's eyes focused on Becky as she stood before them. "The bond that she had with my son, Aiden..." Becky trailed off again, drawing in a shaky breath as a few tears escaped down her cheeks. She brushed them aside and smiled towards her son. "She always said that his birth was what knitted our entire family closer together. Before him, we were too scared to lean on each other, too scared to trust in one another because we'd been burned by someone close to us before. But we came together for that, for him.

Even with distance separating us, we grew stronger as a family."

"I guess what I'm trying to say here," Becky continued, the tears streaming down her face without restraint, "is don't take the people you care about for granted. Don't throw away their love. We're stronger together than we are apart."

Elle let out a strangled sound beside me, the tears she'd fought to hold back finally falling free at Becky's final words as Becky made her way back to her seat and Pastor Bruce positioned himself in front of the altar.

"Before we conclude the funeral service, I'd like to end with a note from Luke 6:37; 'Judge not, and you will not be judged; condemn not, and you will not be condemned; forgive, and you will be forgiven.'"

<hr />

THE BURIAL for Deanna was family only. A huge group of us that planned on attending the reception afterwards at Flanigan's decided to grab something to eat beforehand.

"Let's go to Betty's diner," Gordon suggested to the group at large. The group included my dad, all three of my brothers, a very pregnant Katie, Elle, and Sue.

"Sure, why not?" Elle sighed. "I've got nothing else to do." I knew she was still hurt over Braden walking right past her without so much as a single glance once the funeral services had ended.

"I've got stuff to do at the farm," Dad said. He looked completely out of place, dressed up in his Sunday best. When my mom was alive, Dad used to attend masses every Sunday with her and the boys. After her death, he stopped going and he stopped taking us. The last time he'd set foot in the church was for Ben's wedding and he'd been every bit as uncomfortable then as he was now.

Truthfully, I was surprised that my father had even showed up for the funeral. He'd made his opinion about Brock Miller perfectly clear time and time again over the past week and I didn't think he was ever friendly with Deanna.

"It can't wait until after you've had something to eat?" Sue interjected, arching a brow.

Dad gave her a rare smile and scratched his beard, considering. "I suppose it could." His eyes drifted over to me. The disappointment and anger that had clouded them a few days before had diminished and he looked at me with warmth. "Mind keeping your old man company on the drive there?"

"Sure," I said, giving him a tiny smile. I hadn't really spoken to my father since I'd stormed away from the conversation I'd overheard him having with Sue. I didn't exactly want to talk about any of that today, not with everything else going on, but I didn't want to cause further friction by continuing to ignore him. After all, he was my father. He was always going to be a major part of my life, whether or not he agreed with my choices. We were just going to have to learn how to live with one another when we disagreed.

Katie had been massaging her stomach distractedly while we all debated on whether or not we wanted to come, and she tensed, breathing through her mouth carefully.

"Are you okay?" Ben asked, frowning at the strained look on her face.

"I'm fine." She waved him away. "It's another one of those Braxton Hicks contractions."

"I should get you home," my brother fretted, rubbing her back in slow circular movements.

"I want to go eat," she told him, smiling and shrugging.

He regarded her for a minute then sighed. "Alright, we'll stop by for a bite to eat. Meet you all there?"

Our group divided into separate vehicles. I squeezed Elle's hand in mine briefly before I followed my dad to his truck.

Dad held the key up to the ignition, his hand freezing. He exhaled deeply and turned to look at me. "I don't expect you to understand the love a parent has for their child. Maybe you will one day far into the future, but right now, all you see is me being unfair."

"Dad –"

"Let me talk, Tessa," Dad cut me off, giving me a stern look that booked no room for arguments. "Maybe I am being a little unfair, but you're my little girl and I don't want anything bad happening to you."

The silence stretched on between us for several long seconds. "Dad, you can't protect me from every bad thing out there," I told him, giving him a pained smile as memories of the bush party, and Chris, overcame me. I swallowed hard. "Bad things in life happen to everyone. You've given me more than enough tools to handle the bad things, though, and I have the added bonus of having a lot of good things in my life. I have a family that loves me; you all might drive me nuts, but I know you'll always be there for me. A lot of people don't have that," I remarked, my brows creasing as I thought about the Millers. I looked back at my father with determination. "Brock might break my heart, I might break his heart. We might work, we might not, but that's for me to find out and you can't shelter me from that."

My father was quiet, absorbing my words. He nodded slowly, pursing his lips. "So you care about this boy a lot?"

"Yes."

"What happens when you go to college?" he asked, looking as if he figured I was about to tell him I'd decided to throw away all my academic goals for a boy.

"Brock hasn't changed my decision to go to college." I arched a brow, almost amused. "I don't only care about him. I still care about my future, my dreams and my hopes. I still care about my friends and my family; I just also care about him. We'll make it work long distance if it's meant to be. If it's not, well..." I shrugged, trying to ignore the sick sensation of dread that the thought brought forth.

Dad regarded me for several moments before a proud smile eased the seriousness of his expression. "I'm proud of you, Tessa. I don't give you enough credit. You're a smart girl. A strong girl."

"Does this mean you're going to give him a chance?" I asked, trying to keep the hopefulness from my tone.

"I'll do my best, kiddo," Dad promised, reaching across the seat and rubbing the top of my head like he used to do when I was a little kid.

"Dad!" I laughed, ducking away from his hand and trying to fix my hair. "Can we go now?" I asked, glancing at the time. "I'm starving."

He nodded, his eyes twinkling as he started up his truck and pulled out of the parking spot.

A GOOD HOUR LATER, I walked into the open doors of Flanigan's with Elle by my side. The bar seemed to have gone through a transformation. It was brighter and there were crisp white linen cloths on the tables. Beautiful flower arrangements were placed on each of the tables and booths. Meat and cheese trays, vegetable trays and sandwiches were in abundance on the long table against the far wall. There was a coffee urn and a drink station.

Brock stood by the food table, helping Aiden pick out things for his plate. I glanced around, looking for Braden. I didn't see him anywhere and neither did Elle. I felt her deflate a little beside me before she tossed her shoulders back and took off towards the bar to join Travis, Grady, Ezra and Peter.

I made my way over to Brock, my heart thudding in my

chest when he lifted those metallic eyes. He smiled softly at me, lifting his head a fraction.

"Hi, Aiden," I said, crouching down to give him a hug. He hugged me back, melting into my arms. During the last week, we'd really bonded. When Becky asked me to take him for the day so she and Brock could finalize the funeral details, I'd made sure to make his day a special one that wouldn't be clouded by sadness. We'd gone to my house and spent the majority of the day with the horses. Aiden helped me brush and feed them, and he'd even ridden on Scared Spirit after I'd found my old riding gear from when I was little. The helmet was a little loose, but it had served its purpose well enough for the gentle circles around the fenced-in ring.

Aiden loved it. It was his first time riding a horse and his face had shone with such excitement.

"Hi, Tessa. When can I ride Spirit again?" he asked, his eyes bright with excitement.

"Whenever your mom says it's okay," I told him with a smile. Becky had requested the week off work so she could spend time with her family and grieve. I wasn't sure what her plans were, but she knew I was available to take Aiden whenever she needed the break. "But you're welcome whenever, okay?"

"Okay." Aiden smiled. I straightened up as Brock handed him his plate, watching as he wandered back over to his mom, to sit at one of the booths.

Brock's hand found mine and he gently pulled me towards him. His free hand brushed a strand of hair out of my face and his eyes came to rest upon my lips. "You're beautiful," he told me before his lips gently descended to mine. He kissed me softly, tenderly, just long enough to make my heart rate thrum pleasantly in my chest.

A commotion at the bar broke our moment alone together and I turned my head, seeing Braden slam down his tumbler of whiskey in aggravation.

"Are you seriously going to try to tell me what to do right now, Elle?" he shot out, his eyes flashing with rage.

Elle lifted her chin, her eyes never leaving Braden's face. "I just don't think drinking this much is a good idea."

"Does everything always have to be about you, Elle? What you think and what you want and your plans?" Braden's voice was angry and each word sliced into my friend's heart like a blade.

"Braden!" I said sharply, pulling away from Brock and stomping towards them.

Elle held up a hand, stopping me. She turned her red rimmed eyes back to her boyfriend. "I know you're hurting right now, Braden. But don't lash out at me. Words can't be erased," she told him, her voice cautioning him to tread lightly. Every person in the room knew that Braden held Elle's heart in the palms of his hands and he was dangerously close to crushing it.

The venomous, frantic despair in his eyes made me ache for my friend. He picked his tumbler back up, his eyes never leaving her face. "So don't erase them then," he challenged, tossing it back.

It was the exact moment that Elle's heart completely crumbled. Her eyes welled up with tears that she stubbornly fought to control, and she nodded once with a calm sense of finality before she turned and wordlessly left.

CHAPTER 19

rock

TESSA THREW an angry look across the room at Braden before she followed her friend out of the bar and onto the street. I inhaled deeply through my nose, glancing around the bar. Thankfully, only my old friends and Braden's friends had witnessed his outburst. None of the other guests had shown up from the funeral yet. I was relieved; I knew they surely would have judged us mercilessly for Braden's display.

"Braden Joseph Miller." Becky's voice lashed out across the silence and she stomped towards him angrily. I followed behind her just in case I needed to intervene. Judging by the rage rolling off of Braden in waves, it looked like I'd have to. "How could you treat Elle so grotesquely after everything she's done for you?"

"Whatever. This is fucking bullshit," Braden exploded, his eyes bright with animosity and torment. He tossed back the rest of his drink and stomped off towards the back exit.

Sighing, I followed him, leaving Becky to clean up the awkwardness out front.

I found Braden leaning against the brick wall out back, smoking a cigarette. His red eyes opened when he heard me approach. "Are you going to lecture me too, big bro?" he said, his tone dark and dangerous. He reminded me so much of the kid I used to be, full of anger, disappointment and pain... and unable to direct it in any way but through rage.

It took me a long time to come to terms with my own demons. I knew I wasn't fully there and that it would be an uphill battle for the rest of my life. It was harder before I found Tessa. I didn't really have anyone to keep me accountable. Now I had a taste of something good, something wonderful and I'd be damned if I was going to let my anger fuck it up.

I was just sad my brother couldn't see that. He was letting his rage at the world destroy something incredibly good and pure that he had. He was letting his ugliness spill out and hurt the girl I knew he loved.

He was acting like our old man, but I knew he didn't need me to tell him that. He knew it.

I studied him calmly for a few more seconds, mulling over what I wanted to say. "No, I'm not. I think you already know that you just made a mistake. No need to rub your nose in it." Braden gaped at me. Whatever he'd been expecting me to say, it wasn't that.

"Is she gone?" he asked, his eyes downcast.

"Probably. Why in the hell would she stick around after that?" I demanded, resisting the urge to smack him upside the head.

"Whatever," Braden muttered, swallowing hard. "I'll go in in a few. Let me finish my smoke," he added, still not meeting my eyes.

I left him alone with his thoughts and his remorse.

Tessa wasn't there when I went back inside and neither she

nor Elle came back during the remaining hours of the reception. When everyone had left, I had to force Becky to stop cleaning up, gesturing to a nearly passed out Aiden.

"Take him home," I told her. "I'll finish up here."

Becky glanced at her son, biting her bottom lip guiltily. I knew she felt bad that Braden had taken off without a word to either one of us. He hadn't bothered to come back in for the rest of it. I wasn't exactly surprised, but I knew Becky was worrying herself sick.

"Thanks, Brock." She sighed, giving me a tight smile that didn't reach her eyes. She grabbed her purse and picked up Aiden in her arms. His head lolled against her shoulder, his eyes barely opening at the disruption.

I finished packing away all the food and folded up all the linens. I carried everything out to my truck, including all of the table arrangements and walked back into the bar for one last check. Everything seemed to be back to normal; Mick was behind the bar, preparing for another dart competition night.

I stepped up to the bar, pressing my palms against the smooth wood. "Thanks, Mick. For letting us have the reception here."

"No problem." Mick waved away my words with a rough smile. "It was my pleasure. See you around, kid."

I nodded, tapping my hands against the bar once before I pushed off. I headed to my trailer, feeling a little guilty for the number of times I'd had to leave Hunter over the last week.

I pulled up into the driveway, seeing the old Blazer parked in front of the cabin, an easy smile lifting the corners of my lips at the sight of her. She was sitting on the picnic table, throwing a tennis ball for Hunter as I drove up.

Catching sight of me, Hunter forgot all about the ball. He bolted over to me, almost knocking me over when I climbed out of the cab. I gave him some overdue attention, rubbing his sides and scratching his belly when he finally rolled over onto his back.

"We've been entertaining ourselves," Tessa told me, suppressing a smile.

"I see that." I grinned, straightening up. I stepped around Hunter and made my way over to her, intent on kissing her like I hadn't kissed her in days. I had kissed her, but not the way I'd wanted to. I'd had to be careful, reserved and respectful. Tessa stood up, walking toward me with a heated look in those amber eyes.

I grabbed her ass, pulling her tight against me as I kissed her in a way that would have made Pastor Bruce pass out. I just wanted to dive into her and disappear. She kissed me back, nipping at my bottom lip and sighing against my mouth. She pulled away, giving me a playful look. "Just so you know, I came here because I wanted to invite you over for dinner on Sunday."

"Dinner?" I repeated, frowning. I knew her brothers had eased up about us seeing each other, but I didn't think her dad had done the same.

"Yeah, my dad and I had a nice little chat this afternoon and he's willing to give you a chance."

"How'd you manage that one?" I asked skeptically, figuring it was some kind of trap.

"I think his main issue has always been me getting hurt by you. I told him he can't protect me from every bad thing that may come my way and there are things I'm just going to have to experience myself. I also think he was worried I'd bail on my college plans and stay home, but I told him that wasn't going to happen and he eased up a lot." She shrugged, biting her lip.

I brought my hand up, gently freeing her bottom lip from her teeth. "I'm not going to hurt you," I told her.

"I know that," she whispered, looking up at me with her eyes wide with vulnerability. "I'm not sure how I know that, but I do."

I smiled, framing her face with both my hands. "I can't tell you how much I appreciate all that you've done this past week," I told her, swallowing hard. "You've made this whole process a thousand times more bearable than I ever thought it could be. I love you."

"I love you, too," she whispered as my lips descended upon hers.

PLAYLIST

1. Bow Chicka Wow Wow – Meghan Patrick
2. Come Over – Kenny Chesney
3. Drunk On You – Luke Bryan
4. Cruise – Florida Georgia Line
5. Take a Little Ride – Jason Aldean
6. It Goes Like This – Thomas Rhett
7. Bottoms Up – Brantley Gilbert
8. Sweet Spot – Sara Evans
9. Crash My Party – Luke Bryan
10. This is How We Roll – Florida Georgia Line, Luke Bryan
11. Kick It In The Sticks – Brantley Gilbert
12. Roller Coaster – Luke Bryan
13. Hard to Love – Lee Brice

ABOUT THE AUTHOR

J.C. Hannigan lives in Ontario, Canada with her husband, their two sons, and their dog.
She writes contemporary new adult romance and suspense. Her novels focus on relationships, mental health, social issues, and other life challenges.

Website: www.jchannigan.com
Goodreads: http://bit.ly/jchannigangr
BookBub: https://www.bookbub.com/authors/j-c-hannigan

If you enjoyed this story (or if you didn't), please take a moment to **post a review** on Goodreads, BookBub, your blog, or whichever platform you use.
Reviews help other readers find books, and I appreciate any and all reviews!

Sign up for my newsletter to receive exclusive stories, sneak peeks, and updates: https://landing.mailerlite.com/webforms/landing/q1r0x0

And if you like shenanigans, join my readers group FANnigans! There's exclusive giveaways, monthly live video events, and tons of other perks of becoming a FANnigan!
https://www.facebook.com/groups/FANnigans/

OTHER BOOKS BY J.C. HANNIGAN

Collide Series

Collide

Consumed

Collateral

Damaged Series

Damaged Goods

Reckless Abandon

Rebel Series

Rebel Soul

Rebel Heart

Rebel Song

Standalones

The Key to 19B

Coalescence: A Welder Romance

The Forgotten Flounders Series

Off Beat

Off Limit

www.ingramcontent.com/pod-product-compliance
Lightning Source LLC
Chambersburg PA
CBHW031053020726
47495CB00007B/1861